PUFFIN BOOKS
Editor: Kaye Webb

GHOSTS, SPOOKS AND SPECTRES

In each of these twenty stories and poems there is a ghost or a spectre, but that is all they have in common, for there is such variety in Charles Molin's selection. These spooks don't all rattle chains and appear at the stroke of midnight – each one is a distinct and spine-chilling creation, from the spectre who came to warn the railway signalman in Charles Dickens's brilliant story to Sir Arthur Conan Doyle's dead Indian, who appears to reclaim his lost hand, or Sheridan Le Fanu's story of the little maidservant and the wayward, murdering lady she tends, or W. F. Harvey's terrifyingly original story of the Beast with Five Fingers.

Read this book at your peril, and don't blame us if you can't sleep afterwards ! For readers of eleven and over.

*Cover design
and frontispiece drawing
by Philip Gough*

D1422365

Ghosts,
Spooks and Spectres

*

Edited by Charles Molin

PUFFIN BOOKS
in association with Hamish Hamilton

Puffin Books, Penguin Books Ltd, Harmondsworth, Middlesex, England
Penguin Books Australia Ltd, Ringwood, Victoria, Australia
Penguin Books Canada Ltd, 41 Steelcase Road West, Markham, Ontario, Canada
Penguin Books (N.Z.) Ltd, 182–190 Wairau Road, Auckland 10, New Zealand

—

First published by Hamish Hamilton 1967
Published in Puffin Books 1971
Reprinted 1972, 1973, 1975, 1976

—

Copyright © Hamish Hamilton, 1967

—

Made and printed in Great Britain
by C. Nicholls & Company Ltd
Set in Linotype Pilgrim

This book is sold subject to the condition
that it shall not, by way of trade or otherwise,
be lent, re-sold, hired out, or otherwise circulated
without the publisher's prior consent in any form of
binding or cover other than that in which it is
published and without a similar condition
including this condition being imposed
on the subsequent purchaser

Contents

Introduction		9
The Canterville Ghost	Oscar Wilde	13
Teeny-Tiny	Anonymous	48
The Signal-Man	Charles Dickens	50
The Strange Visitor	Anonymous	67
Madam Crowl's Ghost	J. Sheridan Le Fanu	70
A Ghostly Wife	Anonymous	88
Legend of Hamilton Tighe	Richard Bartram	91
The Phantom Ship	Captain Marryat	95
The Brown Hand	Sir Arthur Conan Doyle	109
The Ghost-Brahman	Anonymous	128
The Ghost-Ship	Richard Middleton	132
The Water Ghost of Harrowby Hall John Kendrick Bangs		145
The Inexperienced Ghost	H. G. Wells	153
The Buggane and the Tailor	Dora Broome	169
Laura	Saki	171
The Betrayal of Nance	R. Blakeborough	177

The Ghost Who Was Afraid of Being Bagged   183
  Anonymous

The Beast with Five Fingers   W. F. Harvey   186

The Night the Ghost Got In   James Thurber   219

The Story of Glam   Andrew Lang   225

Acknowledgements

The editor and publishers are indebted to the following for permission to include copyright stories in this book:

The Trustees of the Estate of Sir Arthur Conan Doyle, John Murray Ltd, London, and Mary Yost Associates, New York, for *The Brown Hand* from THE CONAN DOYLE STORIES.

The Executors of H. G. Wells for *The Inexperienced Ghost* from THE COMPLETE SHORT STORIES OF H. G. WELLS.

Dora Broome for *The Buggane and the Tailor* from FAIRY TALES FROM THE ISLE OF MAN.

Mrs Margaret Harvey, J. M. Dent & Sons Ltd, London, and E. P. Dutton & Co. Inc., New York, for *The Beast with Five Fingers* from the volume with the same title.

Mrs Helen W. Thurber, Executrix of the Estate of James Thurber, for *The Night the Ghost Got In* from THE THURBER CARNIVAL.

Introduction

GHOSTS, unfortunately, behave in rather the same way as people. They seem to get on with the business of being not quite dead in just the same hum-drum way as people get on with being alive. That is to say, most of what they do (and I can mean people or ghosts) does not have a very interesting plot, and does not make a good story. When I began to compile this selection of ghost stories I was not a true believer in the world of visible spirits. I thought, and it seemed reasonable to think, that creatures that had to have so many obviously untrue stories told about them could not exist. But that applies to humans as well. We know that certain people in stories are imaginary; and it is clear that certain ghosts are imaginary (like the Canterville Ghost). But to have imaginary people does not make all people imaginary; and to have imaginary ghosts does not make all ghosts imaginary. The difficulty is that the real ones have, on the whole, such poor plots, and in a ghost story you need story as well as ghost.

As I read book after book, story after story, I began to think 'Yes, this is real,' or 'No, this is unreal' (there is a lot of difference between a real ghost and an unreal one); but my general belief was not changed until I read *The Story of Glam*. I chose it because of the completeness of the story. But the whole book from which it was taken – *Dreams and Ghosts* by Andrew Lang – is full of things that must be true. It is a volume I recommend to people who are not quite sure yet about spectres. After a good long reading in it one evening I dared not go to bed. I heaped up the fire, turned on all the lamps, and sat where I was until really broad daylight.

After that I looked upon ghosts a little differently. Now I want to believe in them. I don't know whether they want to be believed in. If they are anything like their human ancestors, they do want our sympathy and understanding. I have heard, since this book was put together, of frightening things. And things that did not worry me before now have a tinge of fear on them, as if my thoughts had been dipped in pale indigo. In the village where I live there is a ghost. It walks behind people in the street. A mile or two away things have happened in the past few months that I would have explained away before. Not now. I believe that there is a ghost in that particular house and that it used to lead the children downstairs in the night with a candle and then vanish. Their mother would come and send them back to bed, and the children thought for many years that she had called them by name and led them down, only to send them back as soon as they had got cold. They thought it was the strangeness of mothers, not the strangeness of ghosts. In the same house they have woken and found the room full of firewood, or an impression of firewood. They have heard all round the ghosts packing and leaving in a great hurry; but of course the ghosts do not go. They are compelled to pack and leave night after night. What are they doing? Are they commemorating some event in the life of the house when they had to leave in a hurry and in fear?

I believe the man in a Cheshire village who wound the church clock one night, early in this century, and walked down the spiral staircase without a light and met someone coming up who did not stop.

These stories, though, are only a few lines long. They are the jottings of eternity on the margin of life. We do not know what they mean, we do not know what they are saying. On the whole, the actions of ghosts are the actions of people. And, as I said at the beginning, they are mostly rather plotless goings-on, like the lives of humans. Humans have stories written about them. So do ghosts. I believe in humans most of the time, and in ghosts all the time. Now, nervous readers must stop here.

CHARLES MOLIN

Oscar Wilde

The Canterville Ghost

I

WHEN Mr Hiram B. Otis, the American Minister, bought Canterville Chase, everyone told him he was doing a very foolish thing, as there was no doubt at all that the place was haunted. Indeed, Lord Canterville himself, who was a man of the most punctilious honour, had felt it his duty to mention the fact to Mr Otis when they came to discuss terms.

'We have not cared to live in the place ourselves,' said Lord Canterville, 'since my grand-aunt, the Dowager Duchess of Bolton, was frightened into a fit, from which she never really recovered, by two skeleton hands being placed on her shoulders as she was dressing for dinner, and I feel bound to tell you, Mr Otis, that the ghost has been seen by several living members of my family, as well as by the rector of the parish, the Rev. Augustus Dampier, who is a Fellow of King's College, Cambridge. After the unfortunate accident to the Duchess none of our younger servants would stay with us, and Lady Canterville often got very little sleep at night, in consequence of the mysterious noises that came from the corridor and the library.'

'My lord,' answered the Minister, 'I will take the furniture and the ghost at a valuation. I come from a modern country, where we have everything that money can buy; and with all our spry young fellows painting the Old World red, and carrying off your best actresses and prima-donnas, I reckon that if there were such a thing as a ghost in Europe we'd have it at home in a very short time in one of our public museums, or on the road as a show.'

'I fear that the ghost exists,' said Lord Canterville, smiling, 'though it may have resisted the overtures of your enterprising impresarios. It has been well known for three centuries, since 1584 in fact, and always makes its appearance before the death of any member of our family.'

'Well, so does the family doctor for that matter, Lord Canterville. But there is no such thing, sir, as a ghost, and I guess the laws of Nature are not going to be suspended for the British aristocracy.'

'You are certainly very natural in America,' answered Lord Canterville, who did not quite understand Mr Otis's last observation, 'and if you don't mind a ghost in the house, it is all right. Only you must remember I warned you.'

A few weeks after this, the purchase was completed, and at the close of the season the Minister and his family went down to Canterville Chase. Mrs Otis, who, as Miss Lucretia R. Tappan, of West 53rd Street, had been a celebrated New York belle, was now a very handsome, middle-aged woman, with fine eyes and a superb profile. Many American ladies on leaving their native land adopt an appearance of chronic ill-health, under the impression that it is a form of European refinement, but Mrs Otis had never fallen into this error. She had a magnificent constitution, and a really wonderful amount of animal spirits. Indeed, in many respects she was quite English, and was an excellent example of the fact that we have really everything in common with America nowadays, except, of course, language. Her eldest son, christened Washington by his parents in a moment of patriotism, which he never ceased to regret, was a fair-haired, rather good-looking young man, who had qualified himself for American diplomacy by leading the German at the Newport Casino for three successive seasons, and even in London was well known as an excellent dancer. Gardenias and the peerage were his only weaknesses. Otherwise he was extremely sensible. Miss Virginia E. Otis was a little girl of fifteen, lithe and lovely as a fawn, and with a fine freedom in her large blue eyes. She was a wonderful amazon, and had once raced old Lord Bilton on her pony twice round the park, winning by a length and a half, just in front of the Achilles statue, to the huge delight of the young Duke of Cheshire, who proposed for her on the spot, and was sent back to Eton that very night by his guardians, in floods of tears. After Virginia came the twins, who were usually called 'The Stars and Stripes', as they were always getting swished. They were delightful boys, and with the exception of the worthy Minister the only true republicans of the family.

As Canterville Chase is seven miles from Ascot, the nearest railway station, Mr Otis had telegraphed for a waggonette to meet them, and they started on their drive in high spirits. It was a lovely July evening, and the air was delicate with the scent of the pinewoods. Now and then they heard a wood pigeon brooding over its own sweet voice, or saw deep in the rustling fern, the burnished breast of the pheasant. Little squirrels peered at them from the beech-trees as they went by, and the rabbits scudded away through the brushwood and over the mossy knolls, with their white tails in the air. As they entered the avenue of Canterville Chase, however, the sky became suddenly overcast with clouds, a curious stillness seemed to hold the atmosphere, a great flight of rooks passed silently over their heads, and, before they reached the house, some big drops of rain had fallen.

Standing on the steps to receive them was an old woman, neatly dressed in black silk, with a white cap and apron. This was Mrs Umney, the housekeeper, whom Mrs Otis, at Lady Canterville's earnest request, had consented to keep on in her former position. She made them each a low curtsey as they alighted, and said, in a quaint, old-fashioned manner, 'I bid you welcome to Canterville Chase.' Following her, they passed through the fine Tudor hall into the library, a long, low room, panelled in black oak, at the end of which was a large stained-glass window. Here they found tea laid out for them, and, after taking off their wraps, they sat down and began to look round, while Mrs Umney waited on them.

Suddenly Mrs Otis caught sight of a dull red stain on the floor just by the fireplace and, quite unconscious of what it really signified, said to Mrs Umney, 'I am afraid something has been spilt there.'

'Yes, madam,' replied the old housekeeper in a low voice, 'blood has been spilt on that spot.'

'How horrid,' cried Mrs Otis; 'I don't at all care for bloodstains in a sitting-room. It must be removed at once.'

The old woman smiled, and answered in the same low, mysterious voice, 'It is the blood of Lady Eleanore de Canterville, who was murdered on that very spot by her own husband, Sir Simon de Canterville, in 1575. Sir Simon survived her nine years, and disappeared suddenly under very mysterious circumstances. His body has never been discovered, but his guilty spirit still haunts the Chase. The bloodstain has been much admired by tourists and others, and cannot be removed.'

'That is all nonsense,' cried Washington Otis; 'Pinkerton's Champion Stain Remover and Paragon Detergent will clean it up in no time,' and before the terrified housekeeper could interfere he had fallen upon his knees, and was rapidly scouring the floor with a small stick of what looked like a black cosmetic. In a few moments no trace of the bloodstain could be seen.

'I knew Pinkerton would do it,' he exclaimed triumphantly, as he looked round at his admiring family; but no sooner had he said these words than a terrible flash of lightning lit up the sombre room, a fearful peal of thunder made them all start to their feet, and Mrs Umney fainted.

'What a monstrous climate!' said the American Minister calmly, as he lit a long cheroot. 'I guess the old country is so over-populated that they have not enough decent weather for everybody. I have always been of opinion that emigration is the only thing for England.'

'My dear Hiram,' cried Mrs Otis, 'what can we do with a woman who faints?'

'Charge it to her like breakages,' answered the Minister; 'she won't faint after that'; and in a few moments Mrs Umney certainly came to. There was no doubt, however, that she was extremely upset, and she sternly warned Mr Otis to beware of some trouble coming to the house.

'I have seen things with my own eyes, sir,' she said, 'that would make any Christian's hair stand on end, and many and many a night I have not closed my eyes in sleep for the awful things that are done here.' Mr Otis, however, and his wife warmly assured the honest soul that they were not afraid of ghosts, and, after invoking the blessings of Providence on her new master and mistress, and making arrangements for an increase of salary, the old housekeeper tottered off to her own room.

2

The storm raged fiercely all that night, but nothing of particular note occurred. The next morning, however, when they came down to breakfast, they found the terrible stain of blood once again on the floor. 'I don't think it can be the fault of the Paragon Detergent,' said Washington, 'for I have tried it with everything. It must be the ghost.' He accordingly rubbed out the stain a second time, but the second morning it appeared again. The third morning also it was there, though the library had been locked up at night by Mr Otis himself, and the key carried upstairs. The whole family were now quite interested; Mr Otis began to suspect that he had been too dogmatic in his denial of the existence of ghosts. Mrs Otis expressed her intention of joining the Psychical Society, and Washington prepared a long letter to Messrs Myers and Podmore on the subject of the Permanence of Sanguineous Stains when connected with Crime. That night all doubts about the objective existence of phantasmata were removed for ever.

The day had been warm and sunny; and, in the cool of the evening, the whole family went out for a drive. They did not return home till nine o'clock, when they had a light supper. The conversation in no way turned upon ghosts, so there were not even those primary conditions of receptive expectation which so often precede the presentation of psychical phenomena. The subjects discussed, as I have since learned from Mr Otis, were merely such as form the ordinary conversation of cultured Americans of the better class, such as the immense superiority of Miss Fanny Davenport over Sarah Bernhardt as an actress; the difficulty of obtaining green corn, buckwheat cakes, and hominy, even in the best English houses; the importance of Boston in the development of the world-soul; the advantages of the baggage check system in railway travelling; and the sweetness of the New York accent as compared to the London drawl. No mention at all was made of the supernatural, nor was Sir Simon de Canterville alluded to in any way. At eleven o'clock the family retired, and by half-past all the lights were out. Some time after, Mr Otis was awakened by a curious noise in the corridor, outside his room. It sounded like the clank of metal, and seemed to be coming nearer every moment. He got up at once, struck a match, and looked at the time. It was exactly one o'clock. He was quite calm, and felt his pulse, which was not at all feverish. The strange noise still continued, and with it he heard distinctly the sound of footsteps. He put on his slippers, took a small oblong phial out of his dressing-case, and opened the door. Right in front of him he saw, in the wan moonlight, an old man of terrible aspect. His eyes were as red burning coals; long grey hair fell over his shoulders in matted coils; his garments, which were of antique cut, were soiled and ragged, and from his wrists and ankles hung heavy manacles and rusty gyves.

'My dear sir,' said Mr Otis, 'I really must insist on your oiling those chains, and have brought you for that purpose a small bottle of the Tammany Rising Sun Lubricator. It is said to be completely efficacious upon one application, and there are several testimonials to that effect on the wrapper from some of our most eminent native divines. I shall leave it here for you by the bedroom candles, and will be happy to supply you with more should you require it.' With these words the United States Minister laid the bottle down on a marble table, and, closing his door, retired to rest.

For a moment the Canterville ghost stood quite motionless in natural indignation; then, dashing the bottle violently upon the polished floor, he fled down the corridor, uttering hollow groans, and emitting a ghastly green light. Just, however, as he reached the top of the great oak staircase, a door was flung open, two little white-robed figures appeared, and a large pillow whizzed past his head! There was evidently no time to be lost, so, hastily adopting the Fourth Dimension of Space as a means of escape, he vanished through the wainscoting, and the house became quite quiet.

On reaching a small secret chamber in the left wing, he leaned up against a moonbeam to recover his breath, and began to try and realize his position. Never, in a brilliant and uninterrupted career of three hundred years, had he been so grossly insulted. He thought of the Dowager Duchess, whom he had frightened into a fit as she stood before the glass in her lace and diamonds; of the four housemaids who had gone off into hysterics when he merely grinned at them through the curtains of one of the spare bedrooms; of the rector of the parish, whose candle he had blown out as he was coming late one night from the library, and who had been under the care of Sir William Gull ever since, a perfect martyr to nervous disorders; and of old Madame de Tremouillac, who, having wakened up one morning early and seen a skeleton seated in an arm-chair by the fire reading her diary, had been confined to her bed for six weeks with an attack of brain fever, and, on her recovery, had become reconciled to the Church, and broken off her connection with that notorious sceptic, Monsieur de Voltaire. He remembered the terrible night when the wicked Lord Canterville was found choking in his dressing-room, with the knave of diamonds halfway down his throat, and confessed, just before he died, that he had cheated Charles James Fox out of £50,000 at Crockford's by means of that very card, and swore that the ghost had made him swallow it. All his great achievements came back to him again, from the butler who had shot himself in the pantry because he had seen a green hand tapping at the window pane, to the beautiful Lady Stutfield, who was always obliged to wear a black velvet band round her throat to hide the mark of five fingers burnt upon her white skin, and who drowned herself at last in the carp-pond at the end of the King's Walk. With the enthusiastic egotism of the true artist he went over his most celebrated performances, and smiled bitterly to himself as he recalled to mind his last appearance as 'Red Reuben, or the Strangled Babe', his *début* as 'Gaunt Gibeon, the Blood-sucker of Bexley Moor', and the *furore* he had excited one lovely June evening by merely playing ninepins with his own bones upon the lawn-tennis ground. And after all this, some wretched modern Americans were to come and offer him the Rising Sun Lubricator, and throw pillows at his head! It was quite unbearable. Besides, no ghosts in history had ever been treated in this manner. Accordingly, he determined to have vengeance, and remained till daylight in an attitude of deep thought.

3

The next morning when the Otis family met at breakfast, they discussed the ghost at some length. The United States Minister was naturally a little annoyed to find that his present had not been accepted. 'I have no wish,' he said, 'to do the ghost any personal injury, and I must say that, considering the length of time he has been in the house, I don't think it is at all polite to throw pillows at him' – a very just remark, at which, I am sorry to say, the twins burst into shouts of laughter. 'Upon the other hand,' he continued, 'if he really declines to use the Rising Sun Lubricator, we shall have to take his chains from him. It would be quite impossible to sleep, with such a noise going on outside the bedrooms.'

For the rest of the week, however, they were undisturbed, the only thing that excited any attention being the continual renewal of the bloodstain on the library floor. This certainly was very strange, as the door was always locked at night by Mr Otis, and the windows kept closely barred. The chameleon-like colour, also, of the stain excited a good deal of comment. Some mornings it was a dull (almost Indian) red, then it would be vermilion, then a rich purple, and once when they came down for family prayers, according to the simple rites of the Free American Reformed Episcopalian Church, they found it a bright emerald-green. These kaleidoscopic changes naturally amused the party very much, and bets on the subject were freely made every evening. The only person who did not enter into the joke was little Virginia, who, for some unexplained reason, was always a good deal distressed at the sight of the bloodstain, and very nearly cried the morning it was emerald-green.

The second appearance of the ghost was on Sunday night. Shortly after they had gone to bed they were suddenly alarmed by a fearful crash in the hall. Rushing downstairs, they found that a large suit of old armour had become detached from its stand and had fallen on the stone floor, while, seated in a high-backed chair, was the Canterville ghost, rubbing his knees with an expression of acute agony on his face. The twins, having brought their pea-shooters with them, at once discharged two pellets on him, with that accuracy of aim which can only be attained by long and careful practice on a writing-master, while the United States Minister covered him with his revolver, and called upon him, in accordance with Californian etiquette, to hold up his hands! The ghost started up with a wild shriek of rage, and swept through them like a mist, extinguishing Washington Otis's candle as he passed, and so leaving them all in total darkness. On reaching the top of the staircase he recovered himself, and determined to give his celebrated peal of demoniac laughter. This he had on more than one occasion found extremely useful. It was said to have turned Lord Raker's wig grey in a single night, and had certainly made three of Lady Canterville's French governesses give warning before their month was up. He accordingly laughed his most horrible laugh, till the old vaulted roof rang and rang again, but hardly had the fearful echo died away when a door opened, and Mrs Otis came out in a light blue dressing-gown. 'I am afraid you are far from well,' she said, 'and have brought you a bottle of Dr Dobell's tincture. If it is indigestion, you will find it a most excellent remedy.' The ghost glared at her in fury, and began at once to make preparations for turning himself into a large black dog, an accomplishment for which he was justly renowned, and to which the family doctor always attributed the permanent idiocy of Lord Canterville's uncle, the Hon. Thomas Horton. The sound of approaching footsteps, however, made him hesitate in his fell purpose, so he contented himself with becoming faintly phosphorescent and vanished with a deep churchyard groan, just as the twins had come up to him.

On reaching his room he entirely broke down, and became a prey to the most violent agitation. The vulgarity of the twins, and the gross materialism of Mrs Otis were naturally extremely annoying, but what really distressed him most was that he had been unable to wear the suit of mail. He had hoped that even modern Americans would be thrilled by the sight of a Spectre In Armour, if for no more sensible reason, at least out of respect for their national poet, Longfellow, over whose graceful and attractive poetry he himself had whiled away many a weary hour when the Cantervilles were up in town. Besides, it was his own suit. He had worn it with great success at the Kenilworth tournament, and had been highly complimented on it by no less a person than the Virgin Queen herself. Yet when he had put it on, he had been completely overpowered by the weight of the huge breastplate and steel casque, and had fallen heavily on the stone pavement, barking both his knees severely, and bruising the knuckles of his right hand.

For some days after this he was extremely ill, and hardly stirred out of his room at all, except to keep the bloodstain in proper repair. However, by taking great care of himself, he recovered, and resolved to make a third attempt to frighten the United States Minister and his family. He selected Friday, the 17th of August, for his appearance, and spent most of that day in looking over his wardrobe, ultimately deciding in favour of a large slouched hat with a red feather, a winding sheet frilled at the wrists and neck, and a rusty dagger. Towards evening a violent storm of rain came on, and the wind was so high that all the windows and doors in the old house shook and rattled. In fact, it was just such weather as he loved. His plan of action was this. He was to make his way quietly to Washington Otis's room, gibber at him from the foot of the bed, and stab himself three times in the throat to the sound of slow music. He bore Washington a special grudge, being quite aware that it was he who was in the habit of removing the famous Canterville bloodstain, by means of Pinkerton's Paragon Detergent. Having reduced the reckless and foolhardy youth to a condition of abject terror, he was then to proceed to the room occupied by the United States Minister and his wife, and there to place a clammy hand on Mrs Otis's forehead, while he hissed into her trembling husband's ear the awful secrets of the charnel-house. With regard to little Virginia, he had not quite made up his mind. She had never insulted him in any way, and was pretty and gentle. A few hollow groans from the wardrobe, he thought, would be more than sufficient, or, if that failed to wake her, he might grabble at the counterpane with palsy-twitching fingers. As for the twins, he was quite determined to teach them a lesson. The first thing to be done was, of course, to sit upon their chests, so as to produce the stifling sensation of nightmare. Then, as their beds were quite close to each other, to stand between them in the form of a green, icy-cold corpse, till they became paralysed with fear, and finally, to throw off the winding-sheet and crawl round the room, with white bleached bones and one rolling eyeball in the character of 'Dumb Daniel, or the Suicide's Skeleton', a role in which he had on more than one occasion produced a great effect, and which he considered quite equal to his famous part of 'Martin the Maniac, or the Masked Mystery'.

At half-past ten he heard the family going to bed. For some time he was disturbed by wild shrieks of laughter from the twins, who, with the light-hearted gaiety of schoolboys, were evidently amusing themselves before they retired to rest, but at a quarter-past eleven all was still, and, as midnight sounded, he sallied forth. The owl beat against the window panes, the raven croaked from the old yew-tree, and the wind wandered moaning round the house like a lost soul; but the Otis family slept uncon-scious of their doom, and high above the rain and storm he could hear the steady snoring of the Minister for the United States. He stepped stealthily out of the wainscot-ing, with an evil smile on his cruel, wrinkled mouth, and the moon hid her face in a cloud as he stole past the great oriel window, where his own arms and those of his mur-dered wife were blazoned in azure and gold. On and on he glided, like an evil shadow, the very darkness seeming to loathe him as he passed. Once he thought he heard something call, and stopped; but it was only the baying of a dog from the Red Farm, and he went on, muttering strange sixteenth-century curses, and ever and anon brandishing the rusty dagger in the midnight air. Finally he reached the corner of the passage that led to luckless Washington's room. For a moment he paused there, the wind blowing his long grey locks about his head, and twisting into grotesque and fantastic folds the nameless horror of the dead man's shroud. Then the clock struck the quarter, and he felt the time was come. He chuckled to himself, and turned the corner; but no sooner had he done so than, with a piteous wail of terror, he fell back, and hid his blanched face in his long, bony hands. Right in front of him was standing a horrible spectre, motionless as a carven image, and monstrous as a madman's dream! Its head was bald and burnished; its face round, and fat, and white; and hideous laughter seemed to have writhed its features into an eternal grin. From the eyes streamed rays of scarlet light, the mouth was a wide well of fire, and a hideous garment, like to his own, swathed with its silent snows the Titan form. On its breast was a placard with strange writing in antique characters, some scroll of shame it seemed, some record of wild sins, some awful calendar of crime, and, with its right hand, it bore aloft a falchion of gleaming steel.

Never having seen a ghost before, he naturally was terribly frightened, and, after a second hasty glance at the awful phantom, he fled back to his room, tripping up in his long winding-sheet as he sped down the corridor, and finally dropping the rusty dagger into the Minister's jack-boots, where it was found in the morning by the butler. Once in the privacy of his own apartment, he flung himself down on a small pallet-bed, and hid his face under the clothes. After a time, however, the brave old Canterville spirit asserted itself, and he determined to go and speak to the other ghost as soon as it was daylight. Accordingly, just as the dawn was touching the hills with silver, he returned towards the spot where he had first laid eyes on the grisly phantom, feeling that, after all, two ghosts were better than one, and that, by the aid of his new friend, he might safely grapple with the twins. On reaching the spot, however, a terrible sight met his gaze. Something had evidently happened to the spectre, for the light had entirely faded from its hollow eyes, the gleaming falchion had fallen from its hand, and it was leaning up against the wall in a strained and uncomfortable attitude. He rushed forward and seized it in his arms, when, to his horror, the head slipped off and rolled on the floor, the body assumed a recumbent posture, and he found himself clasping a white dimity bed-curtain, with a sweeping-brush, a kitchen cleaver, and a hollow turnip lying at his feet! Unable to understand this curious transformation, he clutched the placard with feverish haste, and there, in the grey morning light, he read these fearful words:

𝔜𝔢 𝔒𝔗𝔌𝔖 𝔊𝔥𝔬𝔰𝔱𝔢.

𝔜𝔢 𝔒𝔫𝔩𝔦𝔢 𝔗𝔯𝔲𝔢 𝔞𝔫𝔡 𝔒𝔯𝔦𝔤𝔦𝔫𝔞𝔩𝔢 𝔖𝔭𝔬𝔬𝔨.

𝔅𝔢𝔴𝔞𝔯𝔢 𝔬𝔣 𝔜𝔢 𝔌𝔪𝔦𝔱𝔞𝔱𝔦𝔬𝔫𝔰.

𝔄𝔩𝔩 𝔬𝔱𝔥𝔢𝔯𝔰 𝔞𝔯𝔢 𝔆𝔬𝔲𝔫𝔱𝔢𝔯𝔣𝔢𝔦𝔱𝔢.

The whole thing flashed across him. He had been tricked, foiled, and outwitted! The old Canterville look came into his eyes; he ground his toothless gums together; and, raising his withered hands high above his head, swore, according to the picturesque phraseology of the antique school, that when Chanticleer had sounded twice his merry horn, deeds of blood would be wrought, and Murder walk abroad with silent feet.

Hardly had he finished this awful oath when, from the red-tiled roof of a distant homestead, a cock crew. He laughed a long, low, bitter laugh, and waited. Hour after hour he waited, but the cock, for some strange reason, did not crow again. Finally, at half-past seven, the arrival of the housemaids made him give up his fearful vigil, and he stalked back to his room, thinking of his vain hope and baffled purpose. There he consulted several books of ancient chivalry, of which he was exceedingly fond, and found that, on every occasion on which his oath had been used, Chanticleer had always crowed a second time. 'Perdition seize the naughty fowl,' he muttered. 'I have seen the day when, with my stout spear, I would have run him through the gorge, and made him crow for me an 'twere in death!' He then retired to a comfortable lead coffin, and stayed there till evening.

4

The next day the ghost was very weak and tired. The terrible excitement of the last four weeks was beginning to have its effect. His nerves were completely shattered, and he started at the slightest noise. For five days he kept his room, and at last made up his mind to give up the point of the bloodstain on the library floor. If the Otis family did not want it, they clearly did not deserve it. They were evidently people on a low, material plane of existence, and quite incapable of appreciating the symbolic value of sensuous phenomena. The question of phantasmic apparitions, and the development of astral bodies, was of course quite a different matter, and really not under his control.

It was his solemn duty to appear in the corridor once a week, and to gibber from the large oriel window on the first and third Wednesday in every month, and he did not see how he could honourably escape from his obligations. It is quite true that his life had been very evil, but, upon the other hand, he was most conscientious in all things connected with the supernatural. For the next three Saturdays, accordingly, he traversed the corridor as usual between midnight and three o'clock, taking every possible precaution against being either heard or seen. He removed his boots, trod as lightly as possible on the old worm-eaten boards, wore a large black velvet cloak, and was careful to use the Rising Sun Lubricator for oiling his chains. I am bound to acknowledge that it was with a good deal of difficulty that he brought himself to adopt this last mode of protection. However, one night, while the family were at dinner, he slipped into Mr Otis's bedroom and carried off the bottle. He felt a little humiliated at first, but afterwards was sensible enough to see that there was a great deal to be said for the invention, and, to a certain degree, it served his purpose. Still, in spite of everything, he was not left unmolested. Strings were continually being stretched across the corridor, over which he tripped in the dark, and on one occasion, while dressed for the part of 'Black Isaac, or the Huntsman of Hogley Woods', he met with a severe fall, through treading on a butter-slide, which the twins had constructed from the entrance of the Tapestry Chamber to the top of the oak staircase. This last insult so enraged him that he resolved to make one final effort to assert his dignity and social position, and determined to visit the insolent young Etonians the next night in his celebrated character of 'Reckless Rupert, or the Headless Earl'.

He had not appeared in this disguise for more than

seventy years; in fact, not since he had so frightened pretty Lady Barbara Modish by means of it that she suddenly broke off her engagement with the present Lord Canterville's grandfather, and ran away to Gretna Green with handsome Jack Castleton, declaring that nothing in the world would induce her to marry into a family that allowed such a horrible phantom to walk up and down the terrace at twilight. Poor Jack was afterwards shot in a duel by Lord Canterville on Wandsworth Common, and Lady Barbara died of a broken heart at Tunbridge Wells before the year was out, so, in every way, it had been a great success. It was, however, an extremely difficult 'make-up', if I may use such a theatrical expression in connection with one of the greatest mysteries of the supernatural, or, to employ a more scientific term, the higher-natural world, and it took him fully three hours to make his preparations. At last everything was ready, and he was very pleased with his appearance. The big leather riding-boots that went with the dress were just a little too large for him, and he could only find one of the two horse-pistols, but, on the whole, he was quite satisfied, and at a quarter-past one he glided out of the wainscoting and crept down the corridor. On reaching the room occupied by the twins, which I should mention was called the Blue Bed Chamber, on account of the colour of its hangings, he found the door just ajar. Wishing to make an effective entrance, he flung it wide open, when a heavy jug of water fell right down on him, wetting him to the skin and just missing his left shoulder by a couple of inches. At the same moment he heard stifled shrieks of laughter proceeding from the four-post bed. The shock to his nervous system was so great that he fled back to his room as hard as he could go, and the next day he was laid up with a severe cold. The only thing that at all consoled him in the whole affair was the fact that he had not brought his head with him, for, had he done so, the consequences might have been very serious.

He now gave up all hope of ever frightening this rude American family, and contented himself, as a rule, with creeping about the passages in list slippers, with a thick red muffler round his throat for fear of draughts, and a small arquebus, in case he should be attacked by the twins. The final blow he received occurred on the 19th of September. He had gone downstairs to the great entrance-hall, feeling sure that there, at any rate, he would be quite unmolested, and was amusing himself by making satirical remarks on the large Saroni photographs of the United States Minister and his wife, which had now taken the place of the Canterville family pictures. He was simply but neatly clad in a long shroud, spotted with churchyard mould, had tied up his jaw with a strip of yellow linen, and carried a small lantern and a sexton's spade. In fact, he was dressed for the character of 'Jonas the Graveless, or the Corpse-Snatcher of Chertsey Barn', one of his most remarkable impersonations, and one which the Cantervilles had every reason to remember, as it was the real origin of their quarrel with their neighbour, Lord Rufford. It was about a quarter-past two o'clock in the morning, and, as far as he could ascertain, no one was stirring. As he was strolling towards the library, however, to see if there were any traces left of the bloodstain, suddenly there leaped out on him from a dark corner two figures, who waved their arms wildly above their heads, and shrieked out 'Boo!' in his ear.

Seized with a panic, which, under the circumstances, was only natural, he rushed for the staircase, but found Washington Otis waiting for him there with the big garden-syringe; and being thus hemmed in by his enemies on every side, and driven almost to bay, he vanished into the great iron stove, which, fortunately for him, was not lit, and had to make his way home through the flues and chimneys, arriving at his own room in a terrible state of dirt, disorder, and despair.

After this he was not seen again on any nocturnal expedition. The twins lay in wait for him on several occasions, and strewed the passages with nutshells every night to the great annoyance of their parents and the servants, but it was of no avail. It was quite evident that his feelings were so wounded that he would not appear. Mr Otis consequently resumed his great work on the history of the Democratic Party, on which he had been engaged for some years; Mrs Otis organized a wonderful clambake, which amazed the whole county; the boys took to lacrosse, euchre, poker, and other American national games; and Virginia rode about the lanes on her pony, accompanied by the young Duke of Cheshire, who had come to spend the last week of his holidays at Canterville Chase. It was generally assumed that the ghost had gone away, and, in fact, Mr Otis wrote a letter to that effect to Lord Canterville, who, in reply, expressed his great pleasure at the news, and sent his best congratulations to the Minister's worthy wife.

The Otises, however, were deceived, for the ghost was still in the house, and though now almost an invalid, was by no means ready to let matters rest, particularly as he heard that among the guests was the young Duke of Cheshire, whose grand-uncle, Lord Francis Stilton, had once bet a hundred guineas with Colonel Carbury that he would play dice with the Canterville ghost, and was found the next morning lying on the floor of the card-room in such a helpless paralytic state that though he lived on to a great age, he was never able to say anything again but 'Double Sixes'. The story was well known at the time, though, of course, out of respect to the feelings of the two noble fami-

very nice of her brothers to starve me to death, though I did kill her.'

'Starve you to death? Oh, Mr Ghost, I mean Sir Simon, are you hungry? I have a sandwich in my case. Would you like it?'

'No, thank you, I never eat anything now; but it is very kind of you, all the same, and you are much nicer than the rest of your horrid, rude, vulgar, dishonest family.'

'Stop!' cried Virginia, stamping her foot, 'it is you who are rude, and horrid, and vulgar, and as for dishonesty, you know you stole the paints out of my box to try and furbish up that ridiculous bloodstain in the library. First you took all my reds, including the vermilion, and I couldn't do any more sunsets, then you took the emerald-green and the chrome-yellow, and finally I had nothing left but indigo and Chinese white, and could only do moonlight scenes, which are always depressing to look at, and not at all easy to paint. I never told on you, though I was very much annoyed, and it was most ridiculous, the whole thing; for who ever heard of emerald-green blood?'

'Well, really,' said the ghost, rather meekly, 'what was I to do? It is a very difficult thing to get real blood nowadays, and, as your brother began it all with his Paragon Detergent, I certainly saw no reason why I should not have your paints. As for colour, that is always a matter of taste: the Cantervilles have blue blood, for instance, the very bluest in England; but I know you Americans don't care for things of this kind.'

'You know nothing about it, and the best thing you can do is to emigrate and improve your mind. My father will be only too happy to give you a free passage, and though there is a heavy duty on spirits of every kind there will be no difficulty about the Custom House, as the officers are all Democrats. Once in New York, you are sure to be a great success. I know lots of people there who would give a hundred thousand dollars to have a grandfather, and much more than that to have a family ghost!'

'I don't think I should like America.'

'I suppose because we have no ruins and no curiosities,' said Virginia satirically.

'No ruins! no curiosities!' answered the ghost; 'You have your navy and your manners.'

'Good evening; I will go and ask papa to get the twins an extra week's holiday.'

'Please don't go, Miss Virginia,' he cried; 'I am so lonely and so unhappy, and I really don't know what to do. I want to go to sleep and I cannot.'

'That's quite absurd! You have merely to go to bed and blow out the candle. It is very difficult sometimes to keep awake, especially at church, but there is no difficulty at all about sleeping. Why, even babies know how to do that, and they are not very clever.'

'I have not slept for three hundred years,' he said sadly, and Virginia's beautiful blue eyes opened in wonder; 'for three hundred years I have not slept, and I am so tired.'

Virginia grew quite grave, and her little lips trembled like rose-leaves. She came towards him, and kneeling down at his side looked up into his old withered face.

'Poor, poor Ghost,' she murmured; 'have you no place where you can sleep?'

'Far away beyond the pine-woods,' he answered, in a low dreamy voice, 'there is a little garden. There the grass grows long and deep, there are the great white stars of the hemlock flower, there the nightingale sings all night long. All night long he sings, and the cold, crystal moon looks down, and the yew-tree spreads out its giant arms over the sleepers.'

Virginia's eyes grew dim with tears, and she hid her face in her hands.

'You mean the Garden of Death,' she whispered.

'Yes, Death. Death must be so beautiful. To lie in the soft brown earth, with the grasses waving over one's head, and listen to silence. To have no yesterday, and no tomorrow. To forget time, to forgive life, to be at peace. You can help me. You can open for me the portals of Death's house, for Love is always with you, and Love is stronger than Death is.'

Virginia trembled, a cold shudder ran through her, and for a few moments there was silence. She felt as if she was in a terrible dream.

Then the ghost spoke again, and his voice sounded like the sighing of the wind.

'Have you ever read the old prophecy on the library window?'

'Oh, often,' cried the little girl, looking up: 'I know it quite well. It is painted in curious black letters, and it is difficult to read. There are only six lines:

> 𝔚hen a golden girl can win
> 𝔓rayer from out the lips of sin,
> 𝔚hen the barren almond bears,
> 𝔄nd a little child gives away its tears,
> 𝔗hen shall all the house be still
> 𝔄nd peace come to 𝔆anterville.

But I don't know what they mean.'

'They mean,' he said sadly, 'that you must weep for me for my sins, because I have no tears, and pray with me for my soul, because I have no faith, and then, if you have always been sweet, and good, and gentle, the Angel of Death will have mercy on me. You will see fearful shapes in darkness, and wicked voices will whisper in your ear, but they will not harm you, for against the purity of a little child the powers of Hell cannot prevail.'

Virginia made no answer, and the ghost wrung his hands in wild despair as he looked down at her bowed golden head. Suddenly she stood up, very pale, and with a strange light in her eyes. 'I am not afraid,' she said firmly, 'and I will ask the Angel to have mercy on you.'

He rose from his seat with a faint cry of joy, and taking her hand bent over it with old-fashioned grace and kissed it. His fingers were as cold as ice, and his lips burned like fire, but Virginia did not falter as he led her across the dusky room. On the faded green tapestry were broidered little huntsmen. They blew their tasselled horns and with their tiny hands waved to her to go back. 'Go back, Virginia,' they cried, 'go back!' but the ghost clutched her hand more tightly, and she shut her eyes against them. Horrible animals with lizard tails and goggle eyes blinked at her from the carven chimneypiece and murmured 'Beware! little Virginia, beware! We may never see you again,' but the ghost glided on more swiftly, and Virginia did not listen. When they reached the end of the room he stopped, and muttered some words she could not understand. She opened her eyes and saw the wall slowly fading away like a mist and a great black cavern in front of her. A bitter cold wind swept round them and she felt something pulling at her dress. 'Quick, quick,' cried the ghost, 'or it will be too late,' and, in a moment, the wainscoting had closed behind them and the Tapestry Chamber was empty.

6

About ten minutes later the bell rang for tea, and, as Virginia did not come down, Mrs Otis sent up one of the footmen to tell her. After a little time he returned and said that he could not find Miss Virginia anywhere. As she was in the habit of going out to the garden every evening to get flowers for the dinner-table, Mrs Otis was not at all alarmed at first, but when six o'clock struck, and Virginia did not appear, she became really agitated and sent the boys out to look for her, while she herself and Mr Otis searched every room in the house. At half-past six the boys came back and said that they could find no trace of their sister anywhere. They were all now in the greatest state of excitement and did not know what to do, when Mr Otis suddenly remembered that, some few days before, he had given a band of gipsies permission to camp in the park. He accordingly at once set off for Blackell Hollow, where he knew they were, accompanied by his eldest son and two of the farm-servants. The little Duke of Cheshire, who was perfectly frantic with anxiety, begged hard to be allowed to go too, but Mr Otis would not allow him, as he was afraid there might be a scuffle. On arriving at the spot, however, he found that the gipsies had gone, and it was evident that their departure had been rather sudden, as the fire was still burning and some plates were lying on the grass. Having sent off Washington and the two men to scour the district, he ran home and despatched telegrams to all the police inspectors in the county, telling them to look out for a little girl who had been kidnapped by tramps or gipsies. He then ordered his horse to be brought round, and, after insisting on his wife and the three boys sitting down to dinner, rode off down the Ascot Road with a groom. He had hardly, however, gone a couple of miles when he heard somebody galloping after him, and, looking round, saw the little Duke coming up on his pony, with his face very flushed and no hat. 'I'm awfully sorry, Mr Otis,' gasped out the boy, 'but I can't eat any dinner as long as Virginia is lost. Please don't be angry with me; if you had let us be engaged last year there would never have been all this trouble. You won't send me back, will you? I can't go! I won't go!'

The Minister could not help smiling at the handsome young scapegrace, and was a good deal touched at his devotion to Virginia, so leaning down from his horse he patted him kindly on the shoulders, and said, 'Well, Cecil, if you won't go back I suppose you must come with me, but I must get you a hat at Ascot.'

'Oh, bother my hat! I want Virginia!' cried the little Duke, laughing, and they galloped on to the railway station. There Mr Otis inquired of the station-master if any one answering the description of Virginia had been seen on the platform, but could get no news of her. The station-master, however, wired up and down the line and assured him that a strict watch would be kept for her, and, after having bought a hat for the little Duke from a linen-draper, who was just putting up his shutters, Mr Otis rode off to Bexley, a village about four miles away, which he was told was a well-known haunt of the gipsies, as there was a large common next to it. Here they roused up the rural policeman, but could get no information from him, and, after riding all over the common, they turned their horses' heads homewards, and reached the Chase about eleven o'clock, dead-tired and almost heart-broken. They found Washington and the twins waiting for them at the gatehouse with lanterns, as the avenue was very dark. Not the slightest trace of Virginia had been discovered. The gipsies had been caught on Brockley meadows, but she was not with them, and they had explained their sudden departure by saying that they had mistaken the date of Chorton Fair and had gone off in a hurry for fear they might be late. Indeed, they had been quite distressed at hearing of Virginia's disappearance, as they were very grateful to Mr Otis for having allowed them to camp in his park, and four of their number had stayed behind to help in the search. The carp-pond had been dragged, and the whole Chase thoroughly gone over, but without any result. It was evident that, for that night at any rate, Virginia was lost to them; and it was in a state of the deepest depression that Mr Otis and the boys walked up to the house, the groom following behind with the two horses and the pony. In the hall they found a group of frightened servants, and lying on a sofa in the library was poor Mrs Otis, almost out of her mind with terror and anxiety, and having her forehead bathed with eau-de-cologne by the old housekeeper. Mr Otis at once insisted on her having something to eat and ordered up supper for the whole party. It was a melancholy meal, as hardly any one spoke, and even the twins were awestruck and subdued, as they were very fond of their sister. When they had finished, Mr Otis, in spite of the entreaties of the little Duke, ordered them all to bed, saying that nothing more could be done that night, and that he would telegraph in the morning to Scotland Yard for some detectives to be sent down immediately. Just as they were passing out of the dining-room, midnight began to boom from the clock tower, and when the last stroke sounded they heard a crash and a sudden shrill cry; a dreadful peal of thunder shook the house, a strain of unearthly music floated through the air, a panel at the top of the staircase flew back with a loud noise, and out on the landing, looking very pale and white, with a little casket in her hand, stepped Virginia. In a moment they had all rushed up to her. Mrs Otis clasped her passionately in her arms, the Duke smothered her with violent kisses, and the twins executed a wild war-dance round the group.

'Good heavens! child, where have you been?' said Mr Otis, rather angrily, thinking that she had been playing some foolish trick on them. 'Cecil and I have been riding all over the country looking for you, and your mother has been frightened to death. You must never play these practical jokes any more.'

'Except on the ghost! Except on the ghost!' shrieked the twins, as they capered about.

'My own darling, thank God you are found; you must never leave my side again,' murmured Mrs Otis, as she kissed the trembling child, and smoothed the tangled gold of her hair.

'Papa,' said Virginia quietly, 'I have been with the ghost. He is dead, and you must come and see him. He had been very wicked, but he was really sorry for all that he had done, and he gave me this box of beautiful jewels before he died.'

The whole family gazed at her in mute amazement, but she was quite grave and serious; and, turning round, she led them through the opening in the wainscoting down a narrow secret corridor, Washington following with a lighted candle which he had caught up from the table. Finally they came to a great oak door, studded with rusty nails. When Virginia touched it, it swung back on its heavy hinges, and they found themselves in a little low room, with a vaulted ceiling, and one tiny grated window. Imbedded in the wall was a huge iron ring, and chained to it was a gaunt skeleton that was stretched out at full length on the stone floor, and seemed to be trying to grasp with its long fleshless fingers an old-fashioned trencher and ewer that were placed just out of its reach. The jug had evidently been once filled with water, as it was covered inside with green mould. There was nothing on the trencher but a pile of dust. Virginia knelt down beside the skeleton, and, folding her little hands together, began to pray silently, while the rest of the party looked on in wonder at the terrible tragedy whose secret was now disclosed to them.

'Hallo!' suddenly exclaimed one of the twins, who had been looking out of the window to try and discover in what wing of the house the room was situated. 'Hallo! the old withered almond-tree has blossomed. I can see the flowers quite plainly in the moonlight.'

'God has forgiven him,' said Virginia gravely, as she rose to her feet, and a beautiful light seemed to illumine her face.

'What an angel you are!' cried the young Duke, and he put his arm round her neck and kissed her.

7

Four days after these curious incidents a funeral started from Canterville Chase at about eleven o'clock at night. The hearse was drawn by eight black horses, each of which carried on its head a great tuft of nodding ostrich-plumes, and the leaden coffin was covered by a rich purple pall, on which was embroidered in gold the Canterville coat-of-arms. By the side of the hearse and the coaches walked the servants with lighted torches, and the whole procession was wonderfully impressive. Lord Canterville was the chief mourner, having come up specially from Wales to attend the funeral, and sat in the first carriage along with little Virginia. Then came the United States Minister and his wife, then Washington and the three boys, and in the last carriage was Mrs Umney. It was generally felt that, as she had been frightened by the ghost for more than fifty years of her life, she had a right to see the last of him. A deep grave had been dug in the corner of the churchyard, just under the old yew-tree, and the service was read in the most impressive manner by the Reverend Augustus Dampier. When the ceremony was over, the servants, according to an old custom observed in the Canterville family, extinguished their torches, and, as the coffin was being lowered into the grave, Virginia stepped forward and laid on it a large cross made of white and pink almond-blossoms. As she did so, the moon came out from behind a cloud, and flooded with its silent silver the little church-yard, and from a distant copse a nightingale began to sing. She thought of the ghost's description of the Garden of Death, her eyes became dim with tears, and she hardly spoke a word during the drive home.

The next morning, before Lord Canterville went up to town, Mr Otis had an interview with him on the subject of the jewels the ghost had given to Virginia. They were perfectly magnificent, especially a certain ruby necklace with old Venetian setting, which was really a superb specimen of sixteenth-century work, and their value was so great that Mr Otis felt considerable scruples about allowing his daughter to accept them.

'My lord,' he said, 'I know that in this country mortmain is held to apply to trinkets as well as to land, and it is quite clear to me that these jewels are, or should be, heirlooms in your family. I must beg you, accordingly, to take them to London with you and to regard them simply as a portion of your property which has been restored to you under certain strange conditions. As for my daughter, she is merely a child, and has yet, I am glad to say, but little interest in such appurtenances of idle luxury. I am also informed by Mrs Otis, who, I may say, is no mean authority upon Art – having had the privilege of spending several winters in Boston when she was a girl – that these gems are of great monetary worth, and if offered for sale would fetch a tall price. Under these circumstances, Lord Canterville, I feel sure that you will recognize how impossible it would be for me to allow them to remain in the possession of any member of my family; and, indeed, all such vain gauds and toys, however suitable or necessary to the dignity of the British aristocracy, would be completely out of place among those who have been brought up on the severe and I believe immortal principles of republican simplicity. Perhaps I should mention that Virginia is very anxious that you should allow her to retain the box as a memento of your unfortunate but misguided ancestor. As it is extremely old, and consequently a good deal out of repair, you may perhaps think fit to comply with her request. For my own part, I confess I am a good deal surprised to find a child of mine expressing sympathy with medievalism in any form, and can only account for it by the fact that Virginia was born in one of your London suburbs shortly after Mrs Otis had returned from a trip to Athens.'

Lord Canterville listened very gravely to the worthy Minister's speech, pulling his grey moustache now and then to hide an involuntary smile, and when Mr Otis had ended, he shook him cordially by the hand and said, 'My dear sir, your charming little daughter rendered my unlucky ancestor, Sir Simon, a very important service, and I and my family are much indebted to her for her marvellous courage and pluck. The jewels are clearly hers and, egad, I believe that if I were heartless enough to take them from her, the wicked old fellow would be out of his grave in a fortnight, leading me the devil of a life. As for their being heirlooms, nothing is an heirloom that is not so mentioned in a will or legal document, and the existence of these jewels has been quite unknown. I assure you I have no more claim on them than your butler, and when Miss Virginia grows up I daresay she will be pleased to have pretty things to wear. Besides, you forget, Mr Otis, that you took the furniture and the ghost at a valuation, and anything that belonged to the ghost passed at once into your possession, as, whatever activity Sir Simon may have shown in the corridor at night, in point of law he was really dead, and you acquired his property by purchase.'

Mr Otis was a good deal distressed at Lord Canterville's refusal, and begged him to reconsider his decision, but the good-natured peer was quite firm, and finally induced the Minister to allow his daughter to retain the present the ghost had given her, and when, in the spring of 1890, the young Duchess of Cheshire was presented at the Queen's first drawing-room on the occasion of her marriage, her jewels were the universal theme of admiration. For Virginia received the coronet, which is the reward of all good little American girls, and was married to her boy-lover as soon as he came of age. They were both so charming and they loved each other so much, that every one was delighted at the match, except the old Marchioness of Dumbleton, who had tried to catch the Duke for one of her seven unmarried daughters, and had given no less than three expensive dinner-parties for that purpose, and, strange to say, Mr Otis himself. Mr Otis was extremely fond of the young Duke personally, but, theoretically, he objected to titles and, to use his own words, 'was not without apprehension lest, amid the enervating influences of a pleasure-loving aristocracy, the true principles of republican simplicity should be forgotten.' His objections, however, were completely overruled, and I believe that when he walked up the aisle of St George's, Hanover Square, with his daughter leaning on his arm, there was not a prouder man in the whole length and breadth of England.

The Duke and Duchess, after the honeymoon was over, went down to Canterville Chase, and on the day after their arrival they walked over in the afternoon to the lonely churchyard by the pine-woods. There had been a great deal of difficulty at first about the inscription on Sir Simon's tombstone, but finally it had been decided to engrave on it simply the initials of the old gentleman's name, and the verse from the library window. The Duchess had brought with her some lovely roses, which she strewed upon the grave, and after they had stood by it for some time they strolled into the ruined chancel of the old abbey. There the Duchess sat down on a fallen pillar, while her husband lay at her feet smoking a cigarette and looking up at her beautiful eyes. Suddenly he threw his cigarette away, took hold of her hand, and said to her, 'Virginia, a wife should have no secrets from her husband.'

'Dear Cecil! I have no secrets from you.'

'Yes, you have,' he answered, smiling, 'you have never told me what happened to you when you were locked up with the ghost.'

'I have never told any one, Cecil,' said Virginia gravely.

'I know that, but you might tell me.'

'Please don't ask me, Cecil, I cannot tell you. Poor Sir Simon! I owe him a great deal. Yes, don't laugh, Cecil, I really do. He made me see what Life is, and what Death signifies, and why Love is stronger than both.'

The Duke rose and kissed his wife lovingly.

'You can have your secret as long as I have your heart,' he murmured.

'You have always had that, Cecil.'

'And you will tell our children some day, won't you?' Virginia blushed.

Anonymous

Teeny-Tiny

ONCE upon a time there was a teeny-tiny woman lived in a teeny-tiny house in a teeny-tiny village. Now, one day this teeny-tiny woman put on her teeny-tiny bonnet, and went out of her teeny-tiny house to take a teeny-tiny walk. And when this teeny-tiny woman had gone a teeny-tiny way she came to a teeny-tiny gate; so the teeny-tiny woman opened the teeny-tiny gate, and went into a teeny-tiny churchyard. And when this teeny-tiny woman had got into the teeny-tiny churchyard, she saw a teeny-tiny bone on a teeny-tiny grave, and the teeny-tiny woman said to her teeny-tiny self, 'This teeny-tiny bone will make me some teeny-tiny soup for my teeny-tiny supper.' So the teeny-tiny woman put the teeny-tiny bone into her teeny-tiny pocket, and went home to her teeny-tiny house.

Now when the teeny-tiny woman got home to her teeny-tiny house she was teeny-tiny tired; so she went up her teeny-tiny stairs to her teeny-tiny bed, and put the teeny-tiny bone into a teeny-tiny cupboard. And when this teeny-tiny woman had been to sleep a teeny-tiny time, she was awakened by a teeny-tiny voice from the teeny-tiny cupboard, which said:

'Give me my bone!'

And this teeny-tiny woman was a teeny-tiny frightened, so she hid her teeny-tiny head under the teeny-tiny clothes and went to sleep again. And when she had been to sleep

48

again a teeny-tiny time, the teeny-tiny voice again cried out from the teeny-tiny cupboard a teeny-tiny louder,

'GIVE ME MY BONE!'

This made the teeny-tiny woman a teeny-tiny more frightened, so she hid her teeny-tiny head a teeny-tiny further under the teeny-tiny clothes. And when the teeny-tiny woman had been to sleep again a teeny-tiny time, the teeny-tiny voice from the teeny-tiny cupboard said again a teeny-tiny louder,

'GIVE ME MY BONE!'

And this teeny-tiny woman was a teeny-tiny bit more frightened, but she put her teeny-tiny head out of the teeny-tiny clothes, and said in her loudest teeny-tiny voice, 'TAKE IT!'

Charles Dickens

The Signal-Man

from ALL THE YEAR ROUND, 1866

'HALLOA! Below there!'

When he heard a voice thus calling to him, he was standing at the door of his box, with a flag in his hand, furled round its short pole. One would have thought, considering the nature of the ground, that he could not have doubted from what quarter the voice came; but, instead of looking up to where I stood on the top of the steep cutting nearly over his head, he turned himself about and looked down the line. There was something remarkable in his manner of doing so, though I could not have said, for my life, what. But, I know it was remarkable enough to attract my notice, even though his figure was foreshortened and shadowed, down in the deep trench, and mine was high above him, so steeped in the glow of an angry sunset that I had shaded my eyes with my hand before I saw him at all.

'Halloa! Below!'

From looking down the line, he turned himself about again, and, raising his eyes, saw my figure high above him.

'Is there any path by which I can come down and speak to you?'

He looked up at me without replying, and I looked down at him without pressing him too soon with a repetition of my idle question. Just then, there came a vague vibration in the earth and air, quickly changing into a violent pulsation, and an oncoming rush that caused me to start back, as though it had force to draw me down. When such vapour as rose to my height from this rapid train, had passed me and was skimming away over the landscape, I looked down again, and saw him re-furling the flag he had shown while the train went by.

I repeated my inquiry. After a pause, during which he seemed to regard me with fixed attention, he motioned with his rolled-up flag towards a point on my level, some two or three hundred yards distant. I called down to him, 'All right!' and made for that point. There, by dint of looking closely about me, I found a rough zig-zag descending path notched out: which I followed.

The cutting was extremely deep, and unusually precipitate. It was made through a clammy stone that became oozier and wetter as I went down. For these reasons, I found the way long enough to give me time to recall a singular air of reluctance or compulsion with which he had pointed out the path.

When I came down low enough upon the zig-zag descent, to see him again, I saw that he was standing between the rails on the way by which the train had lately passed, in an attitude as if he were waiting for me to appear. He had his left hand at his chin, and that left elbow rested on his right hand crossed over his breast. His attitude was one of such expectation and watchfulness, that I stopped for a moment, wondering at it.

I resumed my downward way, and, stepping out upon the level of the railroad and drawing nearer to him, saw that he was a dark sallow man, with a dark beard and rather heavy eyebrows. His post was in as solitary and dismal a place as ever I saw. On either side, a dripping-wet wall of jagged stone, excluding all view but a strip of sky; the perspective one way, only a crooked prolongation of this great dungeon; the shorter perspective in the other direction, terminating in a gloomy red light, and the gloomier entrance to a black tunnel, in whose massive architecture there was a barbarous, depressing, and forbidding air. So little sunlight ever found its way to this spot, that it had an earthy deadly smell; and so much cold wind rushed through it, that it struck chill to me, as if I had left the natural world.

Before he stirred, I was near enough to him to have touched him. Not even then removing his eyes from mine, he stepped back one step, and lifted his hand.

This was a lonesome post to occupy (I said), and it had riveted my attention when I looked down from up yonder. A visitor was a rarity, I should suppose; not an unwelcome rarity, I hoped? In me, he merely saw a man who had been shut up within narrow limits all his life, and who, being at last set free, had a newly-awakened interest in these great works. To such purpose I spoke to him; but I am far from sure of the terms I used, for, besides that I am not happy in opening any conversation, there was something in the man that daunted me.

He directed a most curious look towards the red light near the tunnel's mouth, and looked all about it, as if something were missing from it, and then looked at me.

That light was part of his charge? Was it not?

He answered in a low voice: 'Don't you know it is?'

The monstrous thought came into my mind as I perused the fixed eyes and the saturnine face, that this was a spirit, not a man. I have speculated since, whether there may have been infection in his mind.

In my turn, I stepped back. But in making the action, I detected in his eyes some latent fear of me. This put the monstrous thought to flight.

'You look at me,' I said, forcing a smile, 'as if you had a dread of me.'

'I was doubtful,' he returned, 'whether I had seen you before.'

'Where?'

He pointed to the red light he had looked at.

'There?' I said.

Intently watchful of me, he replied (but without sound), Yes.

'My good fellow, what should I do there? However, be that as it may, I never was there, you may swear.'

'I think I may,' he rejoined. 'Yes. I am sure I may.'

His manner cleared, like my own. He replied to my remarks with readiness, and in well-chosen words. Had he much to do there? Yes; that was to say, he had enough responsibility to bear; but exactness and watchfulness were what was required of him, and of actual work — manual labour he had next to none. To change that signal, to trim those lights, and to turn this iron handle now and then, was all he had to do under that head. Regarding those many long and lonely hours of which I seemed to make so much, he could only say that the routine of his life had shaped itself into that form, and he had grown used to it. He had taught himself a language down here — if only to know it by sight, and to have formed his own crude ideas of its pronunciation, could be called learning it. He had also worked at fractions and decimals, and tried a little algebra; but he was, and had been as a boy, a poor hand at figures. Was it necessary for him when on duty, always to remain in that channel of damp air, and could he never rise into the sunshine from between those high stone walls? Why, that depended upon times and circumstances. Under some conditions there would be less upon the line than under others, and the same held good as to certain hours of the day and night. In bright weather, he did choose occasions for getting a little above these lower shadows; but, being at all times liable to be called by his electric bell, and at such times listening for it with re-doubled anxiety, the relief was less than I would suppose.

He took me into his box, where there was a fire, a desk for an official book in which he had to make certain entries, a telegraphic instrument with its dial face and needles, and the little bell of which he had spoken. On my trusting that he would excuse the remark that he had been well-educated, and (I hoped I might say without offence) perhaps educated above that station, he observed that instances of slight incongruity in such-wise would rarely be found wanting among large bodies of men; that he had heard it was so in workhouses, in the police force, even in that last desperate resource, the army; and that he knew it was so, more or less, in any great railway staff. He had been, when young (if I could believe it, sitting in that hut; he scarcely could), a student of natural philosophy, and had attended lectures; but he had run wild, misused his opportunities, gone down, and never risen again. He had no complaint to offer about that. He had made his bed, and he lay upon it. It was far too late to make another.

All that I have here condensed, he said in a quiet manner, with his grave dark regards divided between me and the fire. He threw in the word 'Sir' from time to time, and especially when he referred to his youth: as though to request me to understand that he claimed to be nothing but what I found him. He was several times interrupted by the little bell, and had to read off messages, and send replies. Once, he had to stand without the door, and display a flag as a train passed, and make some verbal communication to the driver. In the discharge of his duties I observed him to be remarkably exact and vigilant, breaking off his discourse at a syllable, and remaining silent until what he had to do was done.

In a word, I should have set this man down as one of the safest of men to be employed in that capacity, but for the circumstance that while he was speaking to me he twice broke off with a fallen colour, turned his face towards the little bell when it did *not* ring, opened the door of the hut (which was kept shut to exclude the unhealthy damp), and looked out towards the red light near the mouth of the tunnel. On both of those occasions, he came back to the fire with the inexplicable air upon him which I had remarked, without being able to define, when we were so far asunder.

Said I when I rose to leave him: 'You almost make me think that I have met with a contented man.'

(I am afraid I must acknowledge that I said it to lead him on.)

'I believe I used to be so,' he rejoined, in the low voice in which he had first spoken; 'but I am troubled, sir, I am troubled.'

He would have recalled the words if he could. He had said them, however, and I took them up quickly.

'With what? What is your trouble?'

'It is very difficult to impart, sir. It is very, very difficult to speak of. If ever you make me another visit, I will try to tell you.'

'But I expressly intend to make you another visit. Say, when shall it be?'

'I go off early in the morning, and I shall be on again at ten tomorrow night, sir.'

'I will come at eleven.'

He thanked me, and went out at the door with me. 'I'll show my white light, sir,' he said, in his peculiar low voice, 'till you have found the way up. When you have found it, don't call out! And when you are at the top, don't call out!'

His manner seemed to make the place strike colder to me, but I said no more than 'Very well.'

'And when you come down tomorrow night, don't call out! Let me ask you a parting question. What made you cry "Halloa! Below there!" tonight?'

'Heaven knows,' said I. 'I cried something to that effect . . .'

'Not to that effect, sir. Those were the very words. I know them well.'

'Admit those were the very words. I said them, no doubt, because I saw you below.'

'For no other reason?'

'What other reason could I possibly have!'

'You had no feeling that they were conveyed to you in any supernatural way?'

'No.'

He wished me goodnight, and held up his light. I walked by the side of the down line of rails (with a very disagreeable sensation of a train coming behind me), until I found the path. It was easier to mount than to descend, and I got back to my inn without any adventure.

Punctual to my appointment, I placed my foot on the first notch of the zig-zag next night, as the distant clocks were striking eleven. He was waiting for me at the bottom, with his white light on. 'I have not called out,' I said, when we came close together; 'may I speak now?' 'By all means, sir.' 'Goodnight then, and here's my hand.' 'Goodnight, sir, and here's mine.' With that, we walked side by side to his box, entered it, closed the door, and sat down by the fire.

'I have made up my mind, sir,' he began, bending forward as soon as we were seated, and speaking in a tone but a little above a whisper, 'that you shall not have to ask me twice what troubles me. I took you for someone else yesterday evening. That troubles me.'

'That mistake?'

'No. That someone else.'

'Who is it?'

'I don't know.'

'Like me?'

'I don't know. I never saw the face. The left arm is across the face, and the right arm is waved. Violently waved. This way.'

I followed his action with my eyes, and it was the action of an arm gesticulating with the utmost passion and vehemence: 'For God's sake clear the way!'

'One moonlight night,' said the man, 'I was sitting here, when I heard a voice cry "Halloa! Below there!" I started up, looked from that door, and saw this Someone else standing by the red light near the tunnel, waving as I just now showed you. The voice seemed hoarse with shouting, and it cried, "Look out! Look out!" And then again "Halloa! Below there! Look out!" I caught up my lamp, turned it on red, and ran towards the figure, calling, "What's wrong? What has happened? Where?" It stood just outside the blackness of the tunnel. I advanced so close upon it that I wondered at its keeping the sleeve across its eyes. I ran right up at it, and had my hand stretched out to pull the sleeve away, when it was gone.'

'Into the tunnel,' said I.

'No. I ran on into the tunnel, five hundred yards. I stopped and held my lamp above my head, and saw the figures of the measured distance, and saw the wet stains stealing down the walls and trickling through the arch. I ran out again, faster than I had run in (for I had a mortal abhorrence of the place upon me), and I looked all round the red light with my own red light, and I went up the iron ladder to the gallery atop of it, and I came down again, and ran back here. I telegraphed both ways, "An alarm has been given. Is anything wrong?" The answer came back, both ways: "All well."'

Resisting the slow touch of a frozen finger tracing out my spine, I showed him how that this figure must be a deception of his sense of sight, and how that figures, originating in disease of the delicate nerves that minister to the functions of the eye, were known to have often troubled patients, some of whom had become conscious of the nature of their affliction, and had even proved it by experiments upon themselves. 'As to an imaginary cry,' said I, 'do but listen for a moment to the wind in this unnatural valley while we speak so low, and to the wild harp it makes of the telegraph wires!'

That was all very well, he returned, after we had sat listening for a while, and he ought to know something of the wind and the wires, he who so often passed long winter nights there, alone and watching. But he would beg to remark that he had not finished.

I asked his pardon, and he slowly added these words, touching my arm:

'Within six hours after the Appearance, the memorable accident on this line happened, and within ten hours the dead and wounded were brought along through the tunnel over the spot where the figure had stood.'

A disagreeable shudder crept over me, but I did my best against it. It was not to be denied, I rejoined, that this was a remarkable coincidence, calculated deeply to impress his mind. But it was unquestionable that remarkable coincidences did continually occur, and they must be taken into account in dealing with such a subject. Though to be sure I must admit, I added (for I thought I saw that he was going to bring the objection to bear upon me), men of common sense did not allow much for coincidences in making the ordinary calculations of life.

He again begged to remark that he had not finished.

I again begged his pardon for being betrayed into interruptions.

'This,' he said, again laying his hand upon my arm, and glancing over his shoulder with hollow eyes, 'was just a year ago. Six or seven months passed, and I had recovered from the surprise and shock, when one morning, as the day was breaking, I, standing at that door, looked towards the red light, and saw the spectre again.' He stopped, with a fixed look at me.

'Did it cry out?'

'No. It was silent.'

'Did it wave its arm?'

'No. It leaned against the shaft of the light, with both hands before the face. Like this.'

Once more, I followed his action with my eyes. It was an action of mourning. I have seen such an attitude in stone figures on tombs.

'Did you go up to it?'

'I came in and sat down, partly to collect my thoughts, partly because it had turned me faint. When I went to the door again, daylight was above me, and the ghost was gone.'

'But nothing followed? Nothing came of this?'

He touched me on the arm with his forefinger twice or thrice, giving a ghastly nod each time:

'That very day, as a train came out of the tunnel, I noticed, at a carriage window on my side, what looked like a confusion of hands and heads, and something waved. I saw it, just in time to signal the driver, Stop! He shut off, and put his brake on, but the train drifted past here a hundred and fifty yards or more. I ran after it, and, as I went along, heard terrible screams and cries. A beautiful young lady had died instantaneously in one of the compartments, and was brought in here, and laid down on this floor between us.'

Involuntarily, I pushed my chair back, as I looked from the boards at which he pointed, to himself.

'True, sir. True. Precisely as it happened, so I tell it you.'

I could think of nothing to say, to any purpose, and my mouth was very dry. The wind and the wires took up the story with a long lamenting wail.

He resumed. 'Now, sir, mark this, and judge how my mind is troubled. The spectre came back, a week ago. Ever since, it has been there, now and again, by fits and starts.'

'At the light?'

'At the danger-light.'

'What does it seem to do?'

He repeated, if possible with increased passion and vehemence, that former gesticulation of 'For God's sake clear the way!'

Then, he went on. 'I have no peace or rest for it. It calls to me, for many minutes together, in an agonized manner, "Below there! Look out! Look out!" It stands waving to me. It rings my little bell . . .'

I caught at that. 'Did it ring your bell yesterday evening when I was here, and you went to the door?'

'Twice.'

'Why, see,' said I, 'how your imagination misleads you. My eyes were on the bell, and my ears were open to the bell, and if I am a living man, it did *not* ring at those times. No, nor at any other time, except when it was rung in the natural course of physical things by the station communicating with you.'

He shook his head. 'I have never made a mistake as to that, yet, sir. I have never confused the spectre's ring with the man's. The ghost's ring is a strange vibration in the bell that it derives from nothing else, and I have not asserted that the bell stirs to the eye. I don't wonder that you failed to hear it. But *I* heard it.'

'And did the spectre seem to be there, when you looked out?'

'It *was* there.'

'Both times?'

He repeated firmly: 'Both times.'

'Will you come to the door with me, and look for it now?'

He bit his under-lip as though he were somewhat unwilling, but arose. I opened the door, and stood on the step, while he stood in the doorway. There, was the danger-light. There, was the dismal mouth of the tunnel. There, were the high wet stone walls of the cutting. There, were the stars above them.

'Do you see it?' I asked him, taking particular note of his face. His eyes were prominent and strained; but not very much more so, perhaps, than my own had been when I had directed them earnestly towards the same spot.

'No,' he answered. 'It is not there.'

'Agreed,' said I.

We went in again, shut the door, and resumed our seats. I was thinking how best to improve this advantage, if it might be called one, when he took up the conversation in such a matter of course way, so assuming that there could be no serious question of fact between us, that I felt myself placed in the weakest of positions.

'By this time you will fully understand, sir,' he said, 'that what troubles me so dreadfully, is the question, What does the spectre mean?'

I was not sure, I told him, that I did fully understand.

'What is its warning against?' he said, ruminating, with his eyes on the fire, and only by times turning them on me. 'What is the danger? Where is the danger? There is danger overhanging, somewhere on the line. Some dreadful calamity will happen. It is not to be doubted this third time, after what has gone before. But surely this is a cruel haunting of *me*. What can *I* do?'

He pulled out his handkerchief, and wiped the drops from his heated forehead.

'If I telegraph Danger, on either side of me, or on both, I can give no reason for it,' he went on, wiping the palms of his hands. 'I should get into trouble, and do no good. They would think I was mad. This is the way it would work: – Message: "Danger! Take care!" Answer: "What danger? Where?" Message: "Don't know. But for God's sake take care!" They would displace me. What else could they do?'

His pain of mind was most pitiable to see. It was the mental torture of a conscientious man, oppressed beyond endurance by an unintelligible responsibility involving life.

'When it first stood under the danger-light,' he went on, putting his dark hair back from his head, and drawing his hands outward across and across his temples in an extremity of feverish distress, 'why not tell me where that accident was to happen – if it must happen? Why not tell me how it could be averted – if it could have been averted? When on its second coming it hid its face, why not tell me instead: "She is going to die. Let them keep her at home"? If it came, on those two occasions, only to show me that its warnings were true, and so to prepare me for the third, why not warn me plainly now? And I, Lord help me! A mere poor signal-man on this solitary station! Why not go to somebody with credit to be believed, and power to act!'

When I saw him in this state, I saw that for the poor man's sake, as well as for the public safety, what I had to do for the time was to compose his mind. Therefore, setting aside all question of reality or unreality between us, I represented to him that whoever thoroughly discharged his duty, must do well, and that at least it was his comfort that he understood his duty, though he did not understand these confounding Appearances. In this effort I succeeded far better than in the attempt to reason him out of his conviction. He became calm; the occupations incidental to his post as the night advanced, began to make larger demands on his attention; and I left him at two in the morning. I had offered to stay through the night, but he would not hear of it.

That I more than once looked back at the red light as I ascended the pathway, that I did not like the red light, and that I should have slept but poorly if my bed had been under it, I see no reason to conceal. Nor did I like the two sequences of the accident and the dead girl. I see no reason to conceal that, either.

But, what ran most in my thoughts was the consideration how ought I to act, having become the recipient of this disclosure? I had proved the man to be intelligent, vigilant, painstaking, and exact; but how long might he remain so, in his state of mind? Though in a subordinate position, still he held a most important trust, and would I (for instance) like to stake my own life on the chances of his continuing to execute it with precision?

Unable to overcome a feeling that there would be something treacherous in my communicating what he had told me to his superiors in the Company, without first being plain with himself and proposing a middle course to him,

I ultimately resolved to offer to accompany him (otherwise keeping his secret for the present) to the wisest medical practitioner we could hear of in those parts, and to take his opinion. A change in his time of duty would come round next night, he had apprised me, and he would be off an hour or two after sunrise, and on again soon after sunset. I had appointed to return accordingly.

Next evening was a lovely evening, and I walked out early to enjoy it. The sun was not yet quite down when I traversed the field-path near the top of the deep cutting. I would extend my walk for an hour, I said to myself, half an hour on and half an hour back, and it would then be time to go to my signal-man's box.

Before pursuing my stroll, I stepped to the brink, and mechanically looked down, from the point from which I had first seen him. I cannot describe the thrill that seized upon me, when, close at the mouth of the tunnel, I saw the appearance of a man, with his left sleeves across his eyes, passionately waving his right arm.

The nameless horror that oppressed me passed in a moment, for in a moment I saw that this appearance of a man was a man indeed, and that there was a little group of other men standing at a short distance, to whom he seemed to be rehearsing the gesture he made. The danger-light was not yet lighted. Against its shaft, a little low hut, entirely new to me, had been made of some wooden supports and tarpaulin. It looked no bigger than a bed.

With an irresistible sense that something was wrong – with a flashing self-reproachful fear that fatal mischief had come of my leaving the man there, and causing no one to be sent to overlook or correct what he did – I descended the notched path with all the speed I could make.

'What is the matter?' I asked the men.

'Signal-man killed this morning, sir.'

'Not the man belonging to that box?'

'Yes, sir.'

'Not the man I know?'

'You will recognize him, sir, if you knew him,' said the man who spoke for the others, solemnly uncovering his own head and raising an end of the tarpaulin, 'for his face is quite composed.'

'Oh! how did this happen, how did this happen?' I asked, turning from one to another as the hut closed in again.

'He was cut down by an engine, sir. No man in England knew his work better. But somehow he was not clear of the outer rail. It was just at broad day. He had struck the light, and had the lamp in his hand. As the engine came out of the tunnel, his back was towards her, and she cut him down. That man drove her, and was showing how it happened. Show the gentleman, Tom.'

The man, who wore a rough dark dress, stepped back to his former place at the mouth of the tunnel!

'Coming round the curve in the tunnel, sir,' he said, 'I saw him at the end, like as if I saw him down a perspective-glass. There was no time to check speed, and I knew him to be very careful. As he didn't seem to take heed of the whistle, I shut it off when we were running down upon him, and called to him as loud as I could call.'

'What did you say?'

'I said, Below there! Look out! Look out! For God's sake clear the way!'

I started.

'Ah! it was a dreadful time, sir. I never left off calling to him. I put this arm before my eyes, not to see, and I waved this arm to the last; but it was no use.'

Without prolonging the narrative to dwell on any one

of its curious circumstances more than on any other, I may, in closing it, point out the coincidence that the warning of the Engine-driver included, not only the words which the unfortunate Signal-man had repeated to me as haunting him, but also the words which I myself – not he – had attached, and that only in my own mind, to the gesticulation he had imitated.

Anonymous

The Strange Visitor

A WOMAN was sitting at her reel one night;
  And still she sat, and still she reeled, and still she wished
  for company.

In came a pair of broad broad soles, and sat down at the
  fireside;
  And still she sat, and still she reeled, and still she wished
  for company.

In came a pair of small small legs, and sat down on the
  broad broad soles;
  And still she sat, and still she reeled, and still she wished
  for company.

In came a pair of thick thick knees, and sat down on the
  small small legs;
  And still she sat, and still she reeled, and still she wished
  for company.

In came a pair of thin thin thighs, and sat down on the
  thick thick knees;
  And still she sat, and still she reeled, and still she wished
  for company.

In came a pair of huge huge hips, and sat down on the thin
  thin thighs;

And still she sat, and still she reeled, and still she wished
for company.

In came a wee wee waist, and sat down on the huge huge
hips;
And still she sat, and still she reeled, and still she wished
for company.

In came a pair of broad broad shoulders, and sat down on
the wee wee waist;
And still she sat, and still she reeled, and still she wished
for company.

In came a pair of small small arms, and sat down on the
broad broad shoulders;
And still she sat, and still she reeled, and still she wished
for company.

In came a pair of huge huge hands, and sat down on the
small small arms;
And still she sat, and still she reeled, and still she wished
for company.

In came a small small neck, and sat down on the broad
broad shoulders;
And still she sat, and still she reeled, and still she wished
for company.

In came a huge huge head, and sat down on the small small
neck.

'How did you get such broad feet?' quoth the
woman.
'Much tramping, much tramping' (*gruffly*).

'How did you get such small small legs?'
'*Aih-h-h!* – late – and *wee-e-e* – moul' (*whiningly*).

'How did you get such thick thick knees?'
'Much praying, much praying' (*piously*).

'How did you get such thin thin thighs?'
'Aih-h-h! – late – and wee-e-e moul' (*whiningly*).

'How did you get such big big hips?'
'Much sitting, much sitting' (*gruffly*).

'How did you get such a wee wee waist?'
'Aih-h-h! – late – and wee-e-e – moul' (*whiningly*).

'How did you get such broad broad shoulders?'
'With carrying broom, with carrying broom' (*gruffly*).

'How did you get such small small arms?'
'Aih-h-h! – late – and wee-e-e – moul' (*whiningly*).

'How did you get such huge huge hands?'
'Threshing with an iron flail, threshing with an iron flail'
    (*gruffly*).

'How did you get such a small small neck?'
'Aih-h-a! – late – wee-e-e – moul' (*pitifully*).

'How did you get such a huge huge head?'
'Much knowledge, much knowledge' (*keenly*).

'What do you come for?'
'FOR YOU!' (*At the top of the voice, with a wave of the
    arm and a stamp of the feet.*)

J. Sheridan Le Fanu

Madam Crowl's Ghost

Contributed anonymously to All the Year Round in 1870–71, but afterwards incorporated bodily into Chronicles of Golden Friars (1871, vol i) in the story of 'Laura Mildmay', where it is put into the mouth of an old north-country nurse, Mrs Jolliffe.

I'M an old woman now; and I was but thirteen my last birthday, the night I came to Applewale House. My aunt was the housekeeper there, and a sort o' one-horse carriage was down at Lexhoe to take me and my box up to Applewale.

I was a bit frightened by the time I got to Lexhoe, and when I saw the carriage and horse, I wished myself back again with my mother at Hazelden. I was crying when I got into the 'shay' – that's what we used to call it – and old John Mulbery that drove it, and was a good-natured fellow, bought me a handful of apples at the Golden Lion, to cheer me up a bit; and he told me that there was a cur-rant-cake, and tea, and pork-chops, waiting for me, all hot, in my aunt's room at the great house. It was a fine moonlight night and I eat the apples, lookin' out o' the shay winda.

It is a shame for gentlemen to frighten a poor foolish child like I was. I sometimes think it might be tricks. There was two on 'em on the tap o' the coach beside me. And they began to question me after nightfall, when the moon rose, where I was going to. Well, I told them it was to wait on Dame Arabella Crowl, of Applewale House, near by Lexhoe.

'Ho, then,' says one of them, 'you'll not be long there!'

And I looked at him as much as to say, 'Why not?' for I had spoke out when I told them where I was goin', as if 'twas something clever I had to say.

'Because,' says he – 'and don't you for your life tell no one, only watch her and see – she's possessed by the devil, and more an half a ghost. Have you got a Bible?'

'Yes, sir,' says I. For my mother put my little Bible in my box, and I knew it was there: and by the same token, though the print's too small for my ald eyes, I have it in my press to this hour.

As I looked up at him, saying, 'Yes, sir,' I thought I saw him winkin' at his friend; but I could not be sure.

'Well,' says he, 'be sure you put it under your bolster every night, it will keep the ald girl's claws aff ye.'

And I got such a fright when he said that, you wouldn't fancy! And I'd a liked to ask him a lot about the ald lady, but I was too shy, and he and his friend began talkin' together about their own consarns, and dowly enough I got down, as I told ye, at Lexhoe. My heart sank as I drove into the dark avenue. The trees stand very thick and big, as ald as the ald house almost, and four people, with their arms out and finger-tips touchin', barely girds round some of them.

Well, my neck was stretched out o' the winda, looking for the first view o' the great house; and, all at once, we pulled up in front of it.

A great white-and-black house it is, wi' great black beams across and right up it, and gables lookin' out, as white as a sheet, to the moon, and the shadows o' the trees, two or three up and down upon the front, you could count the leaves on them, and all the little diamond-shaped winda-panes, glimmering on the great hall winda, and great shutters, in the old fashion, hinged on the wall outside, boulted across all the rest o' the windas in front, for there was but three or four servants, and the old lady in the house, and most o' t'rooms was locked up.

My heart was in my mouth when I sid the journey was over, and this, the great house afore me, and I sa near my aunt that I never sid till noo, and Dame Crowl, that I was come to wait upon, and was afeard on already.

My aunt kissed me in the hall, and brought me to her room. She was tall and thin, wi' a pale face and black eyes, and long thin hands wi' black mittins on. She was past fifty, and her word was short; but her word was law. I hev no complaints to make of her; but she was a hard woman, and I think she would hev bin kinder to me if I had bin her sister's child in place of her brother's. But all that's o' no consequence noo.

The squire — his name was Mr Chevenix Crowl, he was Dame Crowl's grandson — came down there, by way of seeing that the old lady was well treated, about twice or thrice in the year. I sid him but twice all the time I was at Applewale House.

I can't say but she was well taken care of, notwithstandin', but that was because my aunt and Meg Wyvern, that was her maid, had a conscience, and did their duty by her.

Mrs Wyvern — Meg Wyvern my aunt called her to herself, and Mrs Wyvern to me — was a fat, jolly lass of fifty, a good height and a good breadth, always good-humoured, and walked slow. She had fine wages, but she was a bit stingy, and kept all her fine clothes under lock and key, and wore, mostly, a twilled chocolate cotton, wi' red, and yellow, and green sprigs and balls on it, and it lasted wonderful.

She never gave me nout, not the vally o' a brass thimble, all the time I was there; but she was good-humoured, and always laughin', and she talked no end o' proas over her tea; and, seeing me sa sackless and dowly, she roused me up wi' her laughin' and stories; and I think I liked her better than my aunt – children is so taken wi' a bit o' fun or a story – though my aunt was very good to me, but a hard woman about some things, and silent always.

My aunt took me into her bed-chamber, that I might rest myself a bit while she was settin' the tea in her room. But first she patted me on the shouther, and said I was a tall lass o' my years, and had spired up well, and asked me if I could do plain work and stitchin'; and she looked in my face, and said I was like my father, her brother, that was dead and gone, and she hoped I was a better Christian, and wad na du a' that lids.

It was a hard sayin' the first time I set my foot in her room, I thought.

When I went into the next room, the housekeeper's room – very comfortable, yak (oak) all round – there was a fine fire blazin' away, wi' coal, and peat, and wood, all in a low together, and tea on the table, and hot cake, and smokin' meat; and there was Mrs Wyvern, fat, jolly, and talkin' away, more in an hour than my aunt would in a year.

While I was still at my tea my aunt went upstairs to see Madam Crowl.

'She's agone up to see that old Judith Squailes is awake,' says Mrs Wyvern. 'Judith sits with Madam Crowl when me and Mrs Shutters' – that was my aunt's name – 'is away. She's a troublesome old lady. Ye'll hev to be sharp wi' her, or she'll be into the fire, or out o' t' winda. She goes on wires, she does, old though she be.'

'How old, ma'am?' says I.

'Ninety-three her last birthday, and that's eight months gone,' says she; and she laughed. 'And don't be askin' questions about her before your aunt – mind, I tell ye; just take her as you find her, and that's all.'

'And what's to be my business about her, please ma'am?' says I.

'About the old lady? Well,' says she, 'your aunt, Mrs Shutters, will tell you that; but I suppose you'll hev to sit in the room with your work, and see she's at no mischief, and let her amuse herself with her things on the table, and get her her food or drink as she calls for it, and keep her out o' mischief, and ring the bell hard if she's troublesome.'

'Is she deaf, ma'am?'

'No, nor blind,' says she; 'as sharp as a needle, but she's gone quite aupy, and can't remember nout rightly; and Jack the Giant Killer, or Goody Twoshoes will please her as well as the King's court, or the affairs of the nation.'

'And what did the little girl go away for, ma'am, that went on Friday last? My aunt wrote to my mother she was to go.'

'Yes; she's gone.'

'What for?' says I again.

'She didn't answer Mrs Shutters, I do suppose,' says she. 'I don't know. Don't be talkin'; your aunt can't abide a talkin' child.'

'And please, ma'am, is the old lady well in health?' says I.

'It ain't no harm to ask that,' says she. 'She's torflin' a bit lately, but better this week past, and I dare say she'll last out her hundred years yet. Hish! Here's your aunt coming down the passage.'

In comes my aunt, and begins talkin' to Mrs Wyvern, and I, beginnin' to feel more comfortable and at home like, was walkin' about the room lookin' at this thing and at that. There was pretty old china things on the cupboard, and pictures again the wall; and there was a door open in the wainscot, and I sees a queer old leathern jacket, wi' straps and buckles to it, and sleeves as long as the bed-post, hangin' up inside.

'What's that you're at, child?' says my aunt, sharp enough, turning about when I thought she least minded. 'What's that in your hand?'

'This, ma'am?' says I, turning about with the leathern jacket. 'I don't know what it is, ma'am.'

Pale as she was, the red came up in her cheeks, and her eyes flashed wi' anger, and I think only she had half a dozen steps to take, between her and me, she'd a gov me a sizzup. But she did give me a shake by the shouther, and she plucked the thing out o' my hand, and says she, 'While ever you stay here, don't ye meddle wi' nout that don't belong to ye,' and she hung it up on the pin that was there, and shut the door wi' a bang and locked it fast.

Mrs Wyvern was liftin' up her hands and laughin' all this time, quietly in her chair, rolling herself a bit in it, as she used when she was kinkin'.

The tears was in my eyes, and she winked at my aunt, and says she, dryin' her own eyes that was wet wi' the laughin', 'Tut, the child meant no harm – come here to me, child. It's only a pair o' crutches for lame ducks, and ask us no questions mind, and we'll tell ye no lies; and come here and sit down, and drink a mug o' beer before ye go to your bed.'

My room, mind ye, was upstairs, next to the old lady's, and Mrs Wyvern's bed was near hers in her room and I was to be ready at call, if need should be.

The old lady was in one of her tantrums that night and part of the day before. She used to take fits o' the sulks.

Sometimes she would not let them dress her, and other times she would not let them take her clothes off. She was a great beauty, they said, in her day. But there was no one about Applewale that remembered her in her prime. And she was dreadful fond o' dress, and had thick silks, and stiff satins, and velvets, and laces, and all sorts, enough to set up seven shops at the least. All her dresses was old-fashioned and queer, but worth a fortune.

Well, I went to my bed. I lay for a while awake; for a' things was new to me; and I think the tea was in my nerves, too, for I wasn't used to it, except now and then on a holiday, or the like. And I heard Mrs Wyvern talkin', and I listened with my hand to my ear; but I could not hear Mrs Crowl, and I don't think she said a word.

There was great care took of her. The people at Apple-wale knew that when she died they would every one get the sack; and their situations was well paid and easy.

The doctor come twice a week to see the old lady, and you may be sure they all did as he bid them. One thing was the same every time; they were never to cross or frump her, any way, but to humour and please her in everything.

So she lay in her clothes all that night, and next day, not a word she said, and I was at my needlework all that day, in my own room, except when I went down to my dinner.

I would a liked to see the ald lady, and even to hear her speak. But she might as well a'bin in Lunnon a' the time for me.

When I had my dinner my aunt sent me out for a walk for an hour. I was glad when I came back, the trees was so big, and the place so dark and lonesome, and 'twas a cloudy day, and I cried a deal, thinkin' of home, while I was walkin' alone there. That evening, the candles bein' alight, I was sittin' in my room, and the door was open into Madam Crowl's chamber, where my aunt was. It was, then, for the first time I heard what I suppose was the ald lady talking.

It was a queer noise like, I couldn't well say which, a bird, or a beast, only it had a bleatin' sound in it, and was very small.

I pricked my ears to hear all I could. But I could not make out one word she said. And my aunt answered:

'The evil one can't hurt no one, ma'am, bout the Lord permits.'

Then the same queer voice from the bed says something more that I couldn't make head nor tail on.

And my aunt med answer again: 'Let them pull faces, ma'am, and say what they will; if the Lord be for us, who can be against us?'

I kept listenin' with my ear turned to the door, holdin' my breath, but not another word or sound came in from the room. In about twenty minutes, as I was sittin' by the table, lookin' at the pictures in the old *Æsop's Fables*, I was aware o' something moving at the door, and lookin' up I sid my aunt's face lookin' in at one door, and her hand raised.

'Hish!' says she, very soft, and comes over to me on tiptoe, and she says in a whisper: 'Thank God, she's asleep at last, and don't ye make no noise till I come back, for I'm goin' down to take my cup o' tea, and I'll be back i' noo – me and Mrs Wyvern, and she'll be sleepin' in the room, and you can run down when we come up, and Judith will gie ye yaur supper in my room.'

And with that away she goes.

I kep' looking at the picture-book, as before, listenin' every noo and then, but there was no sound, not a breath, that I could hear; an' I began whisperin' to the pictures and talkin' to myself to keep my heart up, for I was growin' feared in that big room.

And at last up I got, and began walkin' about the room, lookin' at this and peepin' at that, to amuse my mind, ye'll understand. And at last what sud I do but peeps into Madame Crowl's bed-chamber.

A grand chamber it was, wi' a great four-poster, wi' flowered silk curtains as tall as the ceilin', and foldin' down on the floor, and drawn close all round. There was a lookin'-glass, the biggest I ever sid before, and the room was a blaze o' light. I counted twenty-two wax-candles, all alight. Such was her fancy, and no one dared say her nay.

I listened at the door, and gaped and wondered all round. When I heard there was not a breath, and did not see so much as a stir in the curtains, I took heart, and I walked into the room on tiptoe, and looked round again. Then I takes a keek at myself in the big glass; and at last it came in my head, 'Why couldn't I ha' a keek at the ald lady herself in the bed?'

Ye'd think me a fule if ye knew half how I longed to see Dame Crowl, and I thought to myself if I didn't peep now I might wait many a day before I got so gude a chance again.

Well, my dear, I came to the side o' the bed, the curtains bein' close, and my heart a'most failed me. But I took courage, and I slips my finger in between the thick curtains, and then my hand. So I waits a bit, but all was still as death. So, softly, softly I draws the curtain, and there, sure enough, I sid before me, stretched out like the painted lady on the tomb-stean in Lexhoe Church, the famous Dame Crowl, of Applewale House. There she was, dressed out. You never sid the like in they days. Satin and silk, and scarlet and green, and gold and pint lace; by Jen! 'twas a sight! A big powdered wig, half as high as herself, was a-top o' her head, and, wow! — was ever such wrinkles? — and her old baggy throat all powdered white, and her cheeks rouged, and mouse-skin eyebrows, that Mrs Wyvern used to stick on, and there she lay grand and stark, wi' a pair o' clocked silk hose on, and heels to her shoon as tall as nine-pins. Lawk! But her nose was crooked and thin, and half the whites o' her eyes was open. She used to stand, dressed as she was, gigglin' and dribblin' before the lookin'-glass, wi' a fan in her hand, and a big nosegay in her bodice. Her wrinkled little hands was stretched down by her sides, and such long nails, all cut into points, I never sid in my days. Could it ever a bin the fashion for grit fowk to wear their finger-nails so?

Well, I think ye'd a-bin frightened yourself if ye'd a sid such a sight. I couldn't let go the curtain, nor move an inch, nor take my eyes off her; my very heart stood still. And in an instant she opens her eyes, and up she sits, and spins herself round, and down wi' her, wi' a clack on her two tall heels on the floor, facin' me, ogglin' in my face wi' her two great glassy eyes, and a wicked simper wi' her old wrinkled lips, and lang fause teeth.

Well, a corpse is a natural thing; but this was the dreadfullest sight I ever sid. She had her fingers straight out pointin' at me, and her back was crooked, round again wi' age. Says she:

'Ye little limb! what for did ye say I killed the boy? I'll tickle ye till ye're stiff!'

If I'd a thought an instant, I'd a turned about and run. But I couldn't take my eyes off her, and I backed from her as soon as I could; and she came clatterin' after, like a thing on wires, with her fingers pointing to my throat, and she makin' all the time a sound with her tongue like zizz-zizz-zizz.

I kept backin' and backin' as quick as I could, and her fingers was only a few inches away from my throat, and I felt I'd lose my wits if she touched me.

I went back this way, right into the corner, and I gev a yellock, ye'd think saul and body was partin', and that minute my aunt, from the door, calls out wi' a blare, and the ald lady turns round on her, and I turns about, and ran through my room, and down the back stairs, as hard as my legs could carry me.

I cried hearty, I can tell you, when I got down to the housekeeper's room. Mrs Wyvern laughed a deal when I told her what happened. But she changed her key when she heard the ald lady's words.

'Say them again,' says she.

So I told her.

'Ye little limb! What for did ye say I killed the boy? I'll tickle ye till ye're stiff.'

'And did ye say she killed a boy?' says she.

'Not I, ma'am,' says I.

Judith was always up with me, after that, when the two elder women was away from her. I would a jumped out at winda, rather than stay alone in the same room wi' her.

It was about a week after, as well as I can remember, Mrs Wyvern, one day when me and her was alone, told me a thing about Madam Crowl that I did not know before.

She being young, and a great beauty, full seventy years before, had married Squire Crowl of Applewale. But he was a widower, and had a son about nine year old.

There never was tale or tidings of this boy after one mornin'. No one could say where he went to. He was allowed too much liberty, and used to be off in the morning, one day, to the keeper's cottage, and breakfast wi' him, and away to the warren, and not home, mayhap, till evening, and another time down to the lake, and bathe there, and spend the day fishin' there, or paddlin' about in the boat. Well, no one could say what was gone wi' him; only this, that his hat was found by the lake, under a haathorn that grows thar to this day, and 'twas thought he was drowned bathin'. And the squire's son, by his second marriage, by this Madam Crowl that lived sa dreadful lang, came in for the estates. It was his son, the ald lady's grandson, Squire Chevenix Crowl, that owned the estates at the time I came to Applewale.

There was a deal o' talk lang before my aunt's time about it; and 'twas said the step-mother knew more than she was like to let out. And she managed her husband, the ald squire, wi' her whiteheft and flatteries. And as the boy was never seen more, in course of time the thing died out of fowks' minds.

I'm goin' to tell ye noo about what I sid wi' my own een.

I was not there six months, and it was winter-time, when the ald lady took her last sickness.

The doctor was afeard she might a took a fit o' madness, as she did, fifteen years befoore, and was buckled up, many a time, in a strait-waistcoat, which was the very leathern jerkin' I sid in the closet, off my aunt's room.

Well, she didn't. She pined, and windered, and went off, torflin', torflin', quiet enough, till a day or two before her flittin', and then she took to rabblin', and sometimes skirlin' in the bed, ye'd think a robber had a knife to her throat, and she used to work out o' the bed, and not being strong enough, then, to walk or stand, she'd fall on the flure, wi' her ald wizened hands stretched before her face, and skirlin' still for mercy.

Ye may guess I didn't go into the room, and I used to be shiverin' in my bed wi' fear, at her skirlin' and scrafflin' on the flure, and blarin' out words that id make your skin turn blue.

My aunt, and Mrs Wyvern, and Judith Squailes, and a woman from Lexhoe, was always about her. At last she took fits, and they wore her out.

T' sir (parson) was there, and prayed for her; but she was past praying with. I suppose it was right, but none could think there was much good in it, and sa at lang last she made her flittin,' and a' was over, and old Dame Crowl was shrouded and coffined and Squire Chevenix was wrote for. But he was away in France, and the delay was sa lang, that t' sir and doctor both agreed it would not du to keep her langer out o' her place, and no one cared but just them two, and my aunt and the rest o' us, from Apple-wale, to go to the buryin'. So the old lady of Applewale was laid in the vault under Lexhoe Church; and we lived up at the great house till such time as the squire should come to tell his will about us, and pay off such as he chose to discharge.

I was put into another room, two doors away from what was Dame Crowl's chamber, after her death, and this thing happened the night before Squire Chevenix came to Applewale.

The room I was in now was a large square chamber, covered wi' yak pannels, but unfurnished except for my bed, which had no curtains to it, and a chair and a table, or so, that looked nothing at all in such a big room. And the big looking-glass, that the old lady used to keek into and admire herself from head to heel, now that there was na mair o' that wark, was put out of the way, and stood against the wall in my room, for there was shiftin' o' many things in her chambers ye may suppose, when she came to be coffined.

The news had come that day that the squire was to be down next morning at Applewale; and not sorry was I, for I thought I was sure to be sent home again to my mother. And right glad was I, and I was thinkin' of a' at hame, and my sister, Janet, and the kitten and the pymag, and Trimmer the tike, and all the rest, and I got sa fidgetty, I couldn't sleep, and the clock struck twelve, and me wide awake, and the room as dark as pick. My back was turned to the door, and my eyes toward the wall opposite.

Well, it could na be a full quarter-past twelve, when I sees a lightin' on the wall befoore me, as if something took fire behind, and the shadas o' the bed, and the chair, and my gown, that was hangin' from the wall, was dancin' up and down, on the ceilin' beams and the yak pannels; and I turns my head over my shouther quick, thinkin' something must a gone a' fire.

And what sud I see, by Jen! but the likeness o' the ald beldame, bedizened out in her satins and velvets, on her dead body, simperin', wi' her eyes as wide as saucers, and her face like the fiend himself. 'Twas a red light that rose about her in a fuffin low, as if her dress round her feet was blazin'. She was drivin' on right for me, wi' her ald shrivelled hands crooked as if she was goin' to claw me. I could not stir, but she passed me straight by, wi' a blast o' cald air, and I sid her, at the wall, in the alcove as my aunt used to call it, which was a recess where the state bed used to stand in ald times, wi' a door open wide, and her hands gropin' in at somethin' was there. I never sid that door before. And she turned round to me, like a thing on a pivot, flyrin' (grinning), and all at once the room was dark, and I standin' at the far side o' the bed; I don't know how I got there, and I found my tongue at last, and if I did na blare a yellock, rennin' down the gallery and almost pulled Mrs Wyvern's door, off t'hooks, and frightened her half out o' her wits.

Ye may guess I did na sleep that night; and wi' the first light, down wi' me to my aunt, as fast as my two legs cud carry me.

Well, my aunt did na frump or flite me, as I thought she would, but she held me by the hand, and looked hard in my face all the time. And she telt me not to be feared; and says she:

'Hed the appearance a key in its hand?'

'Yes,' says I, bringin' it to mind, 'a big key in a queer brass handle.'

'Stop a bit,' says she, lettin' go ma hand, and openin' the cupboard-door. 'Was it like this?' says she, takin' one out in her fingers and showing it to me, with a dark look in my face.

'That was it,' says I, quick enough.

'Are ye sure?' she says, turnin' it round.

'Sart,' says I, and I felt like I was gain' to faint when I sid it.

'Well, that will do, child,' says she, saftly thinkin', and she locked it up again.

'The squire himself will be here today, before twelve o'clock, and ye must tell him all about it,' says she, thinkin', 'and I suppose I'll be leavin' soon, and so the best thing for the present is, that ye should go home this afternoon, and I'll look out another place for you when I can.'

Fain was I, ye may guess, at that word.

My aunt packed up my things for me, and the three pounds that was due to me, to bring home, and Squire Crowl himself came down to Applewale that day, a handsome man, about thirty years ald. It was the second time I sid him. But this was the first time he spoke to me.

My aunt talked wi' him in the housekeeper's room, and I don't know what they said. I was a bit feared on the squire, he bein' a great gentleman down in Lexhoe, and I darn't go near till I was called. And says he, smilin':

'What's a' this ye a sen, child? it mun be a dream, for ye know there's na sic a thing as a bo or a freet in a' the world. But whatever it was, ma little maid, sit ye down and tell us all about it from first to last.'

Well, so soon as I med an end, he thought a bit, and says he to my aunt:

'I mind the place well. In old Sir Oliver's time lame Wyndel told me there was a door in that recess, to the left, where the lassie dreamed she saw my grandmother open it. He was past eighty when he telt me that, and I but a boy. It's twenty year sen. The plate and jewels used to be kept there, long ago, before the iron closet was made in the arras chamber, and he told me the key had a brass handle, and this ye say was found in the bottom o' the kist where she kept her old fans. Now, would not it be a queer thing if we found some spoons or diamonds forgot there? Ye mun come up wi' us, lassie, and point to the very spot.'

Loth was I, and my heart in my mouth, and fast I held by my aunt's hand as I stept into that awesome room, and showed them both how she came and passed me by, and the spot where she stood, and where the door seemed to open.

There was an ald empty press against the wall then, and shoving it aside, sure enough there was the tracing of a door in the wainscot, and a keyhole stopped with wood, and planed across as smooth as the rest, and the joining of the door all stopped wi' putty the colour o' yak, and, but for the hinges that showed a bit when the press was shoved aside, ye would not consayt there was a door there at all.

'Ha!' says he, wi' a queer smile, 'this looks like it.'

It took some minutes wi' a small chisel and hammer to pick the bit o' wood out o' the keyhole. The key fitted, sure enough, and, wi' a strang twist and a lang skreeak, the boult went back and he pulled the door open.

There was another door inside, stranger than the first, but the lacks was gone, and it opened easy. Inside was a narrow floor and walls and vault o' brick; we could not see what was in it, for 'twas dark as pick.

When my aunt had lighted the candle the squire held it up and stept in.

My aunt stood on tiptoe tryin' to look over his shouther, and I did na see nout.

'Ha! ha!' says the squire, steppin' backward. 'What's that? Gi'ma the poker – quick!' says he to my aunt. And as she went to the hearth I peeps beside his arm, and I sid squat down in the far corner a monkey or a flayin' on the chest, or else the maist shrivelled up, wizzened ald wife that ever was sen on yearth.

'By Jen!' says my aunt, as, puttin' the poker in his hand, she keeked by his shouther, and sid the ill-favoured thing, 'hae a care sir, what ye're doin'. Back wi' ye, and shut to the door!'

But in place o' that he steps in saftly, wi' the poker pointed like a swoord, and he gies it a poke, and down it a' tumbles together, head and a', in a heap o' bayans and dust, little meyar an' a hatful.

'Twas the bayans o' a child; a' the rest went to dust at a touch. They said nout for a while, but he turns round the skull as it lay on the floor.

Young as I was I consayted I knew well enough what they was thinkin' on.

'A dead cat!' says he, pushin' back and blowin' out the can'le, and shuttin' to the door. 'We'll come back, you and me, Mrs Shutters, and look on the shelves by-and-bye. I've other matters first to speak to ye about; and this little girl's goin' hame, ye say. She has her wages, and I mun mak' her a present,' says he, pattin' my shoulder wi' his hand.

And he did gimma a goud pound, and I went aff to Lexhoe about an hour after, and sa hame by the stagecoach, and fain was I to be at hame again; and I never saa ald Dame Crowl o' Applewale, God be thanked, either in appearance or in dream, at-efter. But when I was grown to be

a woman my aunt spent a day and night wi' me at Little-
ham, and she telt me there was na doubt it was the poor
little boy that was missing sa lang sen that was shut up to
die thar in the dark by that wicked beldame, whar his
skirls, or his prayers, or his thumpin' cud na be heard,
and his hat was left by the water's edge, whoever did it, to
mak' belief he was drowned. The clothes, at the first touch,
a' ran into a snuff o' dust in the cell whar the bayans was
found. But there was a handful o' jet buttons, and a knife
with a green handle, together wi' a couple o' pennies the
poor little fella had in his pocket, I suppose, when he was
decoyed in thar, and sid his last o' the light. And there was,
amang the squire's papers, a copy o' the notice that was
prented after he was lost, when the old squire thought he
might 'a run away, or bin took by gipsies, and it said he
had a green-hefted knife wi' him, and that his buttons were
o' cut jet. Sa that is a' I hev to say consarnin' ald Dame
Crowl, o' Applewale House.

Anonymous

A Ghostly Wife

ONCE on a time there lived a Brahman who had married a wife, and who lived in the same house with his mother. Near his house was a tank, on the embankment of which stood a tree, on the boughs of which lived a ghost of the kind called *Sankchinni*.* One night the Brahman's wife had occasion to go to the tank, and as she went she brushed by a *Sankchinni* who stood near; on which the she-ghost got very angry with the woman, seized her by the throat, climbed into her tree, and thrust her into a hole in the trunk. There the woman lay almost dead with fear. The ghost put on the clothes of the woman and went into the house of the Brahman. Neither the Brahman nor his mother had any inkling of the change. The Brahman thought his wife returned from the tank, and the mother thought that it was her daughter-in-law. Next morning the mother-in-law discovered some change in her daughter-in-law. Her daughter-in-law, she knew, was constitutionally weak and languid, and took a long time to do the work of the house. But she had apparently become quite a different person. All of a sudden she had become very active. She now did the work of the house in an incredibly short time. Suspecting nothing, the old woman said nothing either to her son or to her daughter-in-law; on the contrary, she

Sankchinnis or *Sankhachurnis* are female ghosts of white complexion. They usually stand at the dead of night at the foot of trees, and look like sheets of white cloth.

only rejoiced that her daughter-in-law had turned over a
new leaf. But her surprise became every day greater and
greater. The cooking of the household was done in much
less time than before. When the mother-in-law wanted the
daughter-in-law to bring anything from the next room, it
was brought in much less time than was required in walking from one room to the other. The ghost, instead of going inside the next room, would stretch a long arm – for
ghosts can lengthen or shorten any limb of their bodies –
from the door and get the thing. One day the old woman
observed the ghost doing this. She ordered her to bring a
vessel from some distance, and the ghost unconsciously
stretched her hand to several yards' distance, and brought
it in a trice. The old woman was struck with wonder at
the sight. She said nothing to her, but spoke to her son.
Both mother and son began to watch the ghost more nar-
rowly. One day the old woman knew that there was no
fire in the house, and she knew also that her daughter-in-
law had not gone out of doors to get it; and yet, strange to
say, the hearth in the kitchen-room was quite in a blaze.
She went in, and, to her infinite surprise, found that her
daughter-in-law was not using any fuel for cooking, but
had thrust into the oven her foot, which was blazing
brightly. The old mother told her son what she had seen,
and they both concluded that the young woman in the
house was not his real wife but a she-ghost. The son wit-
nessed those very acts of the ghost which his mother had
seen. An *Ojha** was therefore sent for. The exorcist came,
and wanted in the first instance to ascertain whether the
woman was a real woman or a ghost. For this purpose he
lighted a piece of turmeric and set it below the nose of the
supposed woman. Now this was an infallible test, as no
ghost, whether male or female, can put up with the smell

*An exorcist, one who drives away ghosts from possessed persons.

of burnt turmeric. The moment the lighted turmeric was taken near her, she screamed aloud and ran away from the room. It was now plain that she was either a ghost or a woman possessed by a ghost. The woman was caught hold of by main force and asked who she was. At first she refused to make any disclosures, on which the *Ojha* took up his slippers and began belabouring her with them. Then the ghost said with a strong nasal accent – for all ghosts speak through the nose – that she was a *Sankchinni*, that she lived on a tree by the side of the tank, that she had seized the young Brahmani and put her in the hollow of her tree because one night she had touched her, and that if any person went to the hole the woman would be found. The woman was brought from the tree almost dead; the ghost was again shoebeaten, after which process, on her declaring solemnly that she would not again do any harm to the Brahman and his family, she was released from the spell of the *Ojha* and sent away; and the wife of the Brahman recovered slowly. After which the Brahman and his wife lived many years happily together and begat many sons and daughters.

Richard Bartram

Legend of Hamilton Tighe

THE Captain is walking his quarter-deck,
With a troubled brow and a bended neck;
One eye is down through the hatchway cast,
The other turns up to the truck on the mast;
Yet none of the crew may venture to hint
'Our skipper hath gotten a sinister squint!'

The Captain again the letter hath read
Which the bum-boat woman brought out to Spithead –
Still, since the good ship sail'd away,
He reads that letter three times a-day;
Yet the writing is broad and fair to see
As a Skipper may read in his degree,
And the seal is black, and as broad, and as flat,
As his own cockade in his own cock'd hat:
He reads, and he says, as he walks to and fro,
'Curse the old woman – she bothers me so!'

He pauses now, for the topmen hail –
'On the larboard quarter a sail! a sail!'
That grim old Captain he turns him quick,
And bawls through his trumpet for Hairy-faced Dick.
'The breeze is blowing – huzza! huzza!
The breeze is blowing – away! away!

The breeze is blowing – a race! a race!
The breeze is blowing – we near the chase!
Blood will flow, and bullets will fly, –
Oh where will be then young Hamilton Tighe?'

– 'On the foeman's deck, where a man should be,
With his sword in his hand, and his foe at his knee.
Cockswain, or boatswain, or reefer may try,
But the first man on board will be Hamilton Tighe!'

*

Hairy-faced Dick hath a swarthy hue,
Between a gingerbread-nut and a Jew,
And his pigtail is long, and bushy, and thick,
Like a pump-handle stuck on the end of a stick.
Hairy-faced Dick understands his trade;
He stands by the breech of a long carronade,
The linstock glows in his bony hand,
Waiting that grim old Skipper's command.

'The bullets are flying – huzza! huzza!
The bullets are flying – away! away!' –
The brawny boarders mount by the chains,
And are over their buckles in blood and in brains.

On the foeman's deck, where a man should be,
  Young Hamilton Tighe
  Waves his cutlass high,
And *Capitaine Crapaud* bends low at his knee.

Hairy-face Dick, linstock in hand,
Is waiting that grim-looking Skipper's command:
  A wink comes sly
  From that sinister eye –

Hairy-face Dick at once lets fly,
And knocks off the head of young Hamilton Tighe!

There's a lady sits lonely in bower and hall,
Her pages and handmaidens come at her call:
'Now, haste ye, my handmaidens, haste and see
How he sits there and glow'rs with his head on his knee!'

The maidens smile, and, her thought to destroy,
They bring her a little, pale, mealy-faced boy;
And the mealy-faced boy says, 'Mother dear,
Now Hamilton's dead, I've a thousand a-year!'

The lady has donn'd her mantle and hood,
She is bound for shrift at St Mary's Rood:
'Oh! the taper shall burn, and the bell shall toll,
And the mass shall be said for my step-son's soul,
And the tablet fair shall be hung on high,
Orate pro animâ Hamilton Tighe?'

   Her coach and four
   Draws up to the door,
With her groom, and her footman, and half a score more;
The lady steps into her coach alone,
And they hear her sigh, and they hear her groan;
They close the door, and they turn the pin,
But there's One rides with her that never stept in!
All the way there, and all the way back,
The harness strains, and the coach-springs crack,
The horses snort, and plunge, and kick,
Till the coachman thinks he is driving Old Nick;
And the grooms and the footmen wonder, and say
'What makes the old coach so heavy today?'
But the mealy-faced boy peeps in, and sees
A man sitting there with his head on his knees!

'Tis ever the same, – in hall or in bower,
Wherever the place, whatever the hour,
That Lady mutters, and talks to the air,
And her eye is fix'd on an empty chair;
But the mealy-faced boy still whispers with dread,
'She talks to a man with never a head!'

*

Richard Bartram

There's an old Yellow Admiral living at Bath,
As grey as a badger, as thin as a lath;
And his very queer eyes have such very queer leers,
They seem to be trying to peep at his ears;
That old Yellow Admiral goes to the Rooms,
And he plays long whist, but he frets and he fumes,
For all his Knaves stand upside down,
And the Jack of Clubs does nothing but frown;
And the Kings, and the Aces, and all the best trumps
Get into the hands of the other old frumps;
While, close to his partner, a man he sees
Counting the tricks with his head on his knees.

In Ratcliffe Highway there's an old marine store,
And a great black doll hangs out of the door;
There are rusty locks, and dusty bags,
And musty phials, and fusty rags,
And a lusty old woman, call'd Thirsty Nan,
And her crusty old husband's a Hairy-faced man!

That Hairy-faced man is sallow and wan,
And his great thick pigtail is wither'd and gone;
And he cries, 'Take away that lubberly chap
That sits there and grins with his head in his lap!'
And the neighbours say, as they see him look sick,
'What a rum old covey is Hairy-faced Dick!'

That Admiral, Lady, and Hairy-faced man
May say what they please, and may do what they can;
But one thing seems remarkably clear, –
They may die tomorrow, or live till next year, –
But wherever they live, or whenever they die,
They'll never get quit of young Hamilton Tighe!

Captain Marryat

The Phantom Ship

THE ship was ready to sail for Europe; and Philip Vander-decken went on board – hardly caring whither he went. To return to Terneuse was not his object; he could not bear the idea of revisiting the scene of so much happiness and so much misery. Amine's form was engraven on his heart, and he looked forward with impatience to the time when he should be summoned to join her in the land of spirits.

He had awakened as from a dream, after so many years of aberration of intellect. He was no longer the sincere Catholic that he had been; for he never thought of religion without his Amine's cruel fate being brought to his recollection. Still he clung on to the relic – he believed in that – and that only. It was his god – his creed – his everything – the passport for himself and for his father into the next world – the means whereby he should join his Amine – and for hours would he remain holding in his hand that object so valued – gazing upon it – recalling every important event in his life, from the death of his poor mother, and his first sight of Amine; to the last dreadful scene. It was to him a journal of his existence, and on it were fixed all his hopes for the future.

'When! oh, when is it to be accomplished!' was the constant subject of his reveries. 'Blessed, indeed, will be the day when I leave this world of hate, and seek that other in which "the weary are at rest".'

The vessel on board of which Philip was embarked as a passenger was the *Nostra Señora da Monte*, a brig of three hundred tons, bound for Lisbon. The Captain was an old Portuguese, full of superstition, and fond of arrack – a fondness rather unusual with the people of his nation. They sailed from Goa, and Philip was standing abaft, and sadly contemplating the spire of the Cathedral, in which he had last parted with his wife, when his elbow was touched, and he turned round.

'Fellow-passenger again!' said a well-known voice – it was that of the pilot Schriften.

There was no alteration in the man's appearance; he showed no marks of declining years; his one eye glared as keenly as ever.

Philip started, not only at the sight of the man, but at the reminiscences which his unexpected appearance brought to his mind. It was but for a second, and he was again calm and pensive.

'You here again, Schriften?' observed Philip. 'I trust your appearance forebodes the accomplishment of my task.'

'Perhaps it does,' replied the pilot; 'we both are weary.'

Philip made no reply; he did not even ask Schriften in what manner he had escaped from the fort; he was indifferent about it; for he felt that the man had a charmed life.

'Many are the vessels that have been wrecked, Philip Vanderdecken, and many the souls summoned to their account by meeting with your father's ship, while you have been so long shut up,' observed the pilot.

'May our next meeting with him be more fortunate – may it be the last!' replied Philip.

'No, no! rather may he fulfil his doom, and sail till the day of judgement,' replied the pilot with emphasis.

'Vile caitiff! I have a foreboding that you will not have your detestable wish. Away! – leave me! or you shall find that although this head is blanched by misery, this arm has still some power.'

Schriften scowled as he walked away; he appeared to have some fear of Philip, although it was not equal to his hate. He now resumed his former attempts of stirring up the ship's company against Philip, declaring that he was a Jonas, who would occasion the loss of the ship, and that he was connected with *The Flying Dutchman*. Philip very soon observed that he was avoided; and he resorted to counter-statements, equally injurious to Schriften, whom he declared to be a demon. The appearance of Schriften was so much against him, while that of Philip, on the contrary, was so prepossessing, that the people on board hardly knew what to think. They were divided: some were on the side of Philip – some on that of Schriften; the captain and many others looking with equal horror upon both, and longing for the time when they could be sent out of the vessel.

The captain, as we have before observed, was very superstitious, and very fond of his bottle. In the morning he would be sober and pray; in the afternoon he would be drunk, and swear at the very saints whose protection he had invoked but a few hours before.

'May Holy Saint Antonio preserve us, and keep us from temptation,' said he, on the morning after a conversation with the passengers about the Phantom Ship. 'All the saints protect us from harm,' continued he, taking off his hat reverentially, and crossing himself. 'Let me but rid myself of these two dangerous men without accident, and I will offer up a hundred wax candles, of three ounces each, to the shrine of the Virgin, upon my safe anchoring off the tower of Belem.' In the evening he changed his language.

'Now, if that Maldetto Saint Antonio don't help us, may he feel the coals of hell yet; damn him and his pigs too; if he has the courage to do his duty, all will be well; but he is a cowardly wretch, he cares for nobody, and will not help those who call upon him in trouble. Carambo! that for you,' exclaimed the captain, looking at the small shrine of the saint at the bittacle, and snapping his fingers at the image – 'that for you, you useless wretch, who never help us in our trouble. The Pope must canonize some better saints for us, for all we have now are worn out. They could do something formerly, but now I would not give two ounces of gold for the whole calendar; as for you, you lazy old scoundrel,' continued the captain, shaking his fist at poor Saint Antonio.

The ship had now gained off the southern coast of Africa, and was about one hundred miles from the Lagullas coast; the morning was beautiful, a slight ripple only turned over the waves, the breeze was light and steady, and the vessel was standing on a wind, at the rate of about four miles an hour.

'Blessed be the holy saints,' said the captain, who had just gained the deck; 'another little slant in our favour, and we shall lay our course. Again I say, blessed be the holy saints, and particularly our worthy patron Saint Antonio, who has taken under his peculiar protection the *Nostra Señora da Monte*. We have a prospect of fine weather; come, signors, let us down to breakfast, and after breakfast we will enjoy our cigarros upon the deck.'

But the scene was soon changed; a bank of clouds rose up from the eastward, with a rapidity that, to the seamen's eyes, was unnatural, and it soon covered the whole firmament; the sun was obscured, and all was one deep and unnatural gloom; the wind subsided, and the ocean was hushed. It was not exactly dark, but the heavens were covered with one red haze, which gave an appearance as if the world was in a state of conflagration.

In the cabin the increased darkness was first observed by Philip, who went on deck; he was followed by the captain and passengers, who were in a state of amazement. It was unnatural and incomprehensible. 'Now, holy Virgin, protect us – what can this be?' exclaimed the captain in a fright. 'Holy Saint Antonio, protect us – but this is awful.'

'There! there!' shouted the sailors, pointing to the beam of the vessel. Every eye looked over the gunnel to witness what had occasioned such exclamations. Philip, Schriften, and the captain were side by side. On the beam of the ship, not more than two cables' length distant, they beheld, slowly rising out of the water, the tapering masthead and spars of another vessel. She rose, and rose gradually; her top-masts and top-sail yards, with the sails set, next made their appearance; higher and higher she rose up from the element. Her lower masts and rigging, and, lastly, her hull showed itself above the surface. Still she rose up till her ports, with her guns, and at last the whole of her floatage was above water, and there she remained close to them, with her main-yard squared, and hove-to.

'Holy Virgin!' exclaimed the captain, breathless; 'I have known ships to *go down*, but never to *come up* before. Now will I give one thousand candles, of ten ounces each, to the shrine of the Virgin to save us in this trouble. One thousand wax candles! Hear me, blessed lady; ten ounces each. Gentlemen,' cried the captain to the passengers, who stood aghast, 'why don't you promise? Promise, I say; promise, at all events.'

'The Phantom Ship – *The Flying Dutchman*,' shrieked Schriften; 'I told you so, Philip Vanderdecken; there is your father. He! he!'

Philip's eyes had remained fixed on the vessel; he perceived that they were lowering down a boat from her quarter. 'It is possible,' thought he, 'I shall now be permitted!' and Philip put his hand into his bosom and grasped the relic.

The gloom now increased, so that the strange vessel's hull could but just be discovered through the murky atmosphere. The seamen and passengers threw themselves down on their knees, and invoked their saints. The captain ran down for a candle, to light before the image of Saint Antonio, which he took out of its shrine, and kissed with much apparent affection and devotion, and then replaced.

Shortly afterwards the splash of oars was heard alongside, and a voice calling out, 'I say, my good people, give us a rope from forward.'

No one answered, or complied with the request. Schriften only went up to the captain, and told him that if they offered to send letters they must not be received or the vessel would be doomed, and all would perish.

A man now made his appearance from over the gunnel, at the gangway. 'You might as well have let me had a side rope, my hearties,' said he, as he stepped on deck; 'where is the captain?'

'Here,' replied the captain, trembling from head to foot. The man who accosted him appeared a weather-beaten seaman, dressed in a fur cap and canvas petticoats; he held some letters in his hand.

'What do you want?' at last screamed the captain.

'Yes – what do you want?' continued Schriften. 'He! he!'

'What, you here, pilot?' observed the man; 'well – I thought you had gone to Davy's locker, long enough ago.'

'He! he!' replied Schriften, turning away.

'Why the fact is, captain, we have had very foul weather, and we wish to send letters home; I do believe that we shall never get round this Cape.'

'I can't take them,' cried the captain.

'Can't take them! well, it's very odd – but every ship refuses to take our letters; it's very unkind – seamen should have a feeling for brother seamen, especially in distress. God knows, we wish to see our wives and families again; and it would be a matter of comfort to them, if they only could hear from us.'

'I cannot take your letters – the saints preserve us,' replied the captain.

'We have been a long while out,' said the seaman, shaking his head.

'How long?' inquired the captain, not knowing what to say.

'We can't tell; our almanack was blown overboard, and we have lost our reckoning. We never have our latitude exact now, for we cannot tell the sun's declination for the right day.'

'Let *me* see your letters,' said Philip, advancing, and taking them out of the seaman's hands.

'They must not be touched,' screamed Schriften.

'Out, monster!' replied Philip, 'who dares interfere with me?'

'Doomed – doomed – doomed!' shrieked Schriften, running up and down the deck, and then breaking into a wild fit of laughter.

'Touch not the letters,' said the captain, trembling as if in an ague fit.

Philip made no reply, but held his hand out for the letters.

'Here is one from our second mate, to his wife at Amsterdam, who lives on Waser Quay.'

'Waser Quay has long been gone, my good friend; there is now a large dock for ships where it once was,' replied Philip.

'Impossible!' replied the man; 'here is another from the boatswain to his father, who lives in the old market-place.'

'The old market-place has long been pulled down, and there now stands a church upon the spot.'

'Impossible!' replied the seaman; 'here is another from myself to my sweetheart, Vrow Ketser – with money to buy her a new brooch.'

Philip shook his head – 'I remember seeing an old lady of that name buried some thirty years ago.'

'Impossible! I left her young and blooming. Here's one for the house of Slutz & Co., to whom the ship belongs.'

'There's no such house now,' replied Philip; 'but I have heard that many years ago there was a firm of that name.'

'Impossible! you must be laughing at me. Here is a letter from our captain to his son . . .'

'Give it me,' cried Philip, seizing the letter. He was about to break the seal when Schriften snatched it out of his hand, and threw it over the lee gunnel.

'That's a scurvy trick for an old shipmate,' observed the seaman. Schriften made no reply, but catching up the other letters which Philip had laid down on the capstan, he hurled them after the first.

The strange seaman shed tears, and walked again to the side. 'It is very hard – very unkind,' observed he, as he descended; 'the time may come when you may wish that your family should know your situation.' So saying, he disappeared – in a few seconds was heard the sound of the oars, retreating from the ship.

'Holy Saint Antonio!' exclaimed the captain, 'I am lost in wonder and fright. Steward, bring me up the arrack.'

The steward ran down for the bottle; being as much alarmed as his captain, he helped himself before he brought it up to his commander. 'Now,' said the captain, after keeping his mouth for two minutes to the bottle, and draining it to the bottom, 'what is to be done next?'

'I'll tell you,' said Schriften, going up to him. 'That man there has a charm hung round his neck; take it from him and throw it overboard, and your ship will be saved; if not, it will be lost, with every soul on board.'

'Yes, yes, it's all right, depend upon it,' cried the sailors.

'Fools,' replied Philip, 'do you believe that wretch? Did you not hear the man who came on board recognize him, and call him shipmate? He is the party whose presence on board will prove so unfortunate.'

'Yes, yes,' cried the sailors, 'it's all right, the man did call him shipmate.'

'I tell you it's all wrong,' cried Schriften; 'that is the man, let him give up the charm.'

'Yes, yes; let him give up the charm,' cried the sailors, and they rushed upon Philip.

Philip started back to where the captain stood. 'Madmen, know ye what ye are about? It is the holy cross that I wear round my neck. Throw it overboard if you dare, and your souls are lost for ever': and Philip took the relic from his bosom and showed it to the captain.

'No, no, men,' exclaimed the captain, who was now more settled in his nerves; 'that won't do – the saints protect us.'

The seamen, however, became clamorous; one portion were for throwing Schriften overboard, the other for throwing Philip; at last, the point was decided by the captain, who directed the small skiff, hanging astern, to be lowered down, and ordered both Philip and Schriften to get into it. The seamen approved of this arrangement, as it satisfied both parties. Philip made no objection; Schriften screamed and fought, but he was tossed into the boat. There he remained trembling in the stern sheets, while Philip, who had seized the sculls, pulled away from the vessel in the direction of the Phantom Ship.

In a few minutes the vessel which Philip and Schriften had left was no longer to be discerned through the thick haze; the Phantom Ship was still in sight, but at a much greater distance from them than she was before. Philip pulled hard towards her, but although hove-to, she appeared to increase her distance from the boat. For a short time he paused on his oars to regain his breath, when Schriften rose up and took his seat in the stern sheets of the boat. 'You may pull and pull, Philip Vanderdecken,' observed Schriften; 'but you will not gain that ship – no, no, that cannot be – we may have a long cruise together, but you will be as far from your object at the end of it as you are now at the commencement. Why don't you throw me overboard again? You would be all the lighter – He! he!'

'I threw you overboard in a state of frenzy,' replied Philip, 'when you attempted to force from me my relic.'

'And have I not endeavoured to make others take it from you this very day? – Have I not – He! he!'

'You have,' rejoined Philip; 'but I am now convinced, that you are as unhappy as myself, and that in what you are doing, you are only following your destiny, as I am mine. Why and wherefore I cannot tell, but we are both engaged in the same mystery; – if the success of my endeavours depends upon guarding the relic, the success of yours depends upon your obtaining it, and defeating my purpose by so doing. In this matter we are both agents, and you have been, as far as my mission is concerned, my most active enemy. But, Schriften, I have not forgotten, and never will, that you kindly *did advise* my poor Amine; that you prophesied to her what would be her fate, if she did not listen to your counsel; that you were no enemy of hers, although you have been, and are still mine. Although my enemy, for her sake *I forgive you*, and will not attempt to harm you.'

'You do then *forgive your enemy*, Philip Vanderdecken?' replied Schriften, mournfully, 'for such, I acknowledge myself to be.'

'I do, with *all my heart, with all my soul*,' replied Philip.

'Then you have conquered me, Philip Vanderdecken; you have now made me your friend, and your wishes are about to be accomplished. You would know who I am. Listen: – when your father, defying the Almighty's will, in his rage took my life, he was vouchsafed a chance of his doom being cancelled, through the merits of his son. I had also my appeal, which was for *vengeance*; it was granted that I should remain on earth, and thwart your will. That as long as we were enemies, you should not succeed; but that when you had conformed to the highest attribute of Christianity, proved on the holy cross, that of *forgiving your enemy*, your task should be fulfilled. Philip Vanderdecken, you have forgiven your enemy, and both our destinies are now accomplished.

As Schriften spoke, Philip's eyes were fixed upon him. He extended his hand to Philip – it was taken; and as it was pressed, the form of the pilot wasted as it were into the air, and Philip found himself alone.

'Father of Mercy, I thank Thee,' said Philip, 'that my task is done, and that I again may meet my Amine.'

Philip then pulled towards the Phantom Ship, and found that she no longer appeared to leave him; on the contrary, every minute he was nearer and nearer, and at last he threw in his oars, climbed up her sides, and gained her deck.

The crew of the vessel crowded round him.

'Your captain,' said Philip; 'I must speak with your captain.'

'Who shall I say, sir?' demanded one, who appeared to be the first mate.

'Who?' replied Philip. 'Tell him his son would speak to him, his son Philip Vanderdecken.'

Shouts of laughter from the crew followed this answer of Philip's; and the mate, as soon as they ceased, observed with a smile:

'You forget, sir, perhaps you would say his father.'

'Tell him his son, if you please,' replied Philip; 'take no note of grey hairs.'

'Well, sir, here he is coming forward,' replied the mate, stepping aside, and pointing to the captain.

'What is all this?' inquired the captain.

'Are you Philip Vanderdecken, the captain of this vessel?'

'I am, sir,' replied the other.

'You appear not to know me! But how can you? You saw me but when I was only three years old; yet may you remember a letter which you gave to your wife.'

'Ha!' replied the captain; 'and who then are you?'

'Time has stopped with you, but with those who live in the world he stops not! and for those who pass a life of misery, he hurries on still faster. In me, behold your son, Philip Vanderdecken, who has obeyed your wishes; and after a life of such peril and misery as few have passed, has at last fulfilled his vow, and now offers to his father this precious relic that he required to kiss.'

Philip drew out the relic, and held it towards his father. As if a flash of lightning had passed through his mind, the captain of the vessel started back, clasped his hands, fell on his knees, and wept.

'My son, my son!' exclaimed he, rising, and throwing himself into Philip's arms, 'my eyes are opened – the Almighty knows how long they have been obscured.' Embracing each other, they walked aft, away from the men, who were still crowded at the gangway.

'My son, my noble son, before the charm is broken – before we resolve, as we must, into the elements, oh! let me kneel in thanksgiving and contrition: my son, my noble son, receive a father's thanks,' exclaimed Vanderdecken. Then with tears of joy and penitence he humbly addressed himself to that Being whom he once so awfully defied.

The elder Vanderdecken knelt down: Philip did the same; still embracing each other with one arm, while they raised on high the other, and prayed.

For the last time the relic was taken from the bosom of Philip and handed to his father – and his father raised his eyes to heaven and kissed it. And as he kissed it, the long tapering upper spars of the Phantom vessel, the yards and sails that were set, fell into dust, fluttered in the air and sank upon the wave. Then mainmast, foremast bowsprit, everything above the deck, crumbled into atoms and disappeared.

Again he raised the relic to his lips and the work of destruction continued, the heavy iron guns sank through the decks and disappeared; the crew of the vessel (who were looking on) crumbled down into skeletons, and dust, and fragments of ragged garments; and there were none left on board the vessel in the semblance of life but the father and the son.

Once more did he put the sacred emblem to his lips, and the beams and timber separated, the decks of the vessel slowly sank, and the remnants of the hull floated upon the water; and as the father and son – the one young and vigorous, the other old and decrepit – still kneeling, still embracing, with their hands raised to heaven, sank slowly under the deep blue wave, the lurid sky was for a moment illuminated by a lightning cross.

Then did the clouds which obscured the heavens roll away swift as thought – the sun again burst out in all his splendour – the rippling waves appeared to dance with joy. The screaming seagull again whirled in the air, and the scared albatross once more slumbered on the wing. The porpoise tumbled and tossed in his sportive play, the albicore and dolphin leaped from the sparkling sea. All nature smiled as if it rejoiced that the charm was dissolved for ever, and that the Phantom Ship was no more.

Sir Arthur Conan Doyle

The Brown Hand

EVERYONE knows that Sir Dominick Holden, the famous Indian surgeon, made me his heir, and that his death changed me in an hour from a hard-working and impecunious medical man to a well-to-do landed proprietor. Many know also that there were at least five people between the inheritance and me, and that Sir Dominick's selection appeared to be altogether arbitrary and whimsical. I can assure them, however, that they are quite mistaken, and that, although I only knew Sir Dominick in the closing years of his life, there were none the less very real reasons why he should show his goodwill towards me. As a matter of fact, though I say it myself, no man ever did more for another than I did for my Indian uncle. I cannot expect the story to be believed, but it is so singular that I should feel that it was a breach of duty if I did not put it upon record – so here it is, and your belief or incredulity is your own affair.

Sir Dominick Holden, C.B., K.C.S.I., and I don't know what besides, was the most distinguished Indian surgeon of his day. In the Army originally, he afterwards settled down into civil practice in Bombay, and visited as a consultant every part of India. His name is best remembered in connection with the Oriental Hospital, which he founded and supported. The time came, however, when his iron constitution began to show signs of the long strain to which he had subjected it, and his brother practitioners (who were not, perhaps, entirely disinterested upon the point) were unanimous in recommending him to return to England. He held on so long as he could, but at last he developed nervous symptoms of a very pronounced character, and so came back, a broken man, to his native county of Wiltshire. He bought a considerable estate with an ancient manor-house upon the edge of Salisbury Plain, and devoted his old age to the study of Comparative Pathology, which had been his learned hobby all his life, and in which he was a foremost authority.

We of the family were, as may be imagined, much excited by the news of the return of this rich and childless uncle to England. On his part, although by no means exuberant in his hospitality, he showed some sense of his duty to his relations, and each of us in turn had an invitation to visit him. From the accounts of my cousins it appeared to be a melancholy business, and it was with mixed feelings that I at last received my own summons to appear at Rodenhurst. My wife was so carefully excluded in the invitation that my first impulse was to refuse it, but the interests of the children had to be considered, and so, with her consent, I set out one October afternoon upon my visit to Wiltshire, with little thought of what that visit was to entail.

My uncle's estate was situated where the arable land of the plains begins to swell upwards into the rounded chalk hills which are characteristic of the county. As I drove from Dinton Station in the waning light of that autumn day, I was impressed by the weird nature of the scenery. The few scattered cottages of the peasants were so dwarfed by the huge evidences of prehistoric life, that the present appeared to be a dream and the past to be the obtrusive and masterful reality. The road wound through the valleys, formed by a succession of grassy hills, and the summit of each was cut and carved into the most elaborate fortifications, some circular and some square, but all on a scale which has defied the winds and the rains of many centuries. Some call them Roman and some British, but their true origin and the reasons for this particular tract of country being so interlaced with entrenchments have never been finally made clear. Here and there on the long, smooth, olive-coloured slopes there rose small rounded barrows or tumuli. Beneath them lie the cremated ashes of the race which cut so deeply into the hills, but their graves tell us nothing save that a jar full of dust represents the man who once laboured under the sun.

It was through this weird country that I approached my uncle's residence of Rodenhurst, and the house was, as I found, in due keeping with its surroundings. Two broken and weather-stained pillars, each surmounted by a mutilated heraldic emblem, flanked the entrance to a neglected drive. A cold wind whistled through the elms which lined it, and the air was full of the drifting leaves. At the far end, under the gloomy arch of trees, a single yellow lamp burned steadily. In the dim half-light of the coming night I saw a long, low building stretching out two irregular wings, with deep eaves, a sloping gambrel roof, and walls which were criss-crossed with timber balks in the fashion of the Tudors. The cheery light of a fire flickered in the broad, latticed window to the left of the low-porched door, and this, as it proved, marked the study of my uncle, for it was thither that I was led by his butler in order to make my host's acquaintance.

He was cowering over his fire, for the moist chill of an English autumn had set him shivering. His lamp was unlit, and I only saw the red glow of the embers beating upon a huge, craggy face, with a Red Indian nose and cheek, and deep furrows and seams from eye to chin, the sinister marks of hidden volcanic fires. He sprang up at my entrance with something of an old-world courtesy and welcomed me warmly to Rodenhurst. At the same time I was conscious, as the lamp was carried in, that it was a very critical pair of light-blue eyes which looked out at me from under shaggy eyebrows, like scouts beneath a bush, and that this outlandish uncle of mine was carefully reading off my character with all the ease of a practised observer and an experienced man of the world.

For my part I looked at him, and looked again, for I had never seen a man whose appearance was more fitted to hold one's attention. His figure was the framework of a giant, but he had fallen away until his coat dangled straight down in a shocking fashion from a pair of broad and bony shoulders. All his limbs were huge and yet emaciated, and I could not take my gaze from his knobby wrists, and long, gnarled hands. But his eyes – those peering light-blue eyes – they were the most arrestive of any of his peculiarities. It was not their colour alone, nor was it the ambush of hair in which they lurked; but it was the expression which I read in them. For the appearance and bearing of the man were masterful, and one expected a certain corresponding arrogance in his eyes, but instead of that I read the look which tells of a spirit cowed and crushed, the furtive, expectant look of the dog whose master has taken the whip from the rack. I formed my own medical diagnosis upon one glance at those critical and yet appealing eyes. I believed that he was stricken with some mortal ailment, that he knew himself to be exposed to sudden death, and that he lived in terror of it. Such was my judgement – a false one, as the event showed; but I mention it that it may help you to realize the look which I read in his eyes.

My uncle's welcome was, as I have said, a courteous

one, and in an hour or so I found myself seated between him and his wife at a comfortable dinner, with curious pungent delicacies upon the table, and a stealthy, quick-eyed Oriental waiter behind his chair. The old couple had come round to that tragic imitation of the dawn of life when husband and wife, having lost or scattered all those who were their intimates, find themselves face to face and alone once more, their work done, and the end nearing fast. Those who have reached that stage in sweetness and love, who can change their winter into a gentle Indian summer, have come as victors through the ordeal of life. Lady Holden was a small, alert woman, with a kindly eye, and her expression as she glanced at him was a certificate of character to her husband. And yet, though I read a mutual love in their glances, I read also a mutual horror, and recognized in her face some reflection of that stealthy fear which I detected in his. Their talk was sometimes merry and sometimes sad, but there was a forced note in their merriment and a naturalness in their sadness which told me that a heavy heart beat upon either side of me.

We were sitting over our first glass of wine, and the servants had left the room, when the conversation took a turn which produced a remarkable effect upon my host and hostess. I cannot recall what it was which started the topic of the supernatural, but it ended in my showing them that the abnormal in psychical experiences was a subject to which I had, like many neurologists, devoted a great deal of attention. I concluded by narrating my experiences when, as a member of the Psychical Research Society, I had formed one of a committee of three who spent the night in a haunted house. Our adventures were neither exciting nor convincing, but, such as it was, the story appeared to interest my auditors in a remarkable degree. They listened with an eager silence, and I caught a look of intelligence between them which I could not understand. Lady Holden immediately afterwards rose and left the room.

Sir Dominick pushed the cigar-box over to me, and we smoked for some little time in silence. That huge bony hand of his was twitching as he raised it with his cheroot to his lips, and I felt that the man's nerves were vibrating like fiddle-strings. My instincts told me that he was on the verge of some intimate confidence, and I feared to speak lest I should interrupt it. At last he turned towards me with a spasmodic gesture like a man who throws his last scruple to the winds.

'From the little that I have seen of you it appears to me, Dr Hardacre,' said he, 'that you are the very man I have wanted to meet.'

'I am delighted to hear it, sir.'

'Your head seems to be cool and steady. You will acquit me of any desire to flatter you, for the circumstances are too serious to permit of insincerities. You have some special knowledge upon these subjects, and you evidently view them from that philosophical standpoint which robs them of all vulgar terror. I presume that the sight of an apparition would not seriously discompose you?'

'I think not, sir.'

'Would even interest you, perhaps?'

'Most intensely.'

'As a psychical observer, you would probably investigate it in as impersonal a fashion as an astronomer investigates a wandering comet?'

'Precisely.'

He gave a heavy sigh.

'Believe me, Dr Hardacre, there was a time when I could have spoken as you do now. My nerve was a by-word in India. Even the Mutiny never shook it for an instant. And yet you see what I am reduced to – the most timorous man, perhaps, in all this county of Wiltshire. Do not speak too bravely upon this subject, or you may find yourself subjected to as long-drawn a test as I am – a test which can only end in the madhouse or the grave.'

I waited patiently until he should see fit to go farther in his confidence. His preamble had, I need not say, filled me with interest and expectation.

'For some years, Dr Hardacre,' he continued, 'my life and that of my wife have been made miserable by a cause which is so grotesque that it borders upon the ludicrous. And yet familiarity has never made it more easy to bear – on the contrary, as time passes my nerves become more worn and shattered by the constant attrition. If you have no physical fears, Dr Hardacre, I should very much value your opinion upon this phenomenon which troubles us so.'

'For what it is worth my opinion is entirely at your service. May I ask the nature of the phenomenon?'

'I think that your experiences will have a higher evidential value if you are not told in advance what you may expect to encounter. You are yourself aware of the quibbles of unconscious cerebration and subjective impressions with which a scientific sceptic may throw a doubt upon your statement. It would be as well to guard against them in advance.'

'What shall I do, then?'

'I will tell you. Would you mind following me this way?' He led me out of the dining-room and down a long passage until we came to a terminal door. Inside there was a large bare room fitted as a laboratory, with numerous scientific instruments and bottles. A shelf ran along one side, upon which there stood a long line of glass jars containing pathological and anatomical specimens.

'You see that I still dabble in some of my old studies,' said Sir Dominick. 'These jars are the remains of what was once a most excellent collection, but unfortunately I lost the greater part of them when my house was burned down in Bombay in '92. It was a most unfortunate affair for me – in more ways than one. I had examples of many rare conditions, and my splenic collection was probably unique. These are the survivors.'

I glanced over them, and saw that they really were of a very great value and rarity from a pathological point of view: bloated organs, gaping cysts, distorted bones, odious parasites – a singular exhibition of the products of India.

'There is, as you see, a small settee here,' said my host. 'It was far from our intention to offer a guest so meagre an accommodation, but since affairs have taken this turn, it would be a great kindness upon your part if you would consent to spend the night in this apartment. I beg that you will not hesitate to let me know if the idea should be at all repugnant to you.'

'On the contrary,' I said, 'it is most acceptable.'

'My own room is the second on the left, so that if you should feel that you are in need of company a call would always bring me to your side.'

'I trust that I shall not be compelled to disturb you.'

'It is unlikely that I shall be asleep. I do not sleep much. Do not hesitate to summon me.'

And so with this agreement we joined Lady Holden in the drawing-room and talked of lighter things.

It was no affectation upon my part to say that the prospect of my night's adventure was an agreeable one. I have no pretence to greater physical courage than my neighbours, but familiarity with a subject robs it of those vague and undefined terrors which are the most appalling to the imaginative mind. The human brain is capable of only one strong emotion at a time, and if it be filled with curiosity or scientific enthusiasm, there is no room for fear. It is true that I had my uncle's assurance that he had himself originally taken this point of view, but I reflected that the breakdown of his nervous system might be due to his forty years in India as much as to any psychical experiences which had befallen him. I at least was sound in nerve and brain, and it was with something of the pleasurable thrill of anticipation with which the sportsman takes his position beside the haunt of his game that I shut the laboratory door behind me, and partially undressing, lay down upon the rug-covered settee.

It was not an ideal atmosphere for a bedroom. The air was heavy with many chemical odours, that of methylated spirit predominating. Nor were the decorations of my chamber very sedative. The odious line of glass jars with their relics of disease and suffering stretched in front of my very eyes. There was no blind to the window, and a three-quarter moon streamed its white light into the room, tracing a silver square with filigree lattices upon the opposite wall. When I had extinguished my candle this one bright patch in the midst of the general gloom had certainly an eerie and discomposing aspect. A rigid and absolute silence reigned throughout the old house, so that the low swish of the branches in the garden came softly and soothingly to my ears. It may have been the hypnotic lullaby of this gentle susurrus, or it may have been the result of my tiring day, but after many dozings and many efforts to regain my clearness of perception, I fell at last into a deep and dreamless sleep.

I was awakened by some sound in the room, and I instantly raised myself upon my elbow on the couch. Some hours had passed, for the square patch upon the wall had slid downwards and sideways until it lay obliquely at the end of my bed. The rest of the room was in deep shadow. At first I could see nothing. Presently, as my eyes became accustomed to the faint light, I was aware, with a thrill which all my scientific absorption could not entirely prevent, that something was moving slowly along the line of the wall. A gentle, shuffling sound, as of soft slippers, came to my ears, and I dimly discerned a human figure walking stealthily from the direction of the door. As it emerged into the patch of moonlight I saw very clearly what it was and how it was employed. It was a man, short and squat, dressed in some sort of dark-grey gown, which hung straight from his shoulders to his feet. The moon shone upon the side of his face, and I saw that it was chocolate-brown in colour, with a ball of black hair like a woman's at the back of his head. He walked slowly, and his eyes were cast upwards towards the line of bottles which contained those gruesome remnants of humanity. He seemed to examine each jar with attention, and then to pass on to the next. When he had come to the end of the line, immediately opposite my bed, he stopped, faced me, threw up his hands with a gesture of despair, and vanished from my sight.

I have said that he threw up his hands, but I should have said his arms, for as he assumed that attitude of despair I observed a singular peculiarity about his appearance. He had only one hand! As the sleeves drooped down from the up-flung arms I saw the left plainly, but the right ended in a knobby and unsightly stump. In every other way his appearance was so natural, and I had both seen and heard him so clearly, that I could easily have believed that he was an Indian servant of Sir Dominick's who had come into my room in search of something. It was only his sudden disappearance which suggested anything more sinister to me. As it was I sprang from my couch, lit a candle, and examined the whole room carefully. There were no signs of my visitor, and I was forced to conclude that there had really been something outside the normal laws of Nature in his appearance. I lay awake for the remainder of the night, but nothing else occurred to disturb me.

I am an early riser, but my uncle was an even earlier one, for I found him pacing up and down the lawn at the side of the house. He ran towards me in his eagerness when he saw me come out from the door.

'Well, well!' he cried. 'Did you see him?'

'An Indian with one hand?'

'Precisely.'

'Yes, I saw him' – and I told him all that occurred. When I had finished, he led the way into his study.

'We have a little time before breakfast,' said he. 'It will suffice to give you an explanation of this extraordinary affair – so far as I can explain that which is essentially inexplicable. In the first place, when I tell you that for four years I have never passed one single night, either in Bombay, aboard ship, or here in England without my sleep being broken by this fellow, you will understand why it is that I am a wreck of my former self. His programme is always the same. He appears by my bedside, shakes me roughly by the shoulder, passes from my room into the laboratory, walks slowly along the line of my bottles, and then vanishes. For more than a thousand times he has gone through the same routine.'

'What does he want?'

'He wants his hand.'

'His hand?'

'Yes, it came about in this way. I was summoned to Peshawur for a consultation some ten years ago, and while there I was asked to look at the hand of a native who was passing through with an Afghan caravan. The fellow came from some mountain tribe living away at the back of beyond somewhere on the other side of Kaffiristan. He talked a bastard Pushtoo, and it was all I could do to understand him. He was suffering from a soft sarcomatous swelling of one of the metacarpal joints, and I made him realize that it was only by losing his hand that he could hope to save his life. After much persuasion he consented to the operation, and he asked me, when it was over, what fee I demanded. The poor fellow was almost a beggar, so that the idea of a fee was absurd, but I answered in jest that my fee should be his hand, and that I proposed to add it to my pathological collection.

'To my surprise he demurred very much to the suggestion, and he explained that according to his religion it was an all-important matter that the body should be reunited after death, and so make a perfect dwelling for the spirit. The belief is, of course, an old one, and the mummies of the Egyptians arose from an analogous superstition. I answered him that his hand was already off, and asked him how he intended to preserve it. He replied that he would pickle it in salt and carry it about with him. I suggested that it might be safer in my keeping than in his, and that I had better means than salt for preserving it. On realizing that I really intended to keep it carefully, his opposition vanished instantly. "But remember, sahib," said he, "I shall want it back when I am dead." I laughed at the remark, and so the matter ended. I returned to my practice, and he no doubt in the course of time was able to continue his journey to Afghanistan.

'Well, as I told you last night, I had a bad fire in my house at Bombay. Half of it was burned down, and, among other things, my pathological collection was largely destroyed. What you see are the poor remains of it. The hand of the hillman went with the rest, but I gave the matter no particular thought at the time. That was six years ago.

'Four years ago – two years after the fire – I was awakened one night by a furious tugging at my sleeve. I sat up under the impression that my favourite mastiff was trying to arouse me. Instead of this, I saw my Indian patient of long ago, dressed in the long grey gown which was the badge of his people. He was holding up his stump and looking reproachfully at me. He then went over to my bottles, which at that time I kept in my room, and he examined them carefully, after which he gave a gesture of anger and vanished. I realized that he had just died, and that he had come to claim my promise that I should keep his limb in safety for him.

'Well, there you have it all, Dr Hardacre. Every night at the same hour for four years this performance has been repeated. It is a simple thing in itself, but it has worn me out like water dropping on a stone. It has brought a vile insomnia with it, for I cannot sleep now for the expectation of his coming. It has poisoned my old age and that of my wife, who has been the sharer in this great trouble. But there is the breakfast gong, and she will be waiting impatiently to know how it fared with you last night. We are both much indebted to you for your gallantry, for it takes something from the weight of our misfortune when we share it, even for a single night, with a friend, and it reassures us as to our sanity, which we are sometimes driven to question.'

This was the curious narrative which Sir Dominick confided to me – a story which to many would have appeared to be a grotesque impossibility, but which, after my experience of the night before, and my previous knowledge of such things, I was prepared to accept as an absolute fact.

I thought deeply over the matter, and brought the whole range of my reading and experience to bear upon it. After breakfast, I surprised my host and hostess by announcing that I was returning to London by the next train.

'My dear doctor,' cried Sir Dominick in great distress, 'you make me feel that I have been guilty of a gross breach of hospitality in intruding this unfortunate matter upon you. I should have borne my own burden.'

'It is, indeed, that matter which is taking me to London,' I answered; 'but you are mistaken, I assure you, if you think that my experience of last night was an unpleasant one to me. On the contrary, I am about to ask your permission to return in the evening and spend one more night in your laboratory. I am very eager to see this visitor once again.'

My uncle was exceedingly anxious to know what I was about to do, but my fears of raising false hopes prevented me from telling him. I was back in my own consulting-room a little after luncheon, and was confirming my memory of a passage in a recent book upon occultism which had arrested my attention when I read it.

'In the case of earth-bound spirits,' said my authority, 'some one dominant idea obsessing them at the hour of death is sufficient to hold them to this material world. They are the amphibia of this life and of the next, capable of passing from one to the other as the turtle passes from land to water. The causes which may bind a soul so strongly to a life which its body has abandoned are any violent emotion. Avarice, revenge, anxiety, love, and pity have all been known to have this effect. As a rule it springs from some unfulfilled wish, and when the wish has been fulfilled the material bond relaxes. There are many cases upon record which show the singular persistence of these visitors, and also their disappearance when their wishes have been fulfilled, or in some cases when a reasonable compromise has been effected.'

'*A reasonable compromise effected*' – those were the words which I had brooded over all the morning, and which I now verified in the original. No actual atonement could be made here – but a reasonable compromise! I made my way as fast as a train could take me to the Shadwell Seamen's Hospital, where my old friend Jack Hewett was house-surgeon. Without explaining the situation I made him understand exactly what it was that I wanted.

'A brown man's hand!' said he, in amazement. 'What in the world do you want that for?'

'Never mind. I'll tell you some day. I know that your wards are full of Indians.'

'I should think so. But a hand –' He thought a little and then struck a bell.

'Travers,' said he to a student-dresser, 'what became of the hands of the Lascar which we took off yesterday? I mean the fellow from the East India Dock who got caught in the steam winch.'

'They are in the *post-mortem* room, sir.'

'Just pack one of them in antiseptics and give it to Dr Hardacre.'

And so I found myself back at Rodenhurst before dinner with this curious outcome of my day in town. I still said nothing to Sir Dominick, but I slept that night in the laboratory, and I placed the Lascar's hand in one of the glass jars at the end of my couch.

So interested was I in the result of my experiment that sleep was out of the question. I sat with a shaded lamp beside me and waited patiently for my visitor. This time I saw him clearly from the first. He appeared beside the door, nebulous for an instant, and then hardening into as distinct an outline as any living man. The slippers beneath his grey gown were red and heelless, which accounted for the low, shuffling sound which he made as he walked. As on the previous night he passed slowly along the line of bottles until he paused before that which contained the hand. He reached up to it, his whole figure quivering with expectation, took it down, examined it eagerly, and then, with a face which was convulsed with fury and disappointment, he hurled it down on the floor. There was a crash which resounded through the house, and when I looked up the mutilated Indian had disappeared. A moment later my door flew open and Sir Dominick rushed in.

'You are not hurt?' he cried.

'No – but deeply disappointed.'

He looked in astonishment at the splinters of glass, and the brown hand lying upon the floor.

'Good God!' he cried. 'What is this?'

I told him my idea and its wretched sequel. He listened intently, but shook his head.

'It was well thought of,' said he, 'but I fear that there is no such easy end to my sufferings. But one thing I now insist upon. It is that you shall never again upon any pretext occupy this room. My fears that something might have happened to you – when I heard that crash – have been the most acute of all the agonies which I have undergone. I will not expose myself to a repetition of it.'

He allowed me, however, to spend the remainder of that night where I was, and I lay there worrying over the problem and lamenting my own failure. With the first light of morning there was the Lascar's hand still lying upon the floor to remind me of my fiasco. I lay looking at it – and as I lay suddenly an idea flew like a bullet through my head and brought me quivering with excitement out of my couch. I raised the grim relic from where it had fallen.

Yes, it was indeed so. The hand was the *left* hand of the Lascar.

By the first train I was on my way to town, and hurried at once to the Seamen's Hospital. I remembered that both hands of the Lascar had been amputated, but I was terrified lest the precious organ which I was in search of might have been already consumed in the crematory. My suspense was soon ended. It had still been preserved in the *post-mortem* room. And so I returned to Rodenhurst in the evening with my mission accomplished and the material for a fresh experiment.

But Sir Dominick Holden would not hear of my occupying the laboratory again. To all my entreaties he turned a deaf ear. It offended his sense of hospitality, and he could no longer permit it. I left the hand, therefore, as I had done its fellow the night before, and I occupied a comfortable bedroom in another portion of the house, some distance from the scene of my adventures.

But in spite of that my sleep was not destined to be uninterrupted. In the dead of night my host burst into my room, a lamp in his hand. His huge gaunt figure was enveloped in a loose dressing-gown, and his whole appearance might certainly have seemed more formidable to a weak-nerved man than that of the Indian of the night before. But it was not his entrance so much as his expression which amazed me. He had turned suddenly younger by twenty years at the least. His eyes were shining, his features radiant, and he waved one hand in triumph over his head. I sat up astounded, staring sleepily at this extraordinary visitor. But his words soon drove the sleep from my eyes.

'We have done it! We have succeeded!' he shouted. 'My dear Hardacre, how can I ever in this world repay you?'

Sir Arthur Conan Doyle

'You don't mean to say that it is all right?'

'Indeed I do. I was sure that you would not mind being awakened to hear such blessed news.'

'Mind! I should think not indeed. But is it really certain?'

'I have no doubt whatever upon the point. I owe you such a debt, my dear nephew, as I have never owed a man before, and never expected to. What can I possibly do for you that is commensurate? Providence must have sent you to my rescue. You have saved both my reason and my life, for another six months of this must have seen me either in a cell or a coffin. And my wife – it was wearing her out before my eyes. Never could I have believed that any human being could have lifted this burden off me.' He seized my hand and wrung it in his bony grip.

'It was only an experiment – a forlorn hope – but I am delighted from my heart that it has succeeded. But how do you know that it is all right? Have you seen something?'

He seated himself at the foot of my bed.

'I have seen enough,' said he. 'It satisfies me that I shall be troubled no more. What has passed is easily told. You know that at a certain hour this creature always comes to me. Tonight he arrived at the usual time, and aroused me with even more violence than is his custom. I can only surmise that his disappointment of last night increased the bitterness of his anger against me. He looked angrily at me, and then went on his usual round. But in a few minutes I saw him, for the first time since this persecution began, return to my chamber. He was smiling. I saw the gleam of his white teeth through the dim light. He stood facing me at the end of my bed, and three times he made the low Eastern salaam which is their solemn leave-taking. And the third time that he bowed he raised his arms over

Earthfasts

William Mayne

At the dusk of a summer's day, Keith Heseltine and David Wix were still out on Haw Bank, investigating something. There was a new mound in the grass, and it was getting bigger. Then the ground stirred, as if someone were getting out of bed. And with the movement came the sound of drumming; David was trembling all over, and so was Keith, and then they made sense of it. All that had come out of the hill was a boy about their own size, with a drum.

Two hundred years before, Nellie Jack John the drummer boy had gone to explore the passage under the castle, looking for King Arthur with his sleeping knights. Now he had come out again, but time had got mixed up, so that the ancient dead giants were walking about again, and domestic pigs were transformed into dangerous wild swine.

A Wrinkle in Time

Madeleine L'Engle

Charles Wallace Murry, who goes searching through 'a wrinkle in time' for his lost father, finds himself on an evil planet where all life is enslaved by a huge pulsating brain known as IT.

How Charles, his sister Meg, and his friend Calvin find and free his father makes this a very special and exciting mixture of fantasy and science fiction, which all the way through is dominated by the funny and mysterious trio of guardian angels known as Mrs. Whatsit, Mrs. Who, and Mrs. Which. A Newbery Medal winner.

Ghostly Gallery

sel. Alfred Hitchcock

Eleven weird and uncanny ghost stories collected by Alfred Hitchcock, the master of mystery. They include really spooky spinechilling stories, some fanciful ones, and some where the phantoms and apparitions are even treated humorously. Some of the phantoms are true shades of darkness, and others, stranger still, appear in the glare of the sun at noon or deep in the forest shadows – you may see a spook any day of your life.

For fearless readers of ten upwards.

The House of The Nightmare and other Eerie Tales

ed. Kathleen Lines

A little gooseflesh, a pleasurable shiver, may be all you get if you read these sinister, spooky stories by the fireside among your family, doors locked and windows barred and curtains drawn to shut out the night, but don't take the book to bed with you, don't read it alone.

Kathleen Lines is well known for her anthologies for children, and in this book she has collected some of the classic nineteenth-century ghost stories and some in which modern authors have carried on the tradition, even including one which deals with a mysterious prediction made by a computer. Some true ghost stories are also included.

For readers of eleven and over.

his head, and I saw his *two* hands outstretched in the air. So he vanished, and, as I believe, for ever.'

So that is the curious experience which won me the affection and the gratitude of my celebrated uncle, the famous Indian surgeon. His anticipations were realized, and never again was he disturbed by the visits of the restless hillman in search of his lost member. Sir Dominick and Lady Holden spent a very happy old age, unclouded, so far as I know, by any trouble, and they finally died during the great influenza epidemic within a few weeks of each other. In his lifetime he always turned to me for advice in everything which concerned that English life of which he knew so little; and I aided him also in the purchase and development of his estates. It was no great surprise to me, therefore, that I found myself eventually promoted over the heads of five exasperated cousins, and changed in a single day from a hard-working country doctor into the head of an important Wiltshire family. I at least have reason to bless the memory of the man with the brown hand, and the day when I was fortunate enough to relieve Rodenhurst of his unwelcome presence.

Anonymous

The Ghost-Brahman

ONCE on a time there lived a poor Brahman, who not being a Kulin, found it the hardest thing in the world to get married. He went to rich people and begged of them to give him money that he might marry a wife. And a large sum of money was needed, not so much for the expenses of the wedding, as for giving to the parents of the bride. He begged from door to door, flattered many rich folk, and at last succeeded in scraping together the sum needed. The wedding took place in due time; and he brought home his wife to his mother. After a short time he said to his mother – 'Mother, I have no means to support you and my wife; I must therefore go to distant countries to get money somehow or other. I may be away for years, for I won't return till I get a good sum. In the meantime I'll give you what I have; you make the best of it, and take care of my wife.' The Brahman, receiving his mother's blessing, set out on his travels. In the evening of that very day, a ghost assuming the exact appearance of the Brahman came into the house. The newly-married woman, thinking it was her husband, said to him – 'How is it that you have returned so soon? You said you might be away for years; why have you changed your mind?' The ghost said – 'Today is not a lucky day, I have therefore returned home; besides, I have already got some money.' The mother did not doubt but that it was her son. So the ghost lived in the house as if he was its owner, and as if he was the son of the old woman

and the husband of the young woman. As the ghost and the Brahman were exactly like each other in everything, like two peas, the people in the neighbourhood all thought that the ghost was the real Brahman. After some years the Brahman returned from his travels; and what was his surprise when he found another like him in the house. The ghost said to the Brahman – 'Who are you? what business have you to come to my house?' 'Who am I?' replied the Brahman, 'let me ask who you are. This is my house; that is my mother, and this is my wife.' The ghost said – 'Why herein is a strange thing. Everyone knows that this is my house, that is my wife, and yonder is my mother; and I have lived here for years. And you pretend this is your house, and that woman is your wife. Your head must have got turned, Brahman.' So saying the ghost drove away the Brahman from his house. The Brahman became mute with wonder. He did not know what to do. At last he bethought himself of going to the King and of laying his case before him. The King saw the ghost-Brahman as well as the Brahman, and the one was the picture of the other; so he was in a fix, and did not know how to decide the quarrel. Day after day the Brahman went to the King and besought him to give him back his house, his wife, and his mother; and the King, not knowing what to say every time, put him off to the following day. Every day the King tells him to – 'Come tomorrow'; and every day the Brahman goes away from the palace weeping and striking his forehead with the palm of his hand, and saying – 'What a wicked world this is! I am driven from my own house, and another fellow has taken possession of my house and of my wife! And what a King this is! He does not do justice.'

Now, it came to pass that as the Brahman went away every day from the court outside the town, he passed a spot at which a great many cowboys used to play. They

let the cows graze on the meadow, while they themselves met together under a large tree to play. And they played at royalty. One cowboy was elected king; another, prime minister or vizier; another, *kotwal*, or prefect of the police; and others, constables. Every day for several days together they saw the Brahman passing by weeping. One day the cowboy king asked his vizier whether he knew why the Brahman wept every day. On the vizier not being able to answer the question, the cowboy king ordered one of his constables to bring the Brahman to him. One of them went and said to the Brahman – 'The king requires your immediate attendance.' The Brahman replied – 'What for? I have just come from the King, and he put me off till tomorrow. Why does he want me again?' 'It is our king that wants you – our neat-herd king,' rejoined the constable. 'Who is neat-herd king?' asked the Brahman. 'Come and see,' was the reply. The neat-herd king then asked the Brahman why he every day went away weeping. The Brahman then told him his sad story. The neat-herd king, after hearing the whole, said, 'I understand your case; I will give you again all your rights. Only go to the King and ask his permission for me to decide your case.' The Brahman went back to the King of the country, and begged His Majesty to send his case to the neat-herd king, who had offered to decide it. The King, whom the case had greatly puzzled, granted the permission sought. The following morning was fixed for the trial. The neat-herd king, who saw through the whole, brought with him next day a phial with a narrow neck. The Brahman and the ghost-Brahman both appeared at the bar. After a great deal of examination of witnesses and of speech-making, the neat-herd king said – 'Well, I have heard enough. I'll decide the case at once. Here is this phial. Whichever of you will enter into it shall be declared by the court to be the right-

ful owner of the house, the title of which is in dispute. Now, let me see, which of you will enter.' The Brahman said – 'You are a neat-herd, and your intellect is that of a neat-herd. What man can enter into such a small phial?' 'If you cannot enter,' said the neat-herd king, 'then you are not the rightful owner. What do you say, sir, to this?' turning to the ghost-Brahman and addressing him. 'If you can enter into the phial, then the house and the wife and the mother become yours.' 'Of course I will enter,' said the ghost. And true to his word, to the wonder of all, he made himself into a small creature like an insect, and entered into the phial. The neat-herd king forthwith corked up the phial, and the ghost could not get out. Then, addressing the Brahman, the neat-herd king said, 'Throw this phial into the bottom of the sea, and take possession of your house, wife, and mother.' The Brahman did so, and lived happily for many years and begat sons and daughters.

Richard Middleton

The Ghost-Ship

FAIRFIELD is a little village lying near the Portsmouth Road about half-way between London and the sea. Strangers who find it by accident now and then, call it a pretty, old-fashioned place; we who live in it and call it home don't find anything very pretty about it, but we should be sorry to live anywhere else. Our minds have taken the shape of the inn and the church and the green, I suppose. At all events we never feel comfortable out of Fairfield.

Of course the Cockneys, with their vasty houses and noise-ridden streets, can call us rustics if they choose, but for all that Fairfield is a better place to live in than London. Doctor says that when he goes to London his mind is bruised with the weight of the houses, and he was a Cockney born. He had to live there himself when he was a little chap, but he knows better now. You gentlemen may laugh – perhaps some of you come from London way – but it seems to me that a witness like that is worth a gallon of arguments.

Dull? Well, you might find it dull, but I assure you that I've listened to all the London yarns you have spun to-night, and they're absolutely nothing to the things that happen at Fairfield. It's because of our way of thinking and minding our own business. If one of your Londoners were set down on the green of a Saturday night when the ghosts

of the lads who died in the war keep tryst with the lasses who lie in the churchyard, he couldn't help being curious and interfering, and then the ghosts would go somewhere where it was quieter. But we just let them come and go and don't make any fuss, and in consequence Fairfield is the ghostiest place in all England. Why, I've seen a headless man sitting on the edge of the well in broad daylight, and the children playing about his feet as if he were their father. Take my word for it, spirits know when they are well off as much as human beings.

Still, I must admit that the thing I'm going to tell you about was queer even for our part of the world, where three packs of ghost-hounds hunt regularly during the season, and blacksmith's great-grandfather is busy all night shoeing the dead gentlemen's horses. Now that's a thing that wouldn't happen in London, because of their interfering way, but blacksmith he lies up aloft and sleeps as quiet as a lamb. Once when he had a bad head he shouted down to them not to make so much noise, and in the morning he found an old guinea left on the anvil as an apology. He wears it on his watch-chain now. But I must get on with my story; if I start telling you about the queer happenings at Fairfield I'll never stop.

It all came of the great storm in the spring of '97, the year that we had two great storms. This was the first one, and I remember it very well, because I found in the morning that it had lifted the thatch of my pigsty into the widow's garden as clean as a boy's kite. When I looked over the hedge, widow – Tom Lamport's widow that was – was prodding for her nasturtiums with a daisy-grubber. After I had watched her for a little I went down to the *Fox and Grapes* to tell landlord what she had said to me. Landlord he laughed, being a married man and at ease with the sex. 'Come to that,' he said, 'the tempest has blowed

something into my field. A kind of a ship I think it would be.'

I was surprised at that until he explained that it was only a ghost-ship and would do no hurt to the turnips. We argued that it had been blown up from the sea at Portsmouth, and then we talked of something else. There were two slates down at the parsonage and a big tree in Lumley's meadow. It was a rare storm.

I reckon the wind had blown our ghosts all over England. They were coming back for days afterwards with foundered horses and as footsore as possible, and they were so glad to get back to Fairfield that some of them walked up the street crying like little children. Squire said that his great-grandfather's great-grandfather hadn't looked so dead-beat since the battle of Naseby, and he's an educated man.

What with one thing and another, I should think it was a week before we got straight again, and then one afternoon I met the landlord on the green and he had a worried face. 'I wish you'd come and have a look at that ship in my field,' he said to me; 'it seems to me it's leaning real hard on the turnips. I can't bear thinking what the missus will say when she sees it.'

I walked down the lane with him, and sure enough there was a ship in the middle of his field, but such a ship as no man had seen on the water for three hundred years, let alone in the middle of a turnip-field. It was all painted black and covered with carvings, and there was a great bay window in the stern for all the world like the Squire's drawing-room. There was a crowd of little black cannon on deck and looking out of her port-holes, and she was anchored at each end to the hard ground. I have seen the wonders of the world on picture-postcards, but I have never seen anything to equal that.

'She seems very solid for a ghost-ship,' I said, seeing the landlord was bothered.

'I should say it's a betwixt and between,' he answered, puzzling it over, 'but it's going to spoil a matter of fifty turnips, and missus she'll want it moved.' We went up to her and touched the side, and it was as hard as a real ship. 'Now there's folks in England would call that very curious,' he said.

Now I don't know much about ships, but I should think that that ghost-ship weighed a solid two hundred tons, and it seemed to me that she had come to stay, so that I felt sorry for landlord, who was a married man. 'All the horses in Fairfield won't move her out of my turnips,' he said, frowning at her.

Just then we heard a noise on her deck, and we looked up and saw that a man had come out of her front cabin and was looking down at us very peaceably. He was dressed in a black uniform set out with rusty gold lace, and he had a great cutlass by his side in a brass sheath. 'I'm Captain Bartholomew Roberts,' he said, in a gentleman's voice, 'put in for recruits. I seem to have brought her rather far up the harbour.'

'Harbour!' cried landlord; 'why, you're fifty miles from the sea.'

Captain Roberts didn't turn a hair. 'So much as that, is it?' he said coolly. 'Well, it's of no consequence.'

Landlord was a bit upset at this. 'I don't want to be un-neighbourly,' he said, 'but I wish you hadn't brought your ship into my field. You see, my wife sets great store on these turnips.'

The captain took a pinch of snuff out of a fine gold box that he pulled out of his pocket, and dusted his fingers with a silk handkerchief in a very genteel fashion. 'I'm only here for a few months,' he said; 'but if a testimony of my

esteem would pacify your good lady I should be content,' and with the words he loosed a great gold brooch from the neck of his coat and tossed it down to landlord.

Landlord blushed as red as a strawberry. 'I'm not denying she's fond of jewellery,' he said, 'but it's too much for half a sackful of turnips.' And indeed it was a handsome brooch.

The captain laughed. 'Tut, man,' he said, 'it's a forced sale, and you deserve a good price. Say no more about it,' and nodding good day to us, he turned on his heel and went into the cabin. Landlord walked back up the lane like a man with a weight off his mind. 'That tempest has blowed me a bit of luck,' he said; 'the missus will be main pleased with that brooch. It's better than blacksmith's guinea, any day.'

Ninety-seven was Jubilee year, the year of the second Jubilee, you remember, and we had great doings at Fairfield, so that we hadn't much time to bother about the ghost-ship; though anyhow it isn't our way to meddle in things that don't concern us. Landlord, he saw his tenant once or twice when he was hoeing his turnips and passed the time of day, and landlord's wife wore her new brooch to church every Sunday. But we didn't mix much with the ghosts at any time, all except an idiot lad there was in the village, and he didn't know the difference between a man and a ghost, poor innocent! On Jubilee Day, however, somebody told Captain Roberts why the church bells were ringing, and he hoisted a flag and fired off his guns like a loyal Englishman. 'Tis true the guns were shotted, and one of the round shot knocked a hole in Farmer Johnstone's barn, but nobody thought much of that in such a season of rejoicing.

It wasn't till our celebrations were over that we noticed that anything was wrong in Fairfield. 'Twas shoemaker

who told me first about it one morning at the *Fox and Grapes*. 'You know my great-uncle?' he said to me.

'You mean Joshua, the quiet lad,' I answered, knowing him well.

'Quiet!' said shoemaker indignantly. 'Quiet you call him, coming home at three o'clock every morning as drunk as a magistrate and waking up the whole house with his noise.'

'Why, it can't be Joshua!' I said, for I knew him for one of the most respectable young ghosts in the village.

'Joshua it is,' said shoemaker; 'and one of these nights he'll find himself out in the street if he isn't careful.'

This kind of talk shocked me, I can tell you, for I don't like to hear a man abusing his own family, and I could hardly believe that a steady youngster like Joshua had taken to drink. But just then in came butcher Aylwin in such a temper that he could hardly drink his beer. 'The young puppy! The young puppy!' he kept on saying; and it was some time before shoemaker and I found out that he was talking about his ancestor that fell at Senlac.

'Drink?' said shoemaker hopefully, for we all like company in our misfortunes, and butcher nodded grimly.

'The young noodle,' he said, emptying his tankard.

Well, after that I kept my ears open, and it was the same story all over the village. There was hardly a young man among all the ghosts of Fairfield who didn't roll home in the small hours of the morning the worse for liquor. I used to wake up in the night and hear them stumble past my house, singing outrageous songs. The worst of it was that we couldn't keep the scandal to ourselves, and the folk at Greenhill began to talk of 'sodden Fairfield' and taught their children to sing a song about us:

'Sodden Fairfield, sodden Fairfield, has no use for bread-
  and-butter,
Rum for breakfast, rum for dinner, rum for tea, and
  rum for supper!'

We are easy-going in our village, but we didn't like that.

Of course we soon found out where the young fellows
went to get the drink, and landlord was terribly cut up that
his tenant should have turned out so badly, but his wife
wouldn't hear of parting with the brooch, so that he
couldn't give the Captain notice to quit. But as time went
on, things grew from bad to worse, and at all hours of the
day you would see those young reprobates sleeping it off
on the village green. Nearly every afternoon a ghost-wagon
used to jolt down to the ship with a lading of rum, and
though the older ghosts seemed inclined to give the Captain's hospitality the go-by, the youngsters were neither to
hold nor to bind.

So one afternoon when I was taking my nap I heard a
knock at the door, and there was Parson looking very serious, like a man with a job before him that he didn't altogether relish. 'I'm going down to talk to the Captain about
all this drunkenness in the village, and I want you to come
with me,' he said straight out.

I can't say that I fancied the visit much myself, and I
tried to hint to Parson that as, after all, they were only a
lot of ghosts, it didn't very much matter.

'Dead or alive, I'm responsible for their good conduct,'
he said, 'and I'm going to do my duty and put a stop to
this continued disorder. And you are coming with me,
John Simmons.' So I went, Parson being a persuasive kind
of man.

We went down to the ship, and as we approached her I
could see the Captain tasting the air on deck. When he

saw Parson he took off his hat very politely, and I can tell you that I was relieved to find that he had a proper respect for the cloth. Parson acknowledged his salute and spoke out stoutly enough. 'Sir, I should be glad to have a word with you.'

'Come on board, sir; come on board,' said the Captain, and I could tell by his voice that he knew why we were there. Parson and I climbed up an uneasy kind of ladder, and the Captain took us into the great cabin at the back of the ship, where the bay-window was. It was the most wonderful place you ever saw in your life, all full of gold and silver plate, swords with jewelled scabbards, carved oak chairs, and great chests that looked as though they were bursting with guineas. Even Parson was surprised, and he did not shake his head very hard when the Captain took down some silver cups and poured us out a drink of rum. I tasted mine, and I don't mind saying that it changed my view of things entirely. There was nothing betwixt and between about that rum, and I felt that it was ridiculous to blame the lads for drinking too much of stuff like that. It seemed to fill my veins with honey and fire.

Parson put the case squarely to the Captain, but I didn't listen much to what he said; I was busy sipping my drink and looking through the window at the fishes swimming to and fro over landlord's turnips. Just then it seemed the most natural thing in the world that they should be there, though afterwards, of course, I could see that that proved it was a ghost-ship.

But even then I thought it was queer when I saw a drowned sailor float by in the thin air with his hair and beard all full of bubbles. It was the first time I had seen anything quite like that at Fairfield.

All the time I was regarding the wonders of the deep, Parson was telling Captain Roberts how there was no

peace or rest in the village owing to the curse of drunkenness, and what a bad example the youngsters were setting to the older ghosts. The Captain listened very attentively, and only put in a word now and then about boys being boys and young men sowing their wild oats. But when Parson had finished his speech he filled up our silver cups and said to Parson, with a flourish, 'I should be sorry to cause trouble anywhere where I have been made welcome, and you will be glad to hear that I put to sea tomorrow night. And now you must drink me a prosperous voyage.' So we all stood up and drank the toast with honour, and that noble rum was like hot oil in my veins.

After that Captain showed us some of the curiosities he had brought back from foreign parts, and we were greatly amazed, though afterwards I couldn't clearly remember what they were. And then I found myself walking across the turnips with Parson, and I was telling him of the glories of the deep that I had seen through the window of the ship. He turned on me severely. 'If I were you, John Simmons,' he said, 'I should go straight home to bed.' He has a way of putting things that wouldn't occur to an ordinary man, has Parson, and I did as he told me.

Well, next day it came on to blow, and it blew harder and harder, till about eight o'clock at night I heard a noise and looked out into the garden. I dare say you won't believe me, it seems a bit tall even to me, but the wind had lifted the thatch of my pigsty into the widow's garden a second time. I thought I wouldn't wait to hear what widow had to say about it, so I went across the green to the *Fox and Grapes*, and the wind was so strong that I danced along on tip-toe like a girl at the fair. When I got to the inn landlord had to help me shut the door; it seemed as though a dozen goats were pushing against it to come in out of the storm.

'It's a powerful tempest,' he said, drawing the beer. 'I hear there's a chimney down at Dickory End.'

'It's a funny thing how these sailors know about the weather,' I answered. 'When Captain said he was going tonight, I was thinking it would take a capful of wind to carry the ship back to sea, but now here's more than a capful.'

'Ah, yes,' said landlord, 'it's tonight he goes true enough and, mind you, though he treated me handsome over the rent, I'm not sure it's a loss to the village. I don't hold with gentrice who fetch their drink from London instead of helping local traders to get their living.'

'But you haven't got any rum like his,' I said, to draw him out.

His neck grew red above his collar, and I was afraid I'd gone too far, but after a while he got his breath with a grunt.

'John Simmons,' he said, 'if you've come down here this windy night to talk a lot of fool's talk, you've wasted a journey.'

Well, of course, then I had to smooth him down with praising his rum, and Heaven forgive me for swearing it was better than Captain's. For the like of that rum no living lips have tasted save mine and Parson's. But somehow or other I brought landlord round, and presently we must have a glass of his best to prove its quality.

'Beat that if you can!' he cried, and we both raised our glasses to our mouths, only to stop half-way and look at each other in amaze. For the wind that had been howling outside like an outrageous dog had all of a sudden turned as melodious as the carol-boys of a Christmas Eve.

'Surely that's not my Martha,' whispered landlord; Martha being his great-aunt that lived in the loft overhead.

We went to the door, and the wind burst it open so that

the handle was driven clean into the plaster of the wall. But we didn't think about that at the time; for over our heads, sailing very comfortably through the windy stars, was the ship that had passed the summer in landlord's field. Her portholes and her bay-window were blazing with lights, and there was a noise of singing and fiddling on her decks. 'He's gone,' shouted landlord above the storm, 'and he's taken half the village with him.' I could only nod in answer, not having lungs like bellows of leather.

In the morning we were able to measure the strength of the storm, and over and above my pigsty there was damage enough wrought in the village to keep us busy. True it is that the children had to break down no branches for the firing that autumn, since the wind had strewn the woods with more than they could carry away. Many of our ghosts were scattered abroad, but this time very few came back, all the young men having sailed with Captain; and not only ghosts, for a poor half-witted lad was missing, and we reckoned that he had stowed himself away or perhaps shipped as cabin-boy, not knowing any better.

What with the lamentations of the ghost-girls and the grumbling of families who had lost an ancestor, the village was upset for a while, and the funny thing was that it was the folk who had complained most of the carryings-on of the youngsters, who made most noise now that they were gone. I hadn't any sympathy with shoemaker or butcher, who ran about saying how much they missed their lads, but it made me grieve to hear the poor bereaved girls calling their lovers by name on the village green at nightfall. It didn't seem fair to me that they should have lost their men a second time, after giving up life in order to join them, as like as not. Still, not even a spirit can be sorry for ever, and after a few months we made up our minds that

the folk who had sailed in the ship were never coming back, and we didn't talk about it any more.

And then one day, I dare say it would be a couple of years after, when the whole business was quite forgotten, who should come trapesing along the road from Portsmouth but the daft lad who had gone away with the ship, without waiting till he was dead to become a ghost. You never saw such a boy as that in all your life. He had a great rusty cutlass hanging to a string at his waist, and he was tattooed all over in fine colours, so that even his face looked like a girl's sampler. He had a handkerchief in his hand full of foreign shells and old-fashioned pieces of small money, very curious, and he walked up to the well outside his mother's house and drew himself a drink as if he had been nowhere in particular.

The worst of it was that he had come back as soft-headed as he went, and try as we might we couldn't get anything reasonable out of him. He talked a lot of gibberish about keel-hauling and walking the plank and crimson murders – things which a decent sailor should know nothing about, so that it seemed to me that for all his manners Captain had been more of a pirate than a gentleman mariner. But to draw sense out of that boy was as hard as picking cherries off a crab-tree. One silly tale he had that he kept on drifting back to, and to hear him you would have thought that it was the only thing that happened to him in his life. 'We was at anchor,' he would say, 'off an island called the Basket of Flowers, and the sailors had caught a lot of parrots and we were teaching them to swear. Up and down the decks, up and down the decks, and the language they used was dreadful. Then we looked up and saw the masts of the Spanish ship outside the harbour. Outside the harbour they were, so we threw the parrots into the sea and sailed out to fight. And all the parrots

were drowned in the sea and the language they used was dreadful.' That's the sort of boy he was, nothing but silly talk of parrots when we asked him about the fighting. And we never had a chance of teaching him better, for two days after he ran away again, and hasn't been seen since!

That's my story, and I assure you that things like that are happening at Fairfield all the time. The ship has never come back, but somehow as people grow older they seem to think that one of these windy nights she'll come sailing in over the hedges with all the lost ghosts on board. Well, when she comes, she'll be welcome. There's one ghost-lass that has never grown tired of waiting for her lad to return. Every night you'll see her out on the green, straining her poor eyes with looking for the mast-lights among the stars. A faithful lass you'd call her, and I'm thinking you'd be right.

Landlord's field wasn't a penny the worse for the visit, but they do say that since then the turnips that have been grown in it have tasted of rum.

John Kendrick Bangs

The Water Ghost of Harrowby Hall

THE trouble with Harrowby Hall was that it was haunted, and, what was worse, the ghost did not merely appear at the bedside of a person, but remained there for one mortal hour before it disappeared.

It never appeared except on Christmas Eve, and then as the clock was striking twelve. The owners of Harrowby Hall had tried their hardest to rid themselves of the damp and dewy lady who rose up out of the best bedroom floor at midnight, but they had failed. They had tried stopping the clock, so that the ghost would not know when it was midnight; but she made her appearance just the same, and there she would stand until everything about her was thoroughly soaked.

Then the owners of Harrowby Hall closed up every crack in the floor with hemp, and over this were placed layers of tar and canvas; the walls were made waterproof, and the doors and windows likewise, in the hope that the lady would find it difficult to leak into the room, but even this did no good.

The following Christmas Eve she appeared as promptly as before, and frightened the guest of the room quite out of his senses by sitting down beside him, and gazing with her cavernous blue eyes into his. In her long, bony fingers bits of dripping seaweed were entwined, the ends hanging down, and these ends she drew across his forehead until he fainted away. He was found unconscious in his bed the

next morning, simply saturated with sea-water and fright.

The next year the master of Harrowby Hall decided not to have the best spare bedroom opened at all, but the ghost appeared as usual in the room – that is, it was supposed she did, for the hangings were dripping wet the next morning. Finding no one there, she immediately set out to haunt the owner of Harrowby himself. She found him in his own cosy room, congratulating himself upon having outwitted her.

All of a sudden the curl went out of his hair, and he was as wet as if he had fallen into a rain barrel. When he saw before him the lady of the cavernous eyes and seaweed fingers he too fainted, but immediately came to, because the vast amount of water in his hair, trickling down over his face, revived him.

Now it so happened that the master of Harrowby was a brave man. He intended to find out a few things he felt he had a right to know. He would have liked to put on a dry suit of clothes first, but the ghost refused to leave him for an instant until her hour was up. In an effort to warm himself up he turned to the fire; it was an unfortunate move, because it brought the ghost directly over the fire, which immediately was extinguished.

At this he turned angrily to her, and said: 'Far be it from me to be impolite to a woman, madam, but I wish you'd stop your infernal visits to this house. Go and sit out on the lake, if you like that sort of thing; soak in the rain barrel, if you wish; but do not come into a gentleman's house and soak him and his possessions in this way, I beg of you!'

'Henry Hartwick Oglethorpe,' said the ghost, in a gurgling voice, 'you don't know what you are talking about. You do not know that I am compelled to haunt this place year after year by my terrible fate. It is no pleasure for me

to enter this house, and ruin everything I touch. I never aspired to be a shower bath, but it is my doom. Do you know who I am?'

'No, I don't,' returned the master of Harrowby. 'I should say you were the Lady of the Lake!'

'No, I am the Water Ghost of Harrowby Hall, and I have held this highly unpleasant office for two hundred years tonight.'

'How the deuce did you ever come to get elected?' asked the master.

'Through a mistake,' replied the spectre. 'I am the ghost of that fair maiden whose picture hangs over the mantel-piece in the drawing-room.'

'But what made you get the house into such a spot?'

'I was not to blame, sir,' returned the lady. 'It was my father's fault. He built Harrowby Hall, and the room I haunt was to have been mine. My father had it furnished in pink and yellow, knowing well that blue and grey was the only combination of colours I could bear. He did it to spite me, and I refused to live in the room. Then my father said that I could live there or on the lawn, he didn't care which. That night I ran from the house and jumped over the cliff into the sea.'

'That was foolish,' said the master of Harrowby.

'So I've heard,' returned the ghost, 'but I really never realized what I was doing until after I was drowned. I had been drowned a week when a sea nymph came to me. She informed me that I was to be one of her followers, and that my doom was to haunt Harrowby Hall for one hour every Christmas Eve throughout the rest of eternity. I was to haunt that room on such Christmas Eves as I found it occupied; and if it should turn out not to be occupied I was to spend that hour with the head of the house.'

'I'll sell the place.'

'That you cannot do, for then I must appear to any purchaser, and reveal to him the awful secret of the house.'

'Do you mean to tell me that on every Christmas Eve that I don't happen to have somebody in that guest-chamber, you are going to haunt me wherever I may be, taking all the curl out of my hair, putting out my fire, and soaking me through to the skin?' demanded the master.

'Yes, Oglethorpe. And what is more,' said the water ghost, 'it doesn't make the slightest difference where you are. If I find that room empty, wherever you may be I shall douse you with my spectral pres...'

Here the clock struck one, and immediately the ghost faded away. It was perhaps more a trickle than a fading, but as a disappearance it was complete.

'By St George and his Dragon!' cried the master of Harrowby, 'I swear that next Christmas there'll be someone in the spare room, or I spend the night in a bathtub.'

But when Christmas Eve came again the master of Harrowby was in his grave. He never recovered from the cold he caught that awful night. Harrowby Hall was closed, and the heir to the estate was in London. And there to him in his apartment came the water ghost at the appointed hour. Being younger and stronger, however, he survived the shock. Everything in his rooms was ruined – his clocks were rusted; a fine collection of watercolour drawings was entirely washed out. And because the apartments below his were drenched with water soaking through the floors, he was asked by his landlady to leave the apartment immediately.

The story of his family's ghost had gone about; no one would invite him to any party except afternoon teas and receptions, and fathers of daughters refused to allow him to remain in their houses later than eight o'clock at night.

So the heir of Harrowby Hall determined that something must be done.

The thought came to him to have the fireplace in the room enlarged, so that the ghost would evaporate at its first appearance. But he remembered his father's experience with the fire. Then he thought of steampipes. These, he remembered, could lie hundreds of feet deep in water, and still be hot enough to drive the water away in vapour. So the haunted room was heated by steam to a withering degree.

The scheme was only partially successful. The water ghost appeared at the specified time, but hot as the room was, it shortened her visit by no more than five minutes in the hour. And during this time the young master was a nervous wreck, and the room itself was terribly cracked and warped. And worse than this, as the last drop of the water ghost was slowly sizzling itself out on the floor, she whispered that there was still plenty of water where she came from, and that next year would find her as exasperatingly saturating as ever.

It was then that, going from one extreme to the other, the heir of Harrowby hit upon the means by which the water ghost was ultimately conquered, and happiness came once more to the house of Oglethorpe.

The heir provided himself with a warm suit of fur underclothing. Wearing this with the furry side in, he placed over it a tight-fitting rubber garment like a jersey. On top of this he drew on another set of woollen underclothing, and over this was a second rubber garment like the first. Upon his head he wore a light and comfortable diving helmet; and so clad, on the following Christmas Eve he awaited the coming of his tormentor.

It was a bitterly cold night that brought to a close this twenty-fourth day of December. The air outside was still,

but the temperature was below zero. Within all was quiet; the servants of Harrowby Hall awaited with beating hearts the outcome of their master's campaign against his supernatural visitor.

The master himself was lying on the bed in the haunted room, dressed as he had planned and then . . .

The clock clanged out the hour of twelve.

There was a sudden banging of doors. A blast of cold air swept through the halls. The door leading into the haunted chamber flew open, a splash was heard, and the water ghost was seen standing at the side of the heir of Harrowby. Immediately from his clothing there streamed rivulets of water, but deep down under the various garments he wore he was as dry and warm as he could have wished.

'Ha!' said the young master of Harrowby, 'I'm glad to see you.'

'You are the most original man I've met, if that is true,' returned the ghost. 'May I ask where did you get that hat?'

'Certainly, madam,' returned the master, courteously. 'It is a little portable observatory I had made for just such emergencies as this. But tell me, is it true that you are doomed to follow me about for one mortal hour – to stand where I stand, to sit where I sit?'

'That is my happy fate,' returned the lady.

'We'll go out on the lake,' said the master, starting up.

'You can't get rid of me that way,' returned the ghost. 'The water won't swallow me up; in fact, it will just add to my present bulk.'

'Nevertheless,' said the master, 'we will go out on the lake.'

'But my dear sir,' returned the ghost, 'it is fearfully cold out there. You will be frozen hard before you've been out ten minutes.'

'Oh, no, I'll not,' replied the master. 'I am very warmly dressed. Come!' This last in a tone of command that made the ghost ripple.

And they started.

They had not gone far before the water ghost showed signs of distress.

'You walk too slowly,' she said. 'I am nearly frozen. I beg you, hurry!'

'I should like to oblige a lady,' returned the master courteously, 'but my clothes are rather heavy, and a hundred yards an hour is about my speed. Indeed, I think we had better sit down on this snowdrift, and talk matters over.'

'Do not! Do not do so, I beg!' cried the ghost. 'Let us move on. I feel myself growing rigid as it is. If we stop here, I shall be frozen stiff.'

'That, madam,' said the master slowly, seating himself on an ice cake ... 'that is why I have brought you here. We have been on this spot just ten minutes; we have fifty more. Take your time about it, madam, but freeze. That is all I ask of you.'

'I cannot move my right leg now,' cried the ghost, in despair, 'and my overskirt is a solid sheet of ice. Oh, good, kind Mr Oglethorpe, light a fire, and let me go free from these icy fetters.'

'Never, madam. It cannot be. I have you at last.'

'Alas!' cried the ghost, a tear trickling down her frozen cheek. 'Help me, I beg, I congeal!'

'Congeal, madam, congeal!' returned Oglethorpe coldly. 'You are drenched and have drenched me for two hundred and three years, madam. Tonight, you have had your last drench.'

'Ah, but I shall thaw out again, and then you'll see. Instead of the comfortably warm, genial ghost I have been in

the past, sir, I shall be ice water,' cried the lady, threateningly.

'No, you won't either,' returned Oglethorpe; 'for when you are frozen quite stiff, I shall send you to a cold-storage warehouse, and there shall you remain an icy work of art for evermore.'

'But warehouses burn.'

'So they do, but this warehouse cannot burn. It is made of asbestos and surrounding it are fireproof walls, and within those walls the temperature is now and shall be 416 degrees below the zero point; low enough to make an icicle of any flame in this world – or the next,' the master added, with a chuckle.

'For the last time I beseech you. I would go on my knees to you, Oglethorpe, if they were not already frozen. I beg of you do not do . . .'

Here even the words froze on the water ghost's lips and the clock struck one. There was a momentary tremor throughout the ice-bound form, and the moon, coming out from behind a cloud, shone down on the rigid figure of a beautiful woman sculptured in clear, transparent ice. There stood the ghost of Harrowby Hall, conquered by the cold, a prisoner of all time.

The heir of Harrowby had won at last, and today in a large storage house in London stands the frigid form of one who will never again flood the house of Oglethorpe with woe and sea-water.

H. G. Wells

The Inexperienced Ghost

THE scene amidst which Clayton told his last story comes back very vividly to my mind. There he sat, for the greater part of the time, in the corner of the authentic settle by the spacious open fire, and Sanderson sat beside him smoking the Broseley clay that bore his name. There was Evans, and that marvel among actors, Wish, who is also a modest man. We had all come down to the Mermaid Club that Saturday morning, except Clayton, who had slept there overnight – which indeed gave him the opening of his story. We had golfed until golfing was invisible; we had dined, and we were in that mood of tranquil kindliness when men will suffer a story. When Clayton began to tell one, we naturally supposed he was lying. It may be that indeed he was lying – of that the reader will speedily be able to judge as well as I. He began, it is true, with an air of matter-of-fact anecdote, but that we thought was only the incurable artifice of the man.

'I say!' he remarked, after a long consideration of the upward rain of sparks from the log that Sanderson had thumped, 'you know I was alone here last night?'

'Except for the domestics,' said Wish.

'Who sleep in the other wing,' said Clayton. 'Yes. Well –' He pulled at his cigar for some little time as though he still hesitated about his confidence. Then he said, quite quietly, 'I caught a ghost!'

'Caught a ghost, did you?' said Sanderson. 'Where is it?'

And Evans, who admires Clayton immensely and has been four weeks in America, shouted, '*Caught* a ghost, did you, Clayton? I'm glad of it! Tell us all about it right now.'

Clayton said he would in a minute, and asked him to shut the door.

He looked apologetically at me. 'There's no eavesdropping of course, but we don't want to upset our very excellent service with any rumours of ghosts in the place. There's too much shadow and oak panelling to trifle with that. And this, you know, wasn't a regular ghost. I don't think it will come again – ever.'

'You mean to say you didn't keep it?' said Sanderson.

'I hadn't the heart to,' said Clayton.

And Sanderson said he was surprised.

We laughed, and Clayton looked aggrieved. 'I know,' he said, with the flicker of a smile, 'but the fact is it really *was* a ghost, and I'm as sure of it as I am that I am talking to you now. I'm not joking. I mean what I say.'

Sanderson drew deeply at his pipe, with one reddish eye on Clayton, and then emitted a thin jet of smoke more eloquent than many words.

Clayton ignored the comment. 'It is the strangest thing that has ever happened in my life. You know I never believed in ghosts or anything of the sort, before, ever; and then, you know, I bag one in a corner; and the whole business is in my hands.'

He meditated still more profoundly and produced and began to pierce a second cigar with a curious little stabber he affected.

'You talked to it?' asked Wish.

'For the space, probably, of an hour.'

'Chatty?' I said, joining the party of the sceptics.

'The poor devil was in trouble,' said Clayton, bowed

over his cigar-end and with the very faintest note of re-
proof.

'Sobbing?' someone asked.

Clayton heaved a realistic sigh at the memory. 'Good
Lord!' he said; 'yes.' And then, 'Poor fellow! yes.'

'Where did you strike it?' asked Evans, in his best
American accent.

'I never realized,' said Clayton, ignoring him, 'the poor
sort of thing a ghost might be,' and he hung us up again
for a time, while he sought for matches in his pocket and
lit and warmed to his cigar.

'I took an advantage,' he reflected at last.

We were none of us in a hurry. 'A character,' he said,
'remains just the same character for all that it's been disembodied. That's a thing we too often forget. People with
a certain strength or fixity of purpose may have ghosts of
a certain strength and fixity of purpose – most haunting
ghosts, you know, must be as one-idea'd as monomaniacs
and as obstinate as mules to come back again and again.
This poor creature wasn't.' He suddenly looked up rather
queerly, and his eye went round the room. 'I say it,' he
said, 'in all kindliness, but that is the plain truth of the
case. Even at the first glance he struck me as weak.'

He punctuated with the help of his cigar.

'I came upon him, you know, in the long passage. His
back was towards me and I saw him first. Right off I knew
him for a ghost. He was transparent and whitish; clean
through his chest I could see the glimmer of the little window at the end. And not only his physique but his attitude
struck me as being weak. He looked, you know, as though
he didn't know in the slightest whatever he meant to do.
One hand was on the panelling and the other fluttered to
his mouth. Like – *so*!'

'What sort of physique?' said Sanderson.

'Lean. You know that sort of young man's neck that has two great flutings down the back, here and here – so! And a little, meanish head with scrubby hair and rather bad ears. Shoulders bad, narrower than the hips; turn-down collar, ready-made short jacket, trousers baggy and a little frayed at the heels. That's how he took me. I came very quietly up the staircase. I did not carry a light, you know – the candles are on the landing table and there is that lamp – and I was in my list slippers, and I saw him as I came up. I stopped dead at that – taking him in. I wasn't a bit afraid. I think that in most of these affairs one is never nearly so afraid or excited as one imagines one would be. I was surprised and interested. I thought, "Good Lord! Here's a ghost at last! And I haven't believed for a moment in ghosts during the last five-and-twenty years."'

'Um,' said Wish.

'I suppose I wasn't on the landing a moment before he found out I was there. He turned on me sharply, and I saw the face of an immature young man, a weak nose, a scrubby little moustache, a feeble chin. So for an instant we stood – he looking over his shoulder at me – and regarded one another. Then he seemed to remember his high calling. He turned round, drew himself up, projected his face, raised his arms, spread his hands in approved ghost fashion – came towards me. As he did so his little jaw dropped, and he emitted a faint, drawn-out "Boo." No, it wasn't – not a bit dreadful. I'd dined. I'd had a bottle of champagne, and being all alone, perhaps two or three – perhaps even four or five – whiskies, so I was as solid as rocks and no more frightened than if I'd been assailed by a frog. "Boo!" I said. "Nonsense. You don't belong to *this* place. What are you doing here?"'

'I could see him wince. "Boo – oo," he said.

'"Boo – be hanged! Are you a member?" I said; and just to show I didn't care a pin for him I stepped through a corner of him and made to light my candle. "Are you a member?" I repeated, looking at him sideways.

'He moved a little so as to stand clear of me, and his bearing became crestfallen. "No," he said, in answer to the persistent interrogation of my eye; "I'm not a member – I'm a ghost."

'"Well, that doesn't give you the run of the Mermaid Club. Is there anyone you want to see, or anything of that sort?" And doing it as steadily as possible for fear that he should mistake the carelessness of whisky for the distraction of fear, I got my candle alight. I turned on him, holding it. "What are you doing here?" I said.

'He had dropped his hands and stopped his booing, and there he stood, abashed and awkward, the ghost of a weak, silly, aimless young man. "I'm haunting," he said.

'"You haven't any business to," I said in a quiet voice.

'"I'm a ghost," he said, as if in defence.

'"That may be, but you haven't any business to haunt here. This is a respectable private club; people often stop here with nursemaids and children, and, going about in the careless way you do, some poor little mite could easily come upon you and be scared out of her wits. I suppose you didn't think of that?"

'"No, sir," he said, "I didn't."

'"You should have done. You haven't any claim on the place, have you? Weren't murdered here, or anything of that sort?"

'"None, sir; but I thought as it was old and oak-panelled –"

'"That's *no* excuse." I regarded him firmly. "Your coming here is a mistake," I said in a tone of friendly superiority. I feigned to see if I had my matches, and then looked

up at him frankly. "If I were you I wouldn't wait for cock-crow – I'd vanish right away."

'He looked embarrassed. "The fact *is*, sir –" he began.

'"I'd vanish," I said, driving it home.

'"The fact is, sir, that – somehow – I can't."

'"You *can't*?"

'"No, sir. There's something I've forgotten. I've been hanging about here since midnight last night, hiding in the cupboards of the empty bedrooms and things like that. I'm flurried. I've never come haunting before, and it seems to put me out."

'"Put you out?"

'"Yes, sir. I've tried to do it several times, and it doesn't come off. There's some little thing has slipped me, and I can't get back."

'That, you know, rather bowled me over. He looked at me in such an abject way that for the life of me I couldn't keep up quite the high hectoring vein I had adopted. "That's queer," I said, and as I spoke I fancied I heard someone moving about down below. "Come into my room and tell me more about it," I said. I didn't, of course, understand this, and I tried to take him by the arm. But, of course, you might as well have tried to take hold of a puff of smoke! I had forgotten my number, I think; anyhow, I remember going into several bedrooms – it was lucky I was the only soul in that wing – until I saw my traps. "Here we are," I said, and sat down in the armchair; "sit down and tell me all about it. It seems to me you have got yourself into a jolly awkward position, old chap."

'Well, he said he wouldn't sit down; he'd prefer to flit up and down the room if it was all the same to me. And so he did, and in a little while we were deep in a long and serious talk. And presently, you know, something of those whiskies and soda evaporated out of me, and I began to

realize just a little what a thundering rum and weird business it was that I was in. There he was, semi-transparent – the proper conventional phantom, and noiseless except for his ghost of a voice – flitting to and fro in that nice, clean, chintz-hung old bedroom. You could see the gleam of the copper candlesticks through him, and the lights on the brass fender, and the corners of the framed engravings on the wall, and there he was telling me all about this wretched little life of his that had recently ended on earth. He hadn't a particularly honest face, you know, but being transparent, of course, he couldn't avoid telling the truth.'

'Eh?' said Wish, suddenly sitting up in his chair.

'What?' said Clayton.

'Being transparent – couldn't avoid telling the truth – I don't see it,' said Wish.

'*I* don't see it,' said Clayton, with inimitable assurance. 'But it *is* so, I can assure you nevertheless. I don't believe he got once a nail's breadth off the Bible truth. He told me how he had been killed – he went down into a London basement with a candle to look for a leakage of gas – and described himself as a senior English master in a London private school when that release occurred.'

'Poor wretch!' said I.

'That's what I thought, and the more he talked the more I thought it. There he was, purposeless in life and purposeless out of it. He talked of his father and mother and his schoolmaster, and all who had ever been anything to him in the world, meanly. He had been too sensitive, too nervous; none of them had ever valued him properly or understood him, he said. He had never had a real friend in the world, I think; he had never had a success. He had shirked games and failed examinations. "It's like that with some people," he said; "whenever I got into the examination-room or anywhere everything seemed to go." Engaged to be

married of course – to another over-sensitive person, I suppose – when the indiscretion with the gas escape ended his affairs. "And where are you now?" I asked. "Not in –?"

'He wasn't clear on that point at all. The impression he gave me was of a sort of vague, intermediate state, a special reserve for souls too non-existent for anything so positive as either sin or virtue. *I* don't know. He was much too egotistical and unobservant to give me any clear idea of the kind of place, kind of country, there is on the Other Side of Things. Wherever he was, he seems to have fallen in with a set of kindred spirits: ghosts of weak Cockney young men, who were on a footing of Christian names, and among these there was certainly a lot of talk about "going haunting" and things like that. Yes – going haunting! They seemed to think "haunting" a tremendous adventure, and most of them funked it all the time. And so primed, you know, he had come.'

'But really!' said Wish to the fire.

'These are the impressions he gave me, anyhow,' said Clayton, modestly. 'I may, of course, have been in a rather uncritical state, but that was the sort of background he gave to himself. He kept flitting up and down, with his thin voice going – talking, talking about his wretched self, and never a word of clear, firm statement from first to last. He was thinner and sillier and more pointless than if he had been real and alive. Only then, you know, he would not have been in my bedroom here – if he *had* been alive. I should have kicked him out.'

'Of course,' said Evans, 'There *are* poor mortals like that.'

'And there's just as much chance of their having ghosts as the rest of us,' I admitted.

'What gave a sort of point to him, you know, was the fact that he did seem within limits to have found himself

out. The mess he had made of haunting had depressed him terribly. He had been told it would be a "lark": he had come expecting it to be a "lark", and here it was, nothing but another failure added to his record! He proclaimed himself an utter out-and-out failure. He said, and I can quite believe it, that he had never tried to do anything all his life that he hadn't made a perfect mess of – and through all the wastes of eternity he never would. If he had had sympathy, perhaps –. He paused at that, and stood regarding me. He remarked that, strange as it might seem to me, nobody, not anyone, ever, had given him the amount of sympathy I was doing now. I could see what he wanted straight away, and I determined to head him off at once. I may be a brute, you know, but being the Only Real Friend, the recipient of the confidences of one of these egotistical weaklings, ghost or body, is beyond my physical endurance. I got up briskly. "Don't you brood on these things too much," I said. "The thing you've got to do is to get out of this – get out of this sharp. You pull yourself together and *try*." "I can't" he said. "You try," I said, and try he did.'

'Try!' said Sanderson. '*How?*'

'Passes,' said Clayton.

'Passes?'

'Complicated series of gestures and passes with the hands. That's how he had come in and that's how he had to get out again. Lord! what a business I had!'

'But how could *any* series of passes –' I began.

'My dear man,' said Clayton, turning on me and putting a great emphasis on certain words, 'you want *everything* clear. I don't know *how*. All I know is that you *do* – that *he* did, anyhow, at least. After a fearful time, you know, he got his passes right and suddenly disappeared.'

'Did you,' said Sanderson slowly, 'observe the passes?'

'Yes,' said Clayton, and seemed to think. 'It was tremendously queer,' he said. 'There we were, I and this thin vague ghost, in that silent room, in this silent, empty inn, in this silent little Friday-night town. Not a sound except out voices and a faint panting he made when he swung. There was the bedroom candle, and one candle on the dressing-table alight, that was all – sometimes one or other would flare up into a tall, lean, astonished flame for a space. And queer things happened. "I can't," he said; "I shall never –!" And suddenly he sat down on a little chair at the foot of the bed and began to sob and sob. Lord! what a harrowing, whimpering thing he seemed!

'"You pull yourself together," I said, and tried to pat him on the back, and ... my confounded hand went through him! By that time, you know, I wasn't nearly so – massive as I had been on the landing. I got the queerness of it full. I remember snatching back my hand out of him, as it were, with a little thrill, and walking over to the dressing-table. "You pull yourself together," I said to him, "and try." And in order to encourage and help him I began to try as well.'

'What!' said Sanderson, 'the passes?'

'Yes, the passes.'

'But –' I said, moved by an idea that eluded me for a space.

'This is interesting,' said Sanderson, with his finger in his pipe-bowl. 'You mean to say this ghost of yours gave way –'

'Did his level best to give away the whole confounded barrier? *Yes.*'

'He didn't,' said Wish; 'he couldn't. Or you'd have gone there too.'

'That's precisely it,' I said, finding my elusive idea put into words for me.

'That *is* precisely it,' said Clayton, with thoughtful eyes upon the fire.

For just a little while there was silence.

'And at last he did it?' said Sanderson.

'At last he did it. I had to keep him up to it hard, but he did it at last – rather suddenly. He despaired, we had a scene, and then he got up abruptly and asked me to go through the whole performance, slowly, so that he might see. "I believe," he said, "if I could *see* I should spot what was wrong at once." And he did. "I know," he said. "What do you know?" said I. "*I* know," he repeated. Then he said, peevishly, "I *can't* do it, if you look at me – I really *can't*; it's been that, partly, all along. I'm such a nervous fellow that you put me out." Well, we had a bit of an argument. Naturally I wanted to see; but he was as obstinate as a mule, and suddenly I had come over as tired as a dog – he tired me out. "All right," I said, "I won't look at you," and turned towards the mirror, on the wardrobe, by the bed.

'He started off very fast. I tried to follow him by looking in the looking-glass, to see just what it was had hung. Round went his arms and his hands, so, and so, and so, and then with a rush came to the last gesture of all – you stand erect and open out your arms – and so, don't you know, he stood. And then he didn't! He didn't! He wasn't! I wheeled round from the looking-glass to him. There was nothing! I was alone, with the flaring candles and a staggering mind. What had happened? Had anything happened? Had I been dreaming? ... And then, with an absurd note of finality about it, the clock upon the landing discovered the moment was ripe for striking *one*. So! – Ping! And I was as grave and sober as a judge, with all my champagne and whisky gone into the vast serene. Feeling queer, you know – confoundedly *queer*! Queer! Good Lord!'

He regarded his cigar-ash for a moment. 'That's all that happened,' he said.

'And then you went to bed?' asked Evans.

'What else was there to do?'

I looked Wish in the eye. We wanted to scoff, and there was something, something perhaps in Clayton's voice and manner, that hampered our desire.

'And about these passes?' said Sanderson.

'I believe I could do them now.'

'Oh!' said Sanderson, and produced a pen-knife and set himself to grub the dottel out of the bowl of his clay.

'Why don't you do them now?' said Sanderson, shutting his pen-knife with a click.

'That's what I'm going to do,' said Clayton.

'They won't work,' said Evans.

'If they do –' I suggested.

'You know, I'd rather you didn't,' said Wish, stretching out his legs.

'Why?' asked Evans.

'I'd rather he didn't,' said Wish.

'But he hasn't got 'em right,' said Sanderson, plugging too much tobacco into his pipe.

'All the same, I'd rather he didn't,' said Wish.

We argued with Wish. He said that for Clayton to go through those gestures was like mocking a serious matter. 'But you don't believe –?' I said. Wish glanced at Clayton, who was staring into the fire, weighing something in his mind. 'I do – more than half, anyhow, I do,' said Wish.

'Clayton,' said I, 'you're too good a liar for us. Most of it was all right. But that disappearance ... happened to be convincing. Tell us, it's a tale of cock and bull.'

He stood up without heeding me, took the middle of the hearthrug, and faced me. For a moment he regarded his feet thoughtfully, and then for all the rest of the time

his eyes were on the opposite wall, with an intent expression. He raised his two hands slowly to the level of his eyes and so began. . . .

Now, Sanderson is a Freemason, a member of the lodge of the Four Kings, which devotes itself so ably to the study and elucidation of all the mysteries of Masonry past and present, and among the students of this lodge Sanderson is by no means the least. He followed Clayton's motions with a singular interest in his reddish eye. 'That's not bad,' he said, when it was done. 'You really do, you know, put things together, Clayton, in a most amazing fashion. But there's one little detail out.'

'I know,' said Clayton. 'I believe I could tell you which.'

'Well?'

'This,' said Clayton, and did a queer little twist and writhing and thrust of the hands.

'Yes.'

'That, you know, was what *he* couldn't get right,' said Clayton. 'But how do *you* –?'

'Most of this business, and particularly how you invented it, I don't understand at all,' said Sanderson, 'but just that phase – I do.' He reflected. 'These happen to be a series of gestures – connected with a certain branch of esoteric Masonry – Probably you know. Or else – *How*?' He reflected still further. 'I do not see I can do any harm in telling you just the proper twist. After all, if you know, you know; if you don't, you don't.'

'I know nothing,' said Clayton, 'except what the poor devil let out last night.'

'Well, anyhow,' said Sanderson, and placed his church-warden very carefully upon the shelf over the fireplace. Then very rapidly he gesticulated with his hands.

'So?' said Clayton, repeating.

'So,' said Sanderson, and took his pipe in hand again.

'Ah, *now*,' said Clayton, 'I can do the whole thing – right.'

He stood up before the waning fire and smiled at us all. But I think there was just a little hesitation in his smile. 'If I begin –' he said.

'I wouldn't begin,' said Wish.

'It's all right!' said Evans. 'Matter is indestructible. You don't think any jiggery-pokery of this sort is going to snatch Clayton into the world of shades. Not it! You may try, Clayton, so far as I'm concerned, until your arms drop off at the wrists.'

'I don't believe that,' said Wish, and stood up and put his arm on Clayton's shoulder. 'You've made me half believe in that story somehow, and I don't want to see the thing done.'

'Goodness!' said I, 'here's Wish frightened!'

'I am,' said Wish, with real or admirably feigned intensity. 'I believe that if he goes through these motions right he'll *go*.'

'He'll not do anything of the sort,' I cried. 'There's only one way out of this world for men, and Clayton is thirty years from that. Besides.... And such a ghost! Do you think –?'

Wish interrupted me by moving. He walked out from among our chairs and stopped beside the table and stood there. 'Clayton,' he said, 'you're a fool.'

Clayton, with a humorous light in his eyes, smiled back at him. 'Wish,' he said, 'is right and all you others are wrong. I shall go. I shall get to the end of these passes, and as the last swish whistles through the air, Presto! – this hearthrug will be vacant, the room will be blank amazement, and a respectably dressed gentleman of fifteen stone will plump into the world of shades. I'm certain. So will

you be. I decline to argue further. Let the thing be tried.'

'No,' said Wish, and made a step and ceased, and Clayton raised his hands once more to repeat the spirit's passing.

By that time, you know, we were all in a state of tension – largely because of the behaviour of Wish. We sat all of us with our eyes on Clayton – I, at least, with a sort of tight, stiff feeling about me as though from the back of my skull to the middle of my thighs my body had been changed to steel. And there, with a gravity that was imperturbably serene, Clayton bowed and swayed and waved his hands and arms before us. As he drew towards the end one piled up, one tingled in one's teeth. The last gesture, I have said, was to swing the arms out wide open, with the face held up. And when at last he swung out to his closing gesture I ceased even to breathe. It was ridiculous, of course, but you know that ghost-story feeling. It was after dinner, in a queer, old shadowy house. Would he, after all –?

There he stood for one stupendous moment, with his arms open and his upturned face, assured and bright, in the glare of the hanging lamp. We hung through that moment as if it were an age, and then came from all of us something that was half a sigh of infinite relief and half a reassuring 'No!' For visibly – he wasn't going. It was all nonsense. He had told an idle story, and carried it almost to conviction, that was all! ... And then in that moment the face of Clayton changed.

It changed. It changed as a lit house changes when its lights are suddenly extinguished. His eyes were suddenly eyes that were fixed, his smile was frozen on his lips, and he stood there still. He stood there, very gently swaying.

That moment, too, was an age. And then, you know, chairs were scraping, things were falling, and we were all

moving. His knees seemed to give, and he fell forward, and Evans rose and caught him in his arms. . . .

It stunned us all. For a minute I suppose no one said a coherent thing. We believed it, yet could not believe it. . . . I came out of a muddled stupefaction to find myself kneeling beside him, and his vest and shirt were torn open, and Sanderson's hand lay on his heart. . . .

Well – the simple fact before us could very well wait our convenience; there was no hurry for us to comprehend. It lay there for an hour; it lies athwart my memory, black and amazing still, to this day. Clayton had, indeed, passed into the world that lies so near to and so far from our own, and he had gone thither by the only road that mortal man may take. But whether he did indeed pass there by that poor ghost's incantation, or whether he was stricken suddenly by apoplexy in the midst of an idle tale – as the coroner's jury would have us believe – is no matter for my judging; it is just one of those inexplicable riddles that must remain unsolved until the final solution of all things shall come. All I certainly know is that, in the very moment, in the very instant, of concluding those passes, he changed, and staggered, and fell down before us – dead!

Dora Broome

The Buggane and the Tailor

THERE was once a little church called St Trinian's going building at the foot of Greeba mountain. The walls were up, and everything was going well, but the minute a roof was put on it, down came the Buggane that was living on Greeba, and tore it off, r-r-r-p-p! before you could wink.

'I'll not have singin' an' shoutin' on my ground,' said he, and away he went, roaring and ranting, back up the mountain. When this had happened several times, the people got very tired of it, so they went to Tim Kelly, the tailor, who was a bold little fellow, and asked what they should do.

'L'ave him to me,' said Tim, 'an' I'll larn him. The imperance of sin is in that one.' And he laid a wager that he would make a pair of breeches in the church, the first night the roof was on.

He took his needle and thread, scissors and cloth, and sat down cross-legged in the chancel. Everything was very dark and quiet, with only the little candle guttering away beside him. Stitch, stitch, stitch, went the tailor, thinking of the things he'd buy with the wager, when he'd earned it. There wasn't a sound except the whispering of the wind outside.

All night long he worked, and as day was breaking, and the first cock crowed, he began to sew the buttons on. Just then, up from the ground at his feet came the Buggane's

169

big head, the eyes rolling, his hair standing on end, like stubble.

'Do thou see my big head, Tim Kelly?' said he, in a voice like growling thunder.

'Yis, yis,' said Tim. 'Moghrey mie. Moghrey mie – good mornin' Buggane.'

Up came the Buggane's big fist, shaking in Tim's face.

'Do thou see my big fis', Tim Kelly?'

'Yis, yis,' said Tim. 'Traa dy liooar – Time enough, Buggane.'

Up came the Buggane's big foot, with a plump.

'Do thou see my big –'

'Yis, yis,' said Tim. 'Oie-vie, Oie-vie – good-bye, Buggane.' And with that, he threw down his needle and scissors, and away he went, with the breeches dangling over his arm, and the Buggane after him, and Tim never stopped running until he threw himself over the churchyard wall at Marown. The Buggane was so angry he took off his head, and threw it over the wall at Tim's feet, where it burst into flames; then away he went up the mountain, like a big black thunder-cloud.

But the church of St Trinian's wasn't finished, after all, for Tim hadn't sewed the last button on the breeches, and hadn't won his wager. Down came the Buggane, the next night, and r-r-r-p-p! went the roof, and it has been roofless to this day, for the people were taking no more risks. And so you may see it, if you go and look.

Saki

Laura

'You are not really dying, are you?' asked Amanda.

'I have the doctor's permission to live till Tuesday,' said Laura.

'But today is Saturday; this is serious!' gasped Amanda.

'I don't know about it being serious; it is certainly Saturday,' said Laura.

'Death is always serious,' said Amanda.

'I never said I was going to die. I am presumably going to leave off being Laura, but I shall go on being something. An animal of some kind, I suppose. You see, when one hasn't been very good in the life one has just lived, one reincarnates in some lower organism. And I haven't been very good, when one comes to think of it. I've been petty and mean and vindictive and all that sort of thing when circumstances have seemed to warrant it.'

'Circumstances never warrant that sort of thing,' said Amanda hastily.

'If you don't mind my saying so,' observed Laura, 'Egbert is a circumstance that would warrant any amount of that sort of thing. You're married to him – that's different; you've sworn to love, honour, and endure him: I haven't.'

'I don't see what's wrong with Egbert,' protested Amanda.

'Oh, I dare say the wrongness has been on my part,' admitted Laura dispassionately; 'he has merely been the

171

extenuating circumstance. He made a thin, peevish kind of fuss, for instance, when I took the collie puppies from the farm out for a run the other day.'

'They chased his young broods of speckled Sussex and drove two sitting hens off their nests, besides running all over the flower beds. You know how devoted he is to his poultry and garden.'

'Anyhow, he needn't have gone on about it for the entire evening and then have said, "Let's say no more about it" just when I was beginning to enjoy the discussion. That's where one of my petty vindictive revenges came in,' added Laura with an unrepentant chuckle; 'I turned the entire family of speckled Sussex into his seedling shed the day after the puppy episode.'

'How could you?' exclaimed Amanda.

'It came quite easy,' said Laura; 'two of the hens pretended to be laying at the time, but I was firm.'

'And we thought it was an accident!'

'You see,' resumed Laura, 'I really *have* some grounds for supposing that my next incarnation will be in a lower organism. I shall be an animal of some kind. On the other hand, I haven't been a bad sort in my way, so I think I may count on being a nice animal, something elegant and lively, with a love of fun. An otter, perhaps.'

'I can't imagine you as an otter,' said Amanda.

'Well, I don't suppose you can imagine me as an angel, if it comes to that,' said Laura.

Amanda was silent. She couldn't.

'Personally I think an otter life would be rather enjoyable,' continued Laura; 'salmon to eat all the year round, and the satisfaction of being able to fetch the trout in their own homes without having to wait for hours till they condescend to rise to the fly you've been dangling before them; and an elegant svelte figure –'

'Think of the otter hounds,' interposed Amanda; 'how dreadful to be hunted and harried and finally worried to death!'

'Rather fun with half the neighbourhood looking on, and anyhow not worse than this Saturday-to-Tuesday business of dying by inches; and then I should go on into something else. If I had been a moderately good otter I suppose I should get back into human shape of some sort; probably something rather primitive – a little brown, unclothed Nubian boy, I should think.'

'I wish you would be serious,' sighed Amanda; 'you really ought to be if you're only going to live till Tuesday.'

As a matter of fact Laura died on Monday.

'So dreadfully upsetting,' Amanda complained to her uncle-in-law, Sir Lulworth Quayne. 'I've asked quite a lot of people down for golf and fishing, and the rhododendrons are just looking their best.'

'Laura was always inconsiderate,' said Sir Lulworth; 'she was born during Goodwood week, with an Ambassador staying in the house who hated babies.'

'She had the maddest kind of ideas,' said Amanda; 'do you know if there was any insanity in her family?'

'Insanity? No, I never heard of any. Her father lives in West Kensington, but I believe he's sane on all other subjects.'

'She had an idea that she was going to be reincarnated as an otter,' said Amanda.

'One meets with those ideas of reincarnation so frequently, even in the West,' said Sir Lulworth, 'that one can hardly set them down as being mad. And Laura was such an unaccountable person in this life that I should not like to lay down definite rules as to what she might be doing in an after state.'

'You think she really might have passed into some

animal form?' asked Amanda. She was one of those who
shape their opinions rather readily from the standpoint of
those around them.

Just then Egbert entered the breakfast-room, wearing an
air of bereavement that Laura's demise would have been
insufficient, in itself, to account for.

'Four of my speckled Sussex have been killed,' he exclaimed; 'the very four that were to go to the show on
Friday. One of them was dragged away and eaten right in
the middle of that new carnation bed that I've been to
such trouble and expense over. My best flower bed and my
best fowls singled out for destruction; it almost seems
as if the brute that did the deed had special knowledge
how to be as devastating as possible in a short space of
time.'

'Was it a fox, do you think?' asked Amanda.

'Sounds more like a polecat,' said Sir Lulworth.

'No,' said Egbert, 'there were marks of webbed feet all
over the place, and we followed the tracks down to the
stream at the bottom of the garden; evidently an otter.'

Amanda looked quickly and furtively across at Sir Lulworth.

Egbert was too agitated to eat any breakfast, and went
out to superintend the strengthening of the poultry yard
defences.

'I think she might at least have waited till the funeral
was over,' said Amanda in a scandalized voice.

'It's her own funeral, you know,' said Sir Lulworth; 'it's
a nice point in etiquette how far one ought to show respect to one's own mortal remains.'

Disregard for mortuary convention was carried to
further lengths next day; during the absence of the family
at the funeral ceremony the remaining survivors of the
speckled Sussex were massacred. The marauder's line of

retreat seemed to have embraced most of the flower beds on the lawn, but the strawberry beds in the lower garden had also suffered.

'I shall get the otter hounds to come here at the earliest possible moment,' said Egbert savagely.

'On no account! You can't dream of such a thing!' exclaimed Amanda. 'I mean, it wouldn't do, so soon after a funeral in the house.'

'It's a case of necessity,' said Egbert; 'once an otter takes to that sort of thing it won't stop.'

'Perhaps it will go elsewhere now that there are no more fowls left,' suggested Amanda.

'One would think you wanted to shield the beast,' said Egbert.

'There's been so little water in the stream lately,' objected Amanda; 'it seems hardly sporting to hunt an animal when it has so little chance of taking refuge anywhere.'

'Good gracious!' fumed Egbert, 'I'm not thinking about sport. I want to have the animal killed as soon as possible.'

Even Amanda's opposition weakened when, during church time on the following Sunday, the otter made its way into the house, raided half a salmon from the larder and worried it into scaly fragments on the Persian rug in Egbert's studio.

'We shall have it hiding under our beds and biting pieces out of our feet before long,' said Egbert, and from what Amanda knew of this particular otter she felt that the possibility was not a remote one.

On the evening preceding the day fixed for the hunt Amanda spent a solitary hour walking by the banks of the stream, making what she imagined to be hound noises. It was charitably supposed by those who overheard her

performance, that she was practising for farmyard imitations at the forthcoming village entertainment.

It was her friend and neighbour, Aurora Burret, who brought her news of the day's sport.

'Pity you weren't out; we had quite a good day. We found at once, in the pool just below your garden.'

'Did you – kill?' asked Amanda.

'Rather. A fine she-otter. Your husband got rather badly bitten in trying to "tail it". Poor beast, I felt quite sorry for it, it had such a human look in its eyes when it was killed. You'll call me silly, but do you know who the look reminded me of? My dear woman, what is the matter?'

When Amanda had recovered to a certain extent from her attack of nervous prostration Egbert took her to the Nile Valley to recuperate. Change of scene speedily brought about the desired recovery of health and mental balance. The escapades of an adventurous otter in search of a variation of diet were viewed in their proper light. Amanda's normally placid temperament reasserted itself. Even a hurricane of shouted curses, coming from her husband's dressing-room, in her husband's voice, but hardly in his usual vocabulary, failed to disturb her serenity as she made a leisurely toilet one evening in a Cairo hotel.

'What is the matter? What has happened?' she asked in amused curiosity.

'The little beast has thrown all my clean shirts into the bath! Wait till I catch you, you little –'

'What little beast?' asked Amanda, suppressing a desire to laugh; Egbert's language was so hopelessly inadequate to express his outraged feelings.

'A little beast of a naked brown Nubian boy,' spluttered Egbert.

And now Amanda is seriously ill.

R. Blakeborough

The Betrayal of Nance

'I REMEMBER,' mine host began, 'hearing of Nance when I was quite a lad. The grandfather of the driver who brought you here tonight was at one time a hind at Sheriff-Hutton. It was then he fell in love with a farmer's daughter, called "Nance". The lovers were great favourites, and all looked forward to their wedding day. But it was not to be. When the day was actually fixed for their marriage, there came to the village a young dandy, dressed in all the latest o' fashion, who flung his brass about as if it had no end. He looked a gentleman, and he behaved like one, save being honourable, for soon he made love to Nance. Many of the folk told him to his face that Nance was ommaist as good as wed, and that he ought to let her alone. But the young master just laughed at them, saying, "All's fair in love and war." To Nance he flattered and lied, making all sorts of sport of the less-polished Tom. He told Nance that she was born to grace a lady's gown, and not a drudge's apron, and, like many another silly country lass, she listened to his blandishments, till in the end she told Tom she could no longer claim his honest love, and that she had come to feel she could never be happy as a poor man's wife. She bade him forget her, and find some other girl more worthy of his affection.

'Tom begged her to wait until he found out who and what her new lover might be. This Nance promised to do, and Tom left the village next day on his secret mission.

177

Before he returned, however, Nance was wedded and gone — no one knew whither. At first Tom almost lost his wits, but he managed to pull himself together after a few weeks. A year or two before he had driven one of the mail coaches, and, feeling that the roving life would suit him better in his present state of mind, he was soon on the box again tooling a coach between York and Hull. Well then, gentlemen' (mine host continued, looking round as if to call special attention to what he was about to say), 'a twelvemonth after he had started to drive this coach, one summer night he noticed sitting by the roadside a young woman, nursing a baby. He was then about five miles from York, and well up to time. The woman rose as he drew near her, lifting her hands towards him as if in supplication, at the same time in a broken voice begging him to stop. He saw it was Nance, looking wan and weary, with death written upon her face. Did he pull up, gents? Did he take any notice of the wench who had treated him so cruelly? Aye, that he did. He called to the guard to catch hold of the leaders' heads, and was himself soon off the coach and by her side, supporting her fainting form in his strong arms.

'"Nance, my poor lass, what is the matter?" he cried, for she had slipped from his arms on to her knees upon the turnpike. "Get up, my lass," said Tom, his words choked with emotion. "Oh, Tom!" she sobbed, "I am not worthy that you should look at me, but I'm dying, Tom. For the love you once had for me, I . . ."

'But she got no further. Opening the coach door, he said in a voice filled with tears, "Ladies" (there were but two in-inside passengers), "for the love of God, be kind to her; we shall soon be at York, and then I'll see to her comfort. She was once to have been my wife, but . . ." And then Tom broke down, closed the door, and next moment was mak-

ing up lost time. The landlady of the York Tavern (a Mrs
Pulleyn) tended the girl as if she had been her own daughter. Bit by bit Nance told a sad and sordid story of the
scoundrel who, by his lies and flattery, had blinded her
eyes to Tom's true love. She had discovered he was a
gentleman born, but a penniless younger son of a great
family, who, like many others of his type, had turned
highwayman. Moreover, she had found too late he was
already a married man at the time he had wed her. The
moment this terrible fact became known to her – it was all
no news to Tom – she had fled from his house. She had
learnt that a coach driven by Tom would pass along the
York Road, and had patiently waited his coming.

'"You'll care for my bairn when I'm gone, Tom, won't
you?" she pleaded in a feeble whisper, when she had told
her tale of sorrow and shame. "Aye, lass," promised the
kindly-hearted Tom. "I'll be a father to bairn." ... And
Nance knew the promise would be faithfully kept.

'"Tom," she whispered.

'"Aye, lass, what is it?"

'"It's time you went – kiss me afore you go, and whisper you forgive me. We shall not speak to each other again
on earth." Winding her arms about him, she continued:
"But if my spirit be allowed to return, I will always warn
you, your childer – for you must wed some true lass – and
your childer's children, of any coming danger. Good-bye."

'Tom never saw Nance again alive. She died a few hours
after he left her. Now comes the stranger part of the story.
About two years after Nance's death, Tom was sent to
Durham to take charge of a special coach requiring an ex-
tra-skilful driver, and bring it as far as York, where he
would receive further orders. There were just four passengers – all gents of high degree. Tom had a hint given
him that one was a bishop, one a duke, and the other two

were noblemen, all on secret business connected with the King and Parliament. Circumstances arose that these gents could not leave Durham till later than expected, and it was most urgent they should be in York at a certain time. Just after Tom had climbed on to the box one of the gents called to him from the window:

'"Have you made all arrangements, coachman? You have not one minute to waste."

'"Yes sir; there's a post-boy on in front and fresh horses, and the best will be ready with their sheets off at every stage."

'"Right! Then let's hear the crack of your whip, and remember, if you get us into York by eight chimes, there's a guinea apiece from each of us." Up went the window, Tom gave his team their heads, and away they went.

'All went well until they started on their last stage – ten good miles from York. It was there Tom got his first bit of bad news from the driver of a passing chaise. He learnt there was a heavy fog settling over York, which was spreading northward like a sheet every minute. "What's that he says?" asked one of the gentlemen, letting down the window. Tom repeated the bad news, adding, "I have five minutes to spare now, but I shall soon lose what I have gained if the fog has reached but two miles out of York." But the fresh horses were in and away they went. Before they had travelled three miles Tom's heart sank – even then they were driving into the fog, and, if it became worse, it meant creeping along, and all chance of reaching York by eight was gone. Denser and denser it grew, and he dare not keep up the pace he was going much longer, as he was then risking all their lives. It was just as he caught hold of the leaders to steady them Tom saw a figure take its seat by his side. It came to him out of the mist and seemed to take its form from the curling grey land-low

clouds. He instinctively knew it was Nance even before her hands were laid lightly upon the reins. The instant she did so the leaders sprang into a gallop again. On, on they went, the coach swinging from side to side. On, on, faster and yet faster; safely passing the lumbering carrier's waggons pulled up close to the roadside to give room to what for many a long day was spoken of as "the phantom coach," whose horn the guard sounded till the very veins on his forehead were like to burst. At its warning blasts wide open flew the turnpike gates, the toll-gatherer standing filled with wonderment and awe at the flying coach and at the pale faces staring through the open window upon which the light from their lanterns shone for one brief moment. Those within the coach had ceased to expostulate. They had shouted to Tom until they were hoarse to drive more steadily.... On, on they tore through the fog, now so dense that it was impossible to see a yard in front. Tom, however, had now no fear. Against his own hands he felt cold but gentle fingers gripping the reins. Once, and only once, he shouted to the now terrified passengers, "You have no cause to fear, gentlemen, you'll be safe – and in York before eight chimes."

'He heeded not the retort of one of them: "Pull up, you fool; we'd rather be late as dashed to pieces. You shall have your four guineas anyway."

'On the coach rattled, and it was not until the clatter and jolting of the cobble-stones beneath the wheels told Tom that he was actually safe in York city, that he felt the touch of those magic marble hands had vanished. A few moments later his foam-flecked team was drawn up at the sign of narrow Coney Street's Black Swan.

'"You are here, sirs, and a good five minutes to spare," said Tom, wiping his face as he opened the door. "I told you you'd be here in time; and, gentlemen, if you knew

all that I know you would have felt there was no reason to fear." Tom pocketed his four guineas, and, as he walked after his horses up the spacious Swan yard, he murmured, "Poor Nance! poor Nance!"'

Mine host concluded:

'Several times after that Nance helped Tom out of awkward situations, and when the day came for Tom's son to take his father's place, the old man gave him this advice. Said he: "And last of all, Tom – and there's nowt about driving a coach which is of more consequence than this – think on, if ever you are in a fix and you find yourself beat, and Nance comes to your help, let her have her way; trust both coach, cattle, and yourself to her. You'll pull through all right, take my word for it. Think on," continued old Tom, "if she signals you to stop – *stop*, my lad. If ever she takes hold of the ribbons – let *her* drive."

'That is my story, gentlemen, and that explains what Tom meant when he said he had a warning finger pointed to the buck who is now chained by the leg in my yard.'

Anonymous

The Ghost Who Was Afraid of Being Bagged

ONCE on a time there lived a barber who had a wife. They
did not live happily together, as the wife always complained that she had not enough to eat. Many were the curtain lectures which were inflicted upon the poor barber.
The wife used often to say to her mate, 'If you had not
the means to support a wife, why did you marry me?
People who have not means ought not to indulge in the
luxury of a wife. When I was in my father's house I had
plenty to eat, but it seems that I have come to your house
to fast. Widows only fast; I have become a widow in your
lifetime.' She was not content with mere words; she got
very angry one day and struck her husband with the
broomstick of the house. Stung with shame, and abhorring
himself on account of his wife's reproach and beating, he
left his house, with the implements of his craft, and vowed
never to return and see his wife's face again till he had become rich. He went from village to village, and towards
nightfall came to the outskirts of a forest. He laid himself
down at the foot of a tree, and spent many a sad hour in
bemoaning his hard lot.

It so chanced that the tree, at the foot of which the barber was lying down, was dwelt in by a ghost. The ghost,
seeing a human being at the foot of the tree, naturally
thought of destroying him. With this intention the ghost
alighted from the tree, and, with outspread arms and a
gaping mouth, stood like a tall palmyra tree before the

barber, and said, 'Now, barber, I am going to destroy you. Who will protect you?' The barber, though quaking in every limb through fear, and his hair standing erect, did not lose his presence of mind, but, with that promptitude and shrewdness which are characteristic of his fraternity, replied, 'O spirit, you will destroy me! wait a bit and I'll show you how many ghosts I have captured this very night and put into my bag; and right glad am I to find you here, as I shall have one more ghost in my bag.' So saying the barber produced from his bag a small looking-glass, which he always carried about with him along with his razors, his whet-stone, his strop and other utensils, to enable his customers to see whether their beards had been well shaved or not. He stood up, placed the looking-glass right against the face of the ghost, and said, 'Here you see one ghost which I have seized and bagged; I am going to put you also in the bag to keep this ghost company.' The ghost, seeing his own face in the looking-glass, was convinced of the truth of what the barber had said, and was filled with fear. He said to the barber, 'O, sir barber, I'll do whatever you bid me, only do not put me into your bag. I'll give you whatever you want.' The barber said, 'You ghosts are a faithless set, there is no trusting you. You will promise, and not give what you promise.' 'O, sir,' replied the ghost, 'be merciful to me; I'll bring to you whatever you order; and if I do not bring it, then put me into your bag.' 'Very well,' said the barber, 'bring me just now one thousand gold mohurs; and by tomorrow night you must raise a granary in my house, and fill it with paddy. Go and get the gold mohurs immediately: and if you fail to do my bidding you will certainly be put into my bag.' The ghost gladly consented to the conditions. He went away, and in the course of a short time returned with a bag containing a thousand gold mohurs. The barber was delighted

beyond measure at the sight of the gold mohurs. He then told the ghost to see to it that by the following night a granary was erected in his house and filled with paddy.

It was during the small hours of the morning that the barber, loaded with the heavy treasure, knocked at the door of his house. His wife, who reproached herself for having in a fit of rage struck her husband with a broom-stick, got out of bed and unbolted the door. Her surprise was great when she saw her husband pour out of the bag a glittering heap of gold mohurs.

The next night the poor devil, through fear of being bagged, raised a large granary in the barber's house, and spent the live-long night in carrying on his back large packages of paddy till the granary was filled up to the brim. The uncle of this terrified ghost, seeing his worthy nephew carrying on his back loads of paddy, asked what the matter was. The ghost related what had happened. The uncle-ghost then said, 'You fool, you think the barber can bag you! The barber is a cunning fellow; he has cheated you, like a simpleton as you are.' 'You doubt,' said the nephew-ghost, 'the power of the barber! come and see.' The uncle-ghost then went to the barber's house, and peeped into it through a window. The barber, perceiving from the blast of wind which the arrival of the ghost had produced that a ghost was at the window, placed full before it the self-same looking-glass, saying, 'Come now, I'll put you also into the bag.' The uncle-ghost, seeing his own face in the looking-glass, got quite frightened, and promised that very night to raise another granary and to fill it, not this time with paddy, but with rice. So in two nights the barber became a rich man, and lived happily with his wife begetting sons and daughters.

W. F. Harvey

The Beast with Five Fingers

WHEN I was a little boy I once went with my father to call on Adrian Borlsover. I played on the floor with a black spaniel while my father appealed for a subscription. Just before we left my father said, 'Mr Borlsover, may my son here shake hands with you? It will be a thing to look back upon with pride when he grows to be a man.'

I came up to the bed on which the old man was lying and put my hand in his, awed by the still beauty of his face. He spoke to me kindly, and hoped that I should always try to please my father. Then he placed his right hand on my head and asked for a blessing to rest upon me. 'Amen!' said my father, and I followed him out of the room, feeling as if I wanted to cry. But my father was in excellent spirits.

'That old gentleman, Jim,' said he, 'is the most wonderful man in the whole town. For ten years he has been quite blind.'

'But I saw his eyes,' I said. 'They were ever so black and shiny; they weren't shut up like Nora's puppies. Can't he see at all?'

And so I learnt for the first time that a man might have eyes that looked dark and beautiful and shining without being able to see.

'Just like Mrs Tomlinson has big ears,' I said, 'and can't hear at all except when Mr Tomlinson shouts.'

'Jim,' said my father, 'it's not right to talk about a

186

lady's ears. Remember what Mr Borlsover said about pleasing me and being a good boy.'

That was the only time I saw Adrian Borlsover. I soon forgot about him and the hand which he laid in blessing on my head. But for a week I prayed that those dark tender eyes might see.

'His spaniel may have puppies,' I said in my prayers, 'and he will never be able to know how funny they look with their eyes all closed up. Please let old Mr Borlsover see.'

Adrian Borlsover, as my father had said, was a wonderful man. He came of an eccentric family. Borlsovers' sons, for some reason, always seemed to marry very ordinary women, which perhaps accounted for the fact that no Borlsover had been a genius, and only one Borlsover had been mad. But they were great champions of little causes, generous patrons of odd sciences, founders of querulous sects, trustworthy guides to the by-path meadows of erudition.

Adrian was an authority on the fertilization of orchids. He had held at one time the family living at Borlsover Conyers, until a congenital weakness of the lungs obliged him to seek a less rigorous climate in the sunny south-coast watering-place where I had seen him. Occasionally he would relieve one or other of the local clergy. My father described him as a fine preacher, who gave long and inspiring sermons from what many men would have considered unprofitable texts. 'An excellent proof,' he would add, 'of the truth of the doctrine of direct verbal inspiration.'

Adrian Borlsover was exceedingly clever with his hands. His penmanship was exquisite. He illustrated all his scientific papers, made his own woodcuts, and carved the reredos that is at present the chief feature of interest in the

church at Borlsover Conyers. He had an exceedingly clever knack in cutting silhouettes for young ladies and paper pigs and cows for little children, and made more than one complicated wind instrument of his own devising.

When he was fifty years old Adrian Borlsover lost his sight. In a wonderfully short time he had adapted himself to the new conditions of life. He quickly learned to read Braille. So marvellous indeed was his sense of touch that he was still able to maintain his interest in botany. The mere passing of his long supple fingers over a flower was sufficient means for its identification, though occasionally he would use his lips. I have found several letters of his among my father's correspondence. In no case was there anything to show that he was afflicted with blindness, and this in spite of the fact that he exercised undue economy in the spacing of lines. Towards the close of his life the old man was credited with powers of touch that seemed almost uncanny: it has been said that he could tell at once the colour of a ribbon placed between his fingers. My father would neither confirm nor deny the story.

I

Adrian Borlsover was a bachelor. His elder brother George had married late in life, leaving one son, Eustace, who lived in the gloomy Georgian mansion at Borlsover Conyers, where he could work undisturbed in collecting material for his great book on heredity.

Like his uncle, he was a remarkable man. The Borlsovers had always been born naturalists, but Eustace possessed in a special degree the power of systematizing his knowledge. He had received his university education in Germany, and then, after post-graduate work in Vienna and Naples, had travelled for four years in South America and the East, get-

ting together a huge store of material for a new study into the processes of variation.

He lived alone at Borlsover Conyers with Saunders his secretary, a man who bore a somewhat dubious reputation in the district, but whose powers as a mathematician, combined with his business abilities, were invaluable to Eustace.

Uncle and nephew saw little of each other. The visits of Eustace were confined to a week in the summer or autumn: long weeks, that dragged almost as slowly as the bath-chair in which the old man was drawn along the sunny sea front. In their way the two men were fond of each other, though their intimacy would doubtless have been greater had they shared the same religious views. Adrian held to the old-fashioned evangelical dogmas of his early manhood; his nephew for many years had been thinking of embracing Buddhism. Both men possessed, too, the reticence the Borlsovers had always shown, and which their enemies sometimes called hypocrisy. With Adrian it was a reticence as to the things he had left undone; but with Eustace it seemed that the curtain which he was so careful to leave undrawn hid something more than a half-empty chamber.

Two years before his death Adrian Borlsover developed, unknown to himself, the not uncommon power of automatic writing. Eustace made the discovery by accident. Adrian was sitting reading in bed, the forefinger of his left hand tracing the Braille characters, when his nephew noticed that a pencil the old man held in his right hand was moving slowly along the opposite page. He left his seat in the window and sat down beside the bed. The right hand continued to move, and now he could see plainly that they were letters and words which it was forming.

'Adrian Borlsover,' wrote the hand, 'Eustace Borlsover, George Borlsover, Francis Borlsover, Sigismund Borlsover, Adrian Borlsover, Eustace Borlsover, Saville Borlsover. B, for Borlsover. Honesty is the Best Policy. Beautiful Belinda Borlsover.'

'What curious nonsense!' said Eustace to himself.

'King George the Third ascended the throne in 1760,' wrote the hand. 'Crowd, a noun of multitude; a collection of individuals – Adrian Borlsover, Eustace Borlsover.'

'It seems to me,' said his uncle, closing the book, 'that you had much better make the most of the afternoon sunshine and take your walk now.' 'I think perhaps I will,' Eustace answered as he picked up the volume. 'I won't go far, and when I come back I can read to you those articles in *Nature* about which we were speaking.'

He went along the promenade, but stopped at the first shelter, and seating himself in the corner best protected from the wind, he examined the book at leisure. Nearly every page was scored with a meaningless jungle of pencil marks: rows of capital letters, short words, long words, complete sentences, copy-book tags. The whole thing, in fact, had the apearance of a copy-book, and on a more careful scrutiny Eustace thought that there was ample evidence to show that the handwriting at the beginning of the book, good though it was, was not nearly so good as the handwriting at the end.

He left his uncle at the end of October, with a promise to return early in December. It seemed to him quite clear that the old man's power of automatic writing was developing rapidly, and for the first time he looked forward to a visit that combined duty with interest.

But on his return he was at first disappointed. His uncle, he thought, looked older. He was listless too, preferring others to read to him and dictating nearly all his letters.

Not until the day before he left had Eustace an opportunity of observing Adrian Borlsover's new-found faculty.

The old man, propped up in bed with pillows had sunk into a light sleep. His two hands lay on the coverlet, his left hand tightly clasping his right. Eustace took an empty manuscript book and placed a pencil within reach of the fingers of the right hand. They snatched at it eagerly; then dropped the pencil to unloose the left hand from its restraining grasp.

'Perhaps to prevent interference I had better hold that hand,' said Eustace to himself, as he watched the pencil. Almost immediately it began to write.

'Blundering Borlsovers, unnecessarily unnatural, extraordinarily eccentric, culpably curious.'

'Who are you?' asked Eustace, in a low voice.

'Never you mind,' wrote the hand of Adrian.

'Is it my uncle who is writing?'

'Oh, my prophetic soul, mine uncle.'

'Is it anyone I know?'

'Silly Eustace, you'll see me very soon.'

'When shall I see you?'

'When poor old Adrian's dead.'

'Where shall I see you?'

'Where shall you not?'

Instead of speaking his next question, Borlsover wrote it. 'What is the time?'

The fingers dropped the pencil and moved three or four times across the paper. Then, picking up the pencil, they wrote:

'Ten minutes before four. Put your book away, Eustace. Adrian mustn't find us working at this sort of thing. He doesn't know what to make of it, and I won't have poor old Adrian disturbed. *Au revoir*.'

Adrian Borlsover awoke with a start.

'I've been dreaming again,' he said; 'such queer dreams of leaguered cities and forgotten towns. You were mixed up in this one, Eustace, though I can't remember how. Eustace, I want to warn you. Don't walk in doubtful paths. Choose your friends well. Your poor grandfather –'

A fit of coughing put an end to what he was saying, but Eustace saw that the hand was still writing. He managed unnoticed to draw the book away. 'I'll light the gas,' he said, 'and ring for tea.' On the other side of the bed curtain he saw the last sentences that had been written.

'It's too late, Adrian,' he read. 'We're friends already; aren't we, Eustace Borlsover?'

On the following day Eustace Borlsover left. He thought his uncle looked ill when he said good-bye, and the old man spoke despondently of the failure his life had been.

'Nonsense, uncle!' said his nephew. 'You have got over your difficulties in a way not one in a hundred thousand would have done. Everyone marvels at your splendid perseverance in teaching your hand to take the place of your lost sight. To me it's been a revelation of the possibilities of education.'

'Education,' said his uncle dreamily, as if the word had started a new train of thought, 'education is good so long as you know to whom and for what purpose you give it. But with the lower orders of men, the base and more sordid spirits, I have grave doubts as to its results. Well, good-bye, Eustace, I may not see you again. You are a true Borlsover, with all the Borlsover faults. Marry, Eustace. Marry some good, sensible girl. And if by any chance I don't see you again, my will is at my solicitor's. I've not left you any legacy, because I know you're well provided for, but I thought you might like to have my books. Oh, and there's just one other thing. You know, before the end people often lose control over themselves and make absurd

requests. Don't pay any attention to them, Eustace. Good-bye!' and he held out his hand. Eustace took it. It remained in his a fraction of a second longer that he had expected, and gripped him with a virility that was surprising. There was, too, in its touch a subtle sense of intimacy.

'Why, uncle!' he said, 'I shall see you alive and well for many long years to come.'

Two months later Adrian Borlsover died.

2

Eustace Borlsover was in Naples at the time. He read the obituary notice in the *Morning Post* on the day announced for the funeral.

'Poor old fellow!' he said. 'I wonder where I shall find room for all his books.'

The question occurred to him again with greater force when three days later he found himself standing in the library at Borlsover Conyers, a huge room built for use, and not for beauty, in the year of Waterloo by a Borlsover who was an ardent admirer of the great Napoleon. It was arranged on the plan of many college libraries, with tall, projecting bookcases forming deep recesses of dusty silence, fit graves for the old hates of forgotten controversy, the dead passions of forgotten lives. At the end of the room, behind the bust of some unknown eighteenth-century divine, an ugly iron corkscrew stair led to a shelf-lined gallery. Nearly every shelf was full.

'I must talk to Saunders about it,' said Eustace. 'I suppose that it will be necessary to have the billiard-room fitted up with book cases.'

The two men met for the first time after many weeks in the dining-room that evening.

'Hullo!' said Eustace, standing before the fire with his hands in his pockets. 'How goes the world, Saunders? Why these dress togs?' He himself was wearing an old shooting-jacket. He did not believe in mourning, as he had told his uncle on his last visit; and though he usually went in for quiet-coloured ties, he wore this evening one of an ugly red, in order to shock Morton the butler, and to make them thrash out the whole question of mourning for themselves in the servants' hall. Eustace was a true Borlsover. 'The world,' said Saunders, 'goes the same as usual, confoundedly slow. The dress togs are accounted for by an invitation from Captain Lockwood to bridge.'

'How are you getting there?'

'I've told your coachman to drive me in your carriage. Any objection?'

'Oh, dear me, no! We've had all things in common for far too many years for me to raise objections at this hour of the day.'

'You'll find your correspondence in the library,' went on Saunders. 'Most of it I've seen to. There are a few private letters I haven't opened. There's also a box with a rat, or something, inside it that came by the evening post. Very likely it's the six-toed albino. I didn't look, because I didn't want to mess up my things, but I should gather from the way it's jumping about that it's pretty hungry.'

'Oh, I'll see to it,' said Eustace, 'while you and the Captain earn an honest penny.'

Dinner over and Saunders gone, Eustace went into the library. Though the fire had been lit the room was by no means cheerful.

'We'll have all the lights on at any rate,' he said, as he turned the switches. 'And, Morton,' he added, when the butler brought the coffee, 'get me a screwdriver or something to undo this box. Whatever the animal is, he's kick-

ing up the deuce of a row. What is it? Why are you dawd-ling?'

'If you please sir, when the postman brought it he told me that they'd bored the holes in the lid at the post office. There was no breathin' holes in the lid, sir, and they didn't want the animal to die. That is all, sir.'

'It's culpably careless of the man, whoever he was,' said Eustace, as he removed the screws, 'packing an animal like this in a wooden box with no means of getting air. Con-found it all! I meant to ask Morton to bring me a cage to put it in. Now I suppose I shall have to get one myself.'

He placed a heavy book on the lid from which the screws had been removed, and went into the billiard-room. As he came back into the library with an empty cage in his hand he heard the sound of something falling, and then of something scuttling along the floor.

'Bother it! The beast's got out. How in the world am I to find it again in this library!'

To search for it did indeed seem hopeless. He tried to follow the sound of the scuttling in one of the recesses where the animal seemed to be running behind the books in the shelves, but it was impossible to locate it. Eustace resolved to go on quietly reading. Very likely the animal might gain confidence and show itself. Saunders seemed to have dealt in his usual methodical manner with most of the correspondence. There were still the private letters.

What was that? Two sharp clicks and the lights in the hideous candelabra that hung from the ceiling suddenly went out.

'I wonder if something has gone wrong with the fuse,' said Eustace, as he went to the switches by the door. Then he stopped. There was a noise at the other end of the room, as if something was crawling up the iron corkscrew stair. 'If it's gone into the gallery,' he said, 'well and good.' He

hastily turned on the lights, crossed the room, and climbed up the stair. But he could see nothing. His grandfather had placed a little gate at the top of the stair, so that children could run and romp in the gallery without fear of accident. This Eustace closed, and having considerably narrowed the circle of his search, returned to his desk by the fire.

How gloomy the library was! There was no sense of intimacy about the room. The few busts that an eighteenth-century Borlsover had brought back from the grand tour might have been in keeping in the old library. Here they seemed out of place. The made the room feel cold, in spite of the heavy red damask curtains and great gilt cornices.

With a crash two heavy books fell from the gallery to the floor; then, as Borlsover looked, another and yet another.

'Very well; you'll starve for this, my beauty!' he said. 'We'll do some little experiments on the metabolism of rats deprived of water. Go on! Chuck them down! I think I've got the upper hand!' He turned once again to his correspondence. The letter was from the family solicitor. It spoke of his uncle's death and of the valuable collection of books that had been left to him in the will.

'There was one request,' he read, 'which certainly came as a surprise to me. As you know, Mr Adrian Borlsover had left instructions that his body was to be buried in as simple a manner as possible at Eastbourne. He expressed a desire that there should be neither wreaths nor flowers of any kind, and hoped that his friends and relatives would not consider it necessary to wear mourning. The day before his death we received a letter cancelling these instructions. He wished his body to be embalmed (he gave us the address of the men we were to employ – Pennifer, Ludgate Hill), with orders that his right hand was to be sent to you,

stating that it was at your special request. The other arrangements as to the funeral remained unaltered.'

'Good Lord!' said Eustace; 'what in the world was the old boy driving at? And what in the name of all that's holy is that?'

Someone was in the gallery. Someone had pulled the cord attached to one of the blinds, and it had rolled up with a snap. Someone must be in the gallery, for a second blind did the same. Someone must be walking round the gallery, for one after the other the blinds sprang up, letting in the moonlight.

'I haven't got to the bottom of this yet,' said Eustace, 'but I will do so before the night is very much older,' and he hurried up the corkscrew stair. He had just got to the top when the lights went out a second time, and he heard again the scuttling along the floor. Quickly he stole on tip-toe in the dim moonshine in the direction of the noise, feeling as he went for one of the switches. His fingers touched the metal knob at last. He turned on the electric light.

About ten yards in front of him, crawling along the floor, was a man's hand. Eustace stared at it in utter astonishment. It was moving quickly, in the manner of a geometer caterpillar, the fingers humped up one moment, flattened out the next; the thumb appeared to give a crab-like motion to the whole. While he was looking, too surprised to stir, the hand disappeared round the corner. Eustace ran forward. He no longer saw it, but he could hear it as it squeezed its way behind the books on one of the shelves. A heavy volume had been displaced. There was a gap in the row of books where it had got in. In his fear lest it should escape him again, he seized the first book that came to his hand and plugged it into the hole. Then, emptying two shelves of their contents, he took the wooden

boards and propped them up in front to make his barrier doubly sure.

'I wish Saunders was back,' he said; 'one can't tackle this sort of thing alone.' It was after eleven, and there seemed little likelihood of Saunders returning before twelve. He did not dare to leave the shelf unwatched, even to run downstairs to ring the bell. Morton the butler often used to come round about eleven to see that the windows were fastened, but he might not come. Eustace was thoroughly unstrung. At last he heard steps down below.

'Morton!' he shouted; 'Morton!'

'Sir?'

'Has Mr Saunders got back yet?'

'Not yet, sir.'

'Well, bring me some brandy, and hurry up about it. I'm up here in the gallery, you duffer.'

'Thanks,' said Eustace, as he emptied the glass. 'Don't go to bed yet, Morton. There are a lot of books that have fallen down by accident; bring them up and put them back in their shelves.'

Morton had never seen Borlsover in so talkative a mood as on that night. 'Here,' said Eustace, when the books had been put back and dusted, 'you might hold up these boards for me, Morton. That beast in the box got out, and I've been chasing it all over the place.'

'I think I can hear it chewing at the books, sir. They're not valuable, I hope? I think that's the carriage, sir; I'll go and call Mr Saunders.'

It seemed to Eustace that he was away for five minutes, but it could hardly have been more than one when he returned with Saunders. 'All right, Morton, you can go now. I'm up here, Saunders."

'What's all the row?' asked Saunders, as he lounged forward with his hands in his pockets. The luck had been

with him all the evening. He was completely satisfied, both with himself and with Captain Lockwood's taste in wines. 'What's the matter? You look to me to be in an absolute blue funk.'

'That old devil of an uncle of mine,' began Eustace – 'Oh, I can't explain it all. It's his hand that's been playing old Harry all the evening. But I've got it cornered behind these books. You've got to help me catch it.'

'What's up with you, Eustace? What's the game?'

'It's no game, you silly idiot! If you don't believe me take out one of those books and put your hand in and feel.'

'All right,' said Saunders; 'but wait till I've rolled up my sleeve. The accumulated dust of centuries, eh?' He took off his coat, knelt down, and thrust his arm along the shelf.

'There's something there right enough,' he said. 'It's got a funny stumpy end to it, whatever it is, and nips like a crab. Ah, no, you don't!' He pulled his hand out in a flash. 'Shove in a book quickly. Now it can't get out.'

'What was it?' asked Eustace.

'It was something that wanted very much to get hold of me. I felt what seemed like a thumb and forefinger. Give me some brandy.'

'How are we to get it out of there?'

'What about a landing net?'

'No good. It would be too smart for us. I tell you, Saunders, it can cover the ground far faster than I can walk. But I think I see how we can manage it. The two books at the end of the shelf are big ones that go right back against the wall. The others are very thin. I'll take out one at a time, and you slide the rest along until we have it squashed between the end two.'

It certainly seemed to be the best plan. One by one, as they took out the books, the space behind grew smaller

and smaller. There was something in it that was certainly very much alive. Once they caught sight of fingers pressing outward for a way of escape. At last they had it pressed between the two big books.

'There's muscle there, if there isn't flesh and blood,' said Saunders, as he held them together. 'It seems to be a hand right enough, too. I suppose this is a sort of infectious hallucination. I've read about such cases before.'

'Infectious fiddlesticks!' said Eustace, his face white with anger; 'bring the thing downstairs. We'll get it back into the box.'

It was not altogether easy, but they were successful at last. 'Drive in the screws,' said Eustace, 'we won't run any risks. Put the box in this old desk of mine. There's nothing in it that I want. Here's the key. Thank goodness, there's nothing wrong with the lock.'

'Quite a lively evening,' said Saunders. 'Now let's hear more about your uncle.'

They sat up together until early morning. Saunders had no desire for sleep. Eustace was trying to explain and to forget: to conceal from himself a fear that he had never felt before – the fear of walking alone down the long corridor to his bedroom.

3

'Whatever it was,' said Eustace to Saunders on the following morning, 'I propose that we drop the subject. There's nothing to keep us here for the next ten days. We'll motor up to the Lakes and get some climbing.'

'And see nobody all day, and sit bored to death with each other every night. Not for me, thanks. Why not run up to town? Run's the exact word in this case, isn't it? We're both in such a blessed funk. Pull yourself together, Eustace, and let's have another look at the hand.'

'As you like,' said Eustace; 'There's the key.' They went into the library, and opened the desk. The box was as they had left it on the previous night.

'What are you waiting for?' asked Eustace.

'I am waiting for you to volunteer to open the lid. However, since you seem to funk it, allow me. There doesn't seem to be the likelihood of any rumpus this morning, at all events.' He opened the lid and picked out the hand.

'Cold?' asked Eustace.

'Tepid. A bit below blood-heat by the feel. Soft and supple too. If it's the embalming, it's a sort of embalming I've never seen before. Is it your uncle's hand?'

'Oh, yes, it's his all right,' said Eustace. 'I should know those long thin fingers anywhere. Put it back in the box, Saunders. Never mind about the screws. I'll lock the desk, so that there'll be no chance of its getting out. We'll compromise by motoring up to town for a week. If we get off soon after lunch we ought to be at Grantham or Stamford by night.'

'Right,' said Saunders; 'and tomorrow – Oh, well by to-morrow we shall have forgotten all about this beastly thing.'

If when the morrow came they had not forgotten, it was certainly true that at the end of the week they were able to tell a very vivid ghost story at the little supper Eustace gave on Hallow E'en.

'You don't want us to believe that it's true, Mr Borlsover? How perfectly awful!'

'I'll take my oath on it, and so would Saunders here; wouldn't you, old chap?'

'Any number of oaths,' said Saunders. 'It was a long thin hand, you know, and it gripped me just like that.'

'Don't, Mr Saunders! Don't! How perfectly horrid!

Now tell us another one, do. Only a really creepy one, please!'

'Here's a pretty mess!' said Eustace on the following day as he threw a letter across the table to Saunders. 'It's your affair, though. Mrs Merrit, if I understand it, gives a month's notice.'

'Oh, that's quite absurd on Mrs Merrit's part,' Saunders replied. 'She doesn't know what she's talking about. Let's see what she says.'

'DEAR SIR,' he read,

'this is to let you know that I must give you a month's notice as from Tuesday the 13th. For a long time I've felt the place too big for me, but when Jane Parfit, and Emma Laidlaw go off with scarcely as much as an "if you please," after frightening the wits out of the other girls, so that they can't turn out a room by themselves or walk alone down the stairs for fear of treading on half-frozen toads or hearing it run along the passages at night, all I can say is that it's no place for me. So I must ask you, Mr Borlsover, sir, to find a new housekeeper that has no objection to large and lonely houses, which some people do say, not that I believe them for a minute, my poor mother always having been a Wesleyan, are haunted.

'Yours faithfully,
'ELIZABETH MERRIT.

'P.S. – I should be obliged if you would give my respects to Mr Saunders. I hope that he won't run no risks with his cold.'

'Saunders,' said Eustace, 'you've always had a wonderful way with you in dealing with servants. You mustn't let poor old Merrit go.'

'Of course she shan't go,' said Saunders. 'She's probably only angling for a rise in salary. I'll write to her this morning.'

'No; there's nothing like a personal interview. We've had enough of town. We'll go back tomorrow, and you must work your cold for all it's worth. Don't forget that it's got on to the chest, and will require weeks of feeding up and nursing.'

'All right. I think I can manage Mrs Merrit.'

But Mrs Merrit was more obstinate than he had thought. She was very sorry to hear of Mr Saunders's cold, and how he lay awake all night in London coughing; very sorry indeed. She'd change his room for him gladly, and get the south room aired. And wouldn't he have a basin of hot bread and milk last thing at night? But she was afraid that she would have to leave at the end of the month.

'Try her with an increase of salary,' was the advice of Eustace.

It was no use. Mrs Merrit was obdurate, though she knew of a Mrs Handyside who had been housekeeper to Lord Gargrave, who might be glad to come at the salary mentioned.

'What's the matter with the servants, Morton?' asked Eustace that evening, when he brought the coffee into the library. 'What's all this about Mrs Merrit wanting to leave?'

'If you please, sir, I was going to mention it myself. I have a confession to make, sir. When I found your note asking me to open that desk and take out the box with the rat, I broke the lock as you told me, and was glad to do it, because I could hear the animal in the box making a great noise, and I thought it wanted food. So I took out the box, sir, and got a cage, and was going to transfer it, when the animal got away.'

'What in the world are you talking about? I never wrote any such note.'

'Excuse me, sir, it was the note I picked up here on the

floor on the day you and Mr Saunders left. I have it in my pocket now.'

It certainly seemed to be in Eustace's handwriting. It was written in pencil, and began somewhat abruptly.

'Get a hammer, Morton,' he read, 'or some other tool, and break open the lock in the old desk in the library. Take out the box that is inside. You need not do anything else. The lid is already open. Eustace Borlsover.'

'And you opened the desk?'

'Yes, sir; and as I was getting the cage ready the animal hopped out.'

'What animal?'

'The animal inside the box, sir.'

'What did it look like?'

'Well, sir, I couldn't tell you,' said Morton nervously; 'my back was turned, and it was half-way down the room when I looked up.'

'What was its colour?' asked Saunders; 'black?'

'Oh, no, sir, a greyish white. It crept along in a very funny way, sir. I don't think it had a tail.'

'What did you do then?'

'I tried to catch it, but it was no use. So I set the rat-traps and kept the library shut. Then that girl Emma Laidlaw left the door open when she was cleaning, and I think it must have escaped.'

'And you think it was the animal that's been frightening the maids?'

'Well, no, sir, not quite. They said it was – you'll excuse me, sir – a hand that they saw. Emma trod on it once at the bottom of the stairs. She thought then it was a half-frozen toad, only white. And then Parfit was washing up the dishes in the scullery. She wasn't thinking about anything in particular. It was close on dusk. She took her hands out of the water and was drying them absent-minded like on

the roller towel, when she found that she was drying some-one else's hand as well, only colder than hers.'

'What nonsense!' exclaimed Saunders.

'Exactly, sir; that's what I told her; but we couldn't get her to stop.'

'You don't believe all this?' said Eustace, turning sud-denly towards the butler.

'Me, sir? Oh, no, sir! I've not seen anything.'

'Nor heard anything?'

'Well, sir, if you must know, the bells do ring at odd times, and there's nobody there when we go; and when we go round to draw the blinds of a night, as often as not somebody's been there before us. But as I says to Mrs Merrit, a young monkey might do wonderful things, and we all know that Mr Borlsover has had some strange ani-mals about the place.'

'Very well, Morton, that will do.'

'What do you make of it?' asked Saunders when they were alone. 'I mean of the letter he said you wrote.'

'Oh, that's simple enough,' said Eustace. 'See the paper it's written on? I stopped using that years ago, but there were a few odd sheets and envelopes left in the old desk. We never fastened up the lid of the box before locking it in. The hand got out, found a pencil, wrote this note, and shoved it through a crack on to the floor where Morton found it. That's plain as daylight.'

'But the hand couldn't write!'

'Couldn't it? You've not seen it do the things I've seen,' and he told Saunders more of what had happened at East-bourne.

'Well,' said Saunders, 'in that case we have at least an explanation of the legacy. It was the hand which wrote unknown to your uncle that letter to your solicitor, be-queathing itself to you. Your uncle had no more to do

with that request than I. In fact, it would seem that he had some idea of this automatic writing, and feared it.'

'Then if it's not my uncle, what is it?'

'I suppose some people might say that a disembodied spirit had got your uncle to educate and prepare a little body for it. Now it's got into that little body and is off on its own.'

'What are we to do?'

'We'll keep our eyes open,' said Saunders, 'and try to catch it. If we can't do that, we shall have to wait till the bally clockwork runs down. After all, if it's flesh and blood, it can't live for ever.'

For two days nothing happened. Then Saunders saw it sliding down the banister in the hall. He was taken unawares, and lost a full second before he started in pursuit, only to find that the thing had escaped him. Three days later, Eustace, writing alone in the library at night, saw it sitting on an open book at the other end of the room. The fingers crept over the page, feeling the print as if it were reading; but before he had time to get up from his seat, it had taken the alarm and was pulling itself up the curtains. Eustace watched it grimly as it hung on the cornice with three fingers, flicking thumb and forefinger at him in an expression of scornful derision.

'I know what I'll do,' he said. 'If I only get it into the open I'll set the dogs on to it.'

He spoke to Saunders of the suggestion.

'It's a jolly good idea,' he said; 'only we won't wait till we find it out of doors. We'll get the dogs. There are the two terriers and the under-keeper's Irish mongrel that's on to rats like a flash. Your spaniel has not got spirit enough for this sort of game.' They brought the dogs into the house, and the keeper's Irish mongrel chewed up the slippers, and the terriers tripped up Morton as he waited at

table; but all three were welcome. Even false security is better than no security at all.

For a fortnight nothing happened. Then the hand was caught, not by the dogs, but by Mrs Merrit's grey parrot. The bird was in the habit of periodically removing the pins that kept its seed and water tins in place, and of escaping through the holes in the side of the cage. When once at liberty Peter would show no inclination to return, and would often be about the house for days. Now, after six consecutive weeks of captivity, Peter had again discovered a new means of unloosing his bolts and was at large, exploring the tapestried forests of the curtains and singing songs in praise of liberty from cornice and picture rail.

'It's no use your trying to catch him,' said Eustace to Mrs Merrit, as she came into the study one afternoon towards dusk with a step-ladder. 'You'd much better leave Peter alone. Starve him into surrender, Mrs Merrit, and don't leave bananas and seed about for him to peck at when he fancies he's hungry. You're far too soft-hearted.'

'Well, sir, I see he's right out of reach now on that picture rail, so if you wouldn't mind closing the door, sir, when you leave the room, I'll bring his cage in tonight and put some meat inside it. He's that fond of meat, though it does make him pull out his feathers to suck the quills. They do say that if you cook —'

'Never mind, Mrs Merrit,' said Eustace, who was busy writing. 'That will do; I'll keep an eye on the bird.'

There was silence in the room, unbroken but for the continuous whisper of his pen.

'Scratch poor Peter,' said the bird. 'Scratch poor old Peter!'

'Be quiet, you beastly bird!'

'Poor old Peter! Scratch poor Peter, do.'

'I'm more likely to wring your neck if I get hold of you.' He looked up at the picture rail, and there was the hand holding on to a hook with three fingers, and slowly scratching the head of the parrot with the fourth. Eustace ran to the bell and pressed it hard; then across to the window, which he closed with a bang. Frightened by the noise the parrot shook its wings preparatory to flight, and as it did so the fingers of the hand got hold of it by the throat. There was a shrill scream from Peter as he fluttered across the room, wheeling round in circles that ever descended, borne down under the weight that clung to him. The bird dropped at last quite suddenly, and Eustace saw fingers and feathers rolled into an inextricable mass on the floor. The struggle abruptly ceased as finger and thumb squeezed the neck; the bird's eyes rolled up to show the whites, and there was a faint, half-choked gurgle. But before the fingers had time to loose their hold, Eustace had them in his own.

'Send Mr Saunders here at once,' he said to the maid who came in answer to the bell. 'Tell him I want him immediately.'

Then he went with the hand to the fire. There was a ragged gash across the back where the bird's beak had torn it, but no blood oozed from the wound. He noticed with disgust that the nails had grown long and discoloured.

'I'll burn the beastly thing,' he said. But he could not burn it. He tried to throw it into the flames, but his own hands, as if restrained by some old primitive feeling, would not let him. And so Saunders found him pale and irresolute, with the hand still clasped tightly in his fingers.

'I've got it at last,' he said in a tone of triumph.

'Good; let's have a look at it.'

'Not when it's loose. Get me some nails and a hammer and a board of some sort.'

'Can you hold it all right?'

'Yes; the thing's quite limp; tired out with throttling poor old Peter, I should say.'

'And now,' said Saunders when he returned with the things, 'what are we going to do?'

'Drive a nail through it first, so that it can't get away; then we can take our time examining it.'

'Do it yourself,' said Saunders. 'I don't mind helping you with guinea-pigs occasionally when there's something to be learned; partly because I don't fear a guinea-pig's revenge. This thing's different.'

'All right, you miserable skunk. I won't forget the way you've stood by me.'

He took up a nail, and before Saunders had realized what he was doing had driven it through the hand, deep into the board.

'Oh, my aunt,' he giggled hysterically, 'look at it now.' for the hand was writhing in agonized contortions, squirming and wriggling upon the nail like a worm upon the hook.

'Well,' said Saunders, 'you've done it now. I'll leave you to examine it.'

'Don't go, in heaven's name. Cover it up, man, cover it up! Shove a cloth over it! Here!' and he pulled off the antimacassar from the back of a chair and wrapped the board in it. 'Now get the keys from my pocket and open the safe. Chuck the other things out. Oh, Lord, it's getting itself into frightful knots! and open it quick!' He threw the thing in and banged the door.

'We'll keep it there till it dies,' he said. 'May I burn in hell if I ever open the door of that safe again.'

Mrs Merrit departed at the end of the month. Her successor certainly was more successful in the management

of the servants. Early in her rule she declared that she would stand no nonsense, and gossip soon withered and died. Eustace Borlsover went back to his old way of life. Old habits crept over and covered his new experience. He was, if anything, less morose, and showed a greater inclination to take his natural part in country society.

'I shouldn't be surprised if he marries one of these days,' said Saunders. 'Well, I'm in no hurry for such an event. I know Eustace far too well for the future Mrs Borlsover to like me. It will be the same old story again : a long friendship slowly made – marriage – and a long friendship quickly forgotten.'

4

But Eustace Borlsover did not follow the advice of his uncle and marry. He was too fond of old slippers and tobacco. The cooking, too, under Mrs Handyside's management was excellent, and she seemed, too, to have a heaven-sent faculty in knowing when to stop dusting.

Little by little the old life resumed its old power. Then came the burglary. The men, it was said, broke into the house by way of the conservatory. It was really little more than an attempt, for they only succeeded in carrying away a few pieces of plate from the pantry. The safe in the study was certainly found open and empty, but, as Mr Borlsover informed the police inspector, he had kept nothing of value in it during the last six months.

'Then you're lucky in getting off so easily, sir,' the man replied. 'By the way they have gone about their business, I should say they were experienced cracksmen. They must have caught the alarm when they were just beginning their evening's work.'

'Yes,' said Eustace, 'I suppose I am lucky.'

'I've no doubt,' said the inspector, 'that we shall be able to trace the men. I've said that they must have been old hands at the game. The way they got in and opened the safe shows that. But there's one little thing that puzzles me. One of them was careless enough not to wear gloves, and I'm bothered if I know what he was trying to do. I've traced his finger-marks on the new varnish on the window sashes in every one of the downstairs rooms. They are very distinct ones too.'

'Right hand or left, or both?' asked Eustace.

'Oh, right every time. That's the funny thing. He must have been a foolhardy fellow, and I rather think it was him that wrote that.' He took out a slip of paper from his pocket. 'That's what he wrote, sir. "I've got out, Eustace Borlsover, but I'll be back before long." Some gaol bird just escaped, I suppose. It will make it all the easier for us to trace him. Do you know the writing, sir?'

'No,' said Eustace; 'it's not the writing of anyone I know.'

'I'm not going to stay here any longer,' said Eustace to Saunders at luncheon. 'I've got on far better during the last six months than ever I expected, but I'm not going to run the risk of seeing that thing again. I shall go up to town this afternoon. Get Morton to put my things together, and join me with the car at Brighton on the day after tomorrow. And bring the proofs of those two papers with you. We'll run over them together.'

'How long are you going to be away?'

'I can't say for certain, but be prepared to stay for some time. We've stuck to work pretty closely through the summer, and I for one need a holiday. I'll engage the rooms at Brighton. You'll find it best to break the journey at Hitchin. I'll wire to you there at the Crown to tell you the Brighton address.'

The house he chose at Brighton was in a terrace. He had been there before. It was kept by his old college gyp, a man of discreet silence, who was admirably partnered by an excellent cook. The rooms were on the first floor. The two bedrooms were at the back, and opened out of each other. 'Saunders can have the smaller one, though it is the only one with a fireplace,' he said. 'I'll stick to the larger of the two, since it's got a bathroom adjoining. I wonder what time he'll arrive with the car.'

Saunders came about seven, cold and cross and dirty. 'We'll light the fire in the dining-room,' said Eustace, 'and get Prince to unpack some of the things while we are at dinner. What were the roads like?'

'Rotten; swimming with mud, and a beastly cold wind against us all day. And this is July. Dear old England!'

'Yes,' said Eustace, 'I think we might do worse than leave dear old England for a few months.'

They turned in soon after twelve.

'You oughtn't to feel cold, Saunders,' said Eustace, 'when you can afford to sport a great cat-skin lined coat like this. You do yourself very well, all things considered. Look at those gloves, for instance. Who could possibly feel cold when wearing them?'

'They are far too clumsy though for driving. Try them on and see,' and he tossed them through the door on to Eustace's bed, and went on with his unpacking. A minute later he heard a shrill cry of terror. 'Oh, Lord,' he heard, 'it's in the glove! Quick, Saunders, quick!' Then came a smacking thud. Eustace had thrown it from him. 'I've chucked it into the bathroom,' he gasped, 'it's hit the wall and fallen into the bath. Come now if you want to help.' Saunders, with a lighted candle in his hand, looked over the edge of the bath. There it was, old and maimed, dumb and blind, with a ragged hole in the middle, crawling,

staggering, trying to creep up the slippery sides, only to fall back helpless.

'Stay there,' said Saunders. 'I'll empty a collar box or something, and we'll jam it in. It can't get out while I'm away.'

'Yes, it can,' shouted Eustace. 'It's getting out now. It's climbing up the plug chain. No, you brute, you filthy brute, you don't! Come back, Saunders, it's getting away from me. I can't hold it; it's all slippery. Curse its claw! Shut the window, you idiot! The top too, as well as the bottom. You utter idiot! It's got out!' There was the sound of something dropping on to the hard flagstones below, and Eustace fell back fainting.

For a fortnight he was ill.

'I don't know what to make of it,' the doctor said to Saunders. 'I can only suppose that Mr Borlsover has suffered some great emotional shock. You had better let me send someone to help you nurse him. And by all means indulge that whim of his never to be left alone in the dark. I would keep a light burning all night if I were you. But he *must* have more fresh air. It's perfectly absurd this hatred of open windows.'

Eustace, however, would have no one with him but Saunders. 'I don't want the other men,' he said. 'They'd smuggle it in somehow. I know they would.'

'Don't worry about it, old chap. This sort of thing can't go on indefinitely. You know I saw it this time as well as you. It wasn't half so active. It won't go on living much longer, especially after that fall. I heard it hit the flags myself. As soon as you're a bit stronger we'll leave this place; not bag and baggage, but with only the clothes on our backs, so that it won't be able to hide anywhere. We'll escape it that way. We won't give any address, and we

won't have any parcels sent after us. Cheer up, Eustace! You'll be well enough to leave in a day or two. The doctor says I can take you out in a chair tomorrow.'

'What have I done?' asked Eustace. 'Why does it come after me? I'm no worse than other men. I'm no worse than you, Saunders; you know I'm not. It was you who were at the bottom of that dirty business in San Diego, and that was fifteen years ago.'

'It's not that, of course,' said Saunders. 'We are in the twentieth century, and even the parsons have dropped the idea of your old sins finding you out. Before you caught the hand in the library it was filled with pure malevolence – to you and all mankind. After you spiked it through with that nail it naturally forgot about other people, and concentrated its attention on you. It was shut up in the safe, you know, for nearly six months. That gives plenty of time for thinking of revenge.'

Eustace Borlsover would not leave his room, but he thought that there might be something in Saunders's suggestion to leave Brighton without notice. He began rapidly to regain his strength.

'We'll go on the first of September,' he said.

The evening of August 31st was oppressively warm. Though at midday the windows had been wide open, they had been shut an hour or so before dusk. Mrs Prince had long since ceased to wonder at the strange habits of the gentlemen on the first floor. Soon after their arrival she had been told to take down the heavy curtains in the two bedrooms, and day by day the rooms had seemed to grow more bare. Nothing was left lying about.

'Mr Borlsover doesn't like to have any place where dirt can collect,' Saunders had said as an excuse. 'He likes to see into all the corners of the room.'

'Couldn't I open the window just a little?' he said to

Eustace that evening. 'We're simply roasting in here, you know.'

'No, leave well alone. We're not a couple of boarding-school misses fresh from a course of hygiene lectures. Get the chessboard out.'

They sat down and played. At ten o'clock Mrs Prince came to the door with a note. 'I am sorry I didn't bring it before,' she said. 'but it was left in the letter-box.'

'Open it, Saunders, and see if it wants answering.'

It was very brief. There was neither address nor signature.

'Will eleven o'clock tonight be suitable for our last appointment?'

'Who is it from?' asked Borlsover.

'It was meant for me,' said Saunders. 'There's no answer, Mrs Prince,' and he put the paper into his pocket. 'A dunning letter from a tailor; I suppose he must have got wind of our leaving.'

It was a clever lie, and Eustace asked no more questions. They went on with their game.

On the landing outside Saunders could hear the grand-father's clock whispering the seconds, blurting out the quarter-hours.

'Check!' said Eustace. The clock struck eleven. At the same time there was a gentle knocking on the door; it seemed to come from the bottom panel.

'Who's there?' asked Eustace.

There was no answer.

'Mrs Prince, is that you?'

'She is up above,' said Saunders; 'I can hear her walking about the room.'

'Then lock the door; bolt it too. Your move, Saunders.'

While Saunders sat with his eyes on the chessboard,

Eustace walked over to the window and examined the fastenings. He did the same in Saunders's room and the bathroom. There were no doors between the three rooms, or he would have shut and locked them too.

'Now, Saunders,' he said, 'don't stay all night over your move. I've had time to smoke one cigarette already. It's bad to keep an invalid waiting. There's only one possible thing for you to do. What was that?'

'The ivy blowing against the window. There, it's your move now, Eustace.'

'It wasn't the ivy, you idiot. It was someone tapping at the window,' and he pulled up the blind. On the outer side of the window, clinging to the sash, was the hand.

'What is it that it's holding?'

'It's a pocket-knife. It's going to try to open the window by pushing back the fastener with the blade.'

'Well, let it try,' said Eustace. 'Those fasteners screw down; they can't be opened that way. Anyhow, we'll close the shutters. It's your move, Saunders. I've played.'

But Saunders found it impossible to fix his attention on the game. He could not understand Eustace, who seemed all at once to have lost his fear. 'What do you say to some wine?' he asked. 'You seem to be taking things coolly, but I don't mind confessing that I'm in a blessed funk.'

'You've no need to be. There's nothing supernatural about that hand, Saunders. I mean it seems to be governed by the laws of time and space. It's not the sort of thing that vanishes into thin air or slides through oaken doors. And since that's so, I defy it to get in here. We'll leave the place in the morning. I for one have bottomed the depths of fear. Fill your glass, man! The windows are all shuttered, the door is locked and bolted. Pledge me my uncle Adrian! Drink, man! What are you waiting for?'

Saunders was standing with his glass half raised. 'It can

get in,' he said hoarsely; 'it can get in! We've forgotten. There's the fire-place in my bedroom. It will come down the chimney.'

'Quick!' said Eustace, as he rushed into the other room; 'we haven't a minute to lose. What can we do? Light the fire, Saunders. Give me a match, quick!'

'They must be all in the other room. I'll get them.'

'Hurry, man, for goodness' sake! Look in the bookcase! Look in the bathroom! Here, come and stand here; I'll look.'

'Be quick!' shouted Saunders. 'I can hear something!'

'Then plug a sheet from your bed up the chimney. No, here's a match.' He had found one at last that had slipped into a crack in the floor.

'Is the fire laid? Good, but it may not burn. I know — the oil from that old reading-lamp and this cotton-wool. Now the match, quick! Pull the sheet away, you fool! We don't want it now.'

There was a great roar from the grate as the flames shot up. Saunders had been a fraction of a second too late with the sheet. The oil had fallen on to it. It, too, was burning.

'The whole place will be on fire!' cried Eustace, as he tried to beat out the flames with a blanket. 'It's no good! I can't manage it. You must open the door, Saunders, and get help.'

Saunders ran to the door and fumbled with the bolts. The key was stiff in the lock.

'Hurry!' shouted Eustace; 'the whole place is ablaze!'

The key turned in the lock at last. For half a second Saunders stopped to look back. Afterwards he could never be quite sure as to what he had seen, but at the time he thought that something black and charred was creeping slowly, very slowly, from the masses of flames towards Eustace Borlsover. For a moment he thought of returning

to his friend, but the noise and the smell of the burning sent him running down the passage crying, 'Fire! Fire!' He rushed to the telephone to summon help, and then back to the bathroom – he should have thought of that before – for water. As he burst open the bedroom door there came a scream of terror which ended suddenly, and then the sound of a heavy fall.

James Thurber

The Night the Ghost Got In

THE ghost that got into our house on the night of 17
November 1915 raised such a hullabaloo of misunder-
standings that I am sorry I didn't just let it keep on walking, and go to bed. Its advent caused my mother to throw
a shoe through a window of the house next door and
ended up with my grandfather shooting a patrolman. I am
sorry, therefore, as I have said, that I ever paid any attention to the footsteps.

They began about a quarter-past one o'clock in the
morning, a rhythmic, quick-cadenced walking around the
dining-room table. My mother was asleep in one room upstairs, my brother Herman in another; grandfather was in
the attic, in the old walnut bed which, as you will remember, once fell on my father. I had just stepped out of the
bathtub and was busily rubbing myself with a towel when
I heard the steps. They were the steps of a man walking
rapidly around the dining-room table downstairs. The
light from the bathroom shone down the back steps,
which dropped directly into the dining-room; I could see
the faint shine of plates on the plate-rail; I couldn't see the
table. The steps kept going round and round the table; at
regular intervals a board creaked, when it was trod upon.
I supposed at first that it was my father or my brother Roy,
who had gone to Indianapolis but were expected home at
any time. I suspected next that it was a burglar. It did not
enter my mind until later that it was a ghost.

After the walking had gone on for perhaps three minutes, I tiptoed to Herman's room. 'Psst!' I hissed, in the dark, shaking him. 'Awp,' he said, in the low hopeless tone of a despondent beagle – he always half suspected that something would 'get him' in the night. I told him who I was. 'There's something downstairs!' I said. He got up and followed me to the head of the back staircase. We listened together. There was no sound. The steps had ceased. Herman looked at me in some alarm: I had only the bath towel around my waist. He wanted to go back to bed, but I gripped his arm. 'There's something down there!' I said. Instantly the steps began again, circled the dining-room table like a man running, and started up the stairs towards us, heavily, two at a time. The light still shone palely down the stairs; we saw nothing coming; we only heard the steps. Herman rushed to his room and slammed the door. I slammed shut the door at the stairs top and held my knee against it. After a long minute, I slowly opened it again. There was nothing there. There was no sound. None of us ever heard the ghost again.

The slamming of the doors had aroused mother: she peered out of her room. 'What on earth are you boys doing?' she demanded. Herman ventured out of his room. 'Nothing,' he said, gruffly, but he was, in colour, a light green. 'What was all that running around downstairs?' said mother. So she had heard the steps, too! We just looked at her. 'Burglars!' she shouted intuitively. I tried to quiet her by starting lightly downstairs.

'Come on, Herman,' I said.

'I'll stay with mother,' he said. 'She's all excited.'

I stepped back on to the landing.

'Don't either of you go a step,' said mother. 'We'll call the police.' Since the phone was downstairs, I didn't see how we were going to call the police – nor did I want the

police – but mother made one of her quick, incomparable decisions. She flung up a window of her bedroom, which faced the bedroom windows of the house of a neighbour, picked up a shoe, and whammed it through a pane of glass across the narrow space that separated the two houses. Glass tinkled into the bedroom occupied by a retired engraver named Bodwell and his wife. Bodwell had been for some years in rather a bad way and was subject to mild 'attacks'. Most everybody we knew or lived near had *some* kind of attacks.

It was now about two o'clock of a moonless night; clouds hung black and low. Bodwell was at the window in a minute, shouting, frothing a little shaking his fist. 'We'll sell the house and go back to Peoria,' we could hear Mrs Bodwell saying. It was some time before mother 'got through' to Bodwell. 'Burglars!' she shouted. 'Burglars in the house!' Herman and I hadn't dared to tell her that it was not burglars but ghosts, for she was even more afraid of ghosts than of burglars. Bodwell at first thought that she meant there were burglars in his house, but finally he quieted down and called the police for us over an extension phone by his bed. After he had disappeared from the window, mother suddenly made as if to throw another shoe, not because there was further need of it but, as she later explained, because the thrill of heaving a shoe through a window glass had enormously taken her fancy. I prevented her.

The police were on hand in a commendably short time: a Ford sedan full of them, two on motor-cycles, and a patrol wagon with about eight in it and a few reporters. They began banging at our front door. Flashlights shot streaks of gleam up and down the walls, across the yard, down the walk between our house and Bodwell's. 'Open up!' cried a hoarse voice. 'We're men from Headquarters!' I wanted

to go down and let them in, since there they were, but mother wouldn't hear of it. 'You haven't a stitch on,' she pointed out. 'You'd catch your death.' I wound the towel around me again. Finally the cops put their shoulders to our big heavy front door with its thick bevelled glass and broke it in: I could hear a rending of wood and a splash of glass on the floor of the hall. Their lights played all over the living-room and criss-crossed nervously in the dining-room, stabbed into hallways, shot up the front stairs and finally up the back. They caught me standing in my towel at the top. A heavy policeman bounded up the steps. 'Who are you?' he demanded. 'I live here,' I said. 'Well, what-tsa matta, ya hot?' he asked. It was, as a matter of fact, cold; I went to my room and pulled on some trousers. On my way out, a cop stuck a gun into my ribs. 'Whatta you doin' here?' he demanded. 'I live here,' I said.

The officer in charge reported to mother. 'No sign of no-body, lady,' he said. 'Musta got away – whatt'd he look like?' 'There were two or three of them,' mother said, 'whooping and carrying on and slamming doors.' 'Funny,' said the cop. 'All ya windows and doors was locked on the inside tight as a tick.'

Downstairs, we could hear the tromping of the other police. Police were all over the place; doors were yanked open, drawers were yanked open, windows were shot up and pulled down, furniture fell with dull thumps. A half-dozen policemen emerged out of the darkness of the front hallway upstairs. They began to ransack the floor: pulled beds away from walls, tore clothes off hooks in the closets, pulled suitcases and boxes off shelves. One of them found an old zither that Roy had won in a pool tournament. 'Looky here, Joe,' he said strumming it with a big paw. The cop named Joe took it and turned it over. 'What is it?' he asked me. 'It's an old zither our guinea pig used to

sleep on,' I said. It was true that a pet guinea pig we once had would never sleep anywhere except on the zither, but I should never have said so. Joe and the other cop looked at me a long time. They put the zither back on a shelf.

'No sign o' nuthin',' said the cop who had first spoken to mother. 'This guy,' he explained to the others, jerking a thumb at me, 'was nekked. The lady seems historical.' They all nodded, but said nothing; just looked at me. In the small silence we all heard a creaking in the attic. Grandfather was turning over in bed. 'What's 'at?' snapped Joe. Five or six cops sprang for the attic door before I could intervene or explain. I realized that it would be bad if they burst in on grandfather unannounced, or even announced. He was going through a phase in which he believed that General Meade's men, under steady hammering by Stonewall Jackson, were beginning to retreat and even desert.

When I got to the attic, things were pretty confused. Grandfather had evidently jumped to the conclusion that the police were deserters from Meade's army, trying to hide away in his attic. He bounded out of bed wearing a long flannel nightgown over long woollen underwear, a night-cap, and a leather jacket around his chest. The cops must have realized at once that the indignant white-haired old man belonged in the house, but they had no chance to say so. 'Back, ye cowardly dogs!' roared grandfather. 'Back t' the lines, ye goddam lily-livered cattle!' With that, he fetched the officer who found the zither a flat-handed smack alongside his head that sent him sprawling. The others beat a retreat, but not fast enough; grandfather grabbed Zither's gun from its holster and let fly. The report seemed to crack the rafters; smoke filled the attic. A cop cursed and shot his hand to his shoulder. Somehow, we all finally got downstairs again and locked the door against

the old gentleman. He fired once or twice more in the darkness and then went back to bed. 'That was grandfather,' I explained to Joe, out of breath. 'He thinks you're deserters.' 'I'll say he does,' said Joe.

The cops were reluctant to leave without getting their hands on somebody besides grandfather; the night had been distinctly a defeat for them. Furthermore, they obviously didn't like the 'layout', something looked – and I can see their viewpoint – phony. They began to poke into things again. A reporter, a thin-faced, wispy man, came up to me. I had put on one of mother's blouses, not being able to find anything else. The reporter looked at me with mingled suspicion and interest. 'Just what the hell is the real lowdown here, Bud?' he asked. I decided to be frank with him. 'We had ghosts,' I said. He gazed at me a long time as if I were a slot machine into which he had, without results, dropped a nickel. Then he walked away. The cops followed him, the one grandfather shot holding his now-bandaged arm, cursing and blaspheming. 'I'm gonna get my gun back from that old bird,' said the zither-cop. 'Yeh,' said Joe. 'You – and who else?' I told them I would bring it to the station house the next day.

'What was the matter with that one policeman?' mother asked, after they had gone. 'Grandfather shot him,' I said. 'What for?' she demanded. I told her he was a deserter. 'Of all things!' said mother. 'He was such a nice-looking young man.'

Grandfather was fresh as a daisy and full of jokes at breakfast next morning. We thought at first he had forgotten all about what had happened, but he hadn't. Over his third cup of coffee, he glared at Herman and me. 'What was the idee of all them cops tarryhootin' round the house last night?' he demanded. He had us there.

Andrew Lang

The Story of Glam

THERE was a man named Thorhall, who lived at Thorhall-stead in Forsaela-dala, which lies in the north of Iceland. He was a fairly wealthy man, especially in cattle, so that no one round about had so much livestock as he had. He was not a chief, however, but an honest and worthy yeoman.

Now this man's place was greatly haunted, so that he could scarcely get a shepherd to stay with him, and although he asked the opinion of many as to what he ought to do, he could find none to give him advice of any worth.

One summer at the Althing, or yearly assembly of the people, Thorhall went to the booth of Skafti, the law man, who was the wisest of men and gave good counsel when his opinion was asked. He received Thorhall in a friendly way, because he knew he was a man of means, and asked him what news he had.

'I would have some good advice from you,' said Thorhall.

'I am little able to give that,' said Skafti; 'but what is the matter?'

'This is the way of it,' said Thorhall, 'I have had very bad luck with my shepherds of late. Some of them get injured, and others will not serve out their time; and now no one that knows how the case stands will take the place at all.'

'Then there must be some evil spirit there,' said Skafti, 'when men are less willing to herd your sheep, than those of others. Now since you have asked my advice, I will get a shepherd for you. Glam is his name, he belongs to Sweden, and came out here last summer. He is big and strong, but not very well liked by most people.'

Thorhall said that he did not mind that, if he looked well after the sheep. Skafti answered that there was no hope of other men doing it, if Glam could not, seeing he was so strong and stout-hearted. Their talk ended there, and Thorhall left the booth.

This took place just at the breaking up of the assembly. Thorhall missed two of his horses, and went to look for them in person, from which it may be seen that he was no proud man. He went up to the mountain ridge, and south along the fell that is called Armann's fell. There he saw a man coming down from the wood, leading a horse laden with bundles of brushwood. They soon met each other and Thorhall asked his name. He said he was called Glam. He was tall of body, and of strange appearance; his eyes were blue and staring, and his hair wolf-grey in colour. Thorhall was a little startled when he saw him, and was certain that this was the man he had been told about.

'What work are you best fitted for?' he asked. Glam said that he was good at keeping sheep in winter.

'Will you look after *my* sheep?' said Thorhall. 'Skafti has put you into my hands.'

'On this condition only will I take service with you,' said Glam, 'that I have my own free will, for I am ill-tempered if anything does not please me.'

'That will not harm me,' said Thorhall, 'and I should like you to come to me.'

'I will do so,' said Glam; 'but is there any trouble at your place?'

'It is believed to be haunted,' said Thorhall.

'I am not afraid of such bugbears,' said Glam, 'and think that it will be all the livelier for that.'

'You will need all your boldness,' said Thorhall. 'It is best not to be too frightened for one's self there.'

After this they made a bargain between them, and Glam was to come when the winter nights began. Then they parted, and Thorhall found his horses where he had just newly looked for them, and rode home, after thanking Skafti for his kindness.

The summer passed, and Thorhall heard nothing of the shepherd, nor did anyone know the least about him, but at the time appointed he came to Thorhall-stead. The yeoman received him well, but the others did not like him, and the goodwife least of all. He began his work among the sheep which gave him little trouble, for he had a loud, hoarse voice, and the flock all ran together whenever he shouted. There was a church at Thorhall-stead, but Glam would never go to it nor join in the service. He was unbelieving, surly, and difficult to deal with, and everyone felt a dislike towards him.

So time went on till it came to Christmas Eve. On that morning Glam rose early and called for his food. The goodwife answered: 'It is not the custom of Christian people to eat on this day, for tomorrow is the first day of Christmas, and we ought to fast today.' Glam replied: 'You have many foolish fashions that I see no good in. I cannot see that men are any better off now than they were when they never troubled themselves about such things. I think it was a far better life when men were heathens; and now I want my food, and no nonsense.' The goodwife answered: 'I am sure you will come to sorrow today if you act thus perversely.'

Glam bade her bring his food at once, or it would be the

227

worse for her. She was afraid to refuse, and after he had eaten he went out in a great rage.

The weather was very bad. It was dark and gloomy all round; snowflakes fluttered about; loud noises were heard in the air, and it grew worse and worse as the day wore on. They heard the shepherd's voice during the forenoon, but less of him as the day passed. Then the snow began to drift, and by evening there was a violent storm. People came to the service in church, and the day wore on to evening, but still Glam did not come home. There was some talk among them of going to look for him, but no search was made on account of the storm and the darkness.

All Christmas Eve Glam did not return, and in the morning men went to look for him. They found the sheep scattered in the fens, beaten down by the storm, or up on the hills. Thereafter they came to a place in the valley where the snow was all trampled, as if there had been a terrible struggle there, for stones and frozen earth were torn up all round about. They looked carefully round the place, and found Glam lying a short distance off, quite dead. He was black in colour, and swollen up as big as an ox. They were horrified at the sight, and shuddered in their hearts. However, they tried to carry him to the church, but could get him no further than to the edge of a cleft, a little lower down; so they left him there and went home and told their master what had happened.

Thorhall asked them what had been the cause of Glam's death. They said that they had traced footprints as large as though the bottom of a cask had been set down in the snow leading from where the trampled place was up to the cliffs at the head of the valley, and all along the track there were huge bloodstains. From this they guessed that the evil spirit which lived there must have killed Glam, but had re-

ceived so much hurt that it had died, for nothing was ever seen of it after.

The second day of Christmas they tried again to bring Glam to the church. They yoked horses to him, but after they had come down the slope and reached level ground they could drag him no further, and he had to be left there.

On the third day a priest went with them, but Glam was not to be found, although they searched for him all day. The priest refused to go a second time, and the shepherd was found at once when the priest was not present. So they gave over their attempts to take him to the church, and buried him on the spot.

Soon after this they became aware that Glam was not lying quiet, and great damage was done by him, for many that saw him fell into a swoon, or lost their reason. Immediately after Yule men believed that they saw him about the farm itself, and grew terribly frightened, so that many of them ran away. After this Glam began to ride on the house-top by night, and nearly shook it to pieces, and then he walked about almost night and day. Men hardly dared to go up into the valley, even although they had urgent business there, and everyone in the district thought great harm of the matter.

In spring, Thorhall got new men, and started his farm again, while Glam's walkings began to grow less frequent as the days grew longer. So time went on, until it was mid-summer. That summer a ship from Norway came into Huna-water (a firth to the north of Thorhall-stead), and had on board a man called Thorgaut. He was foreign by birth, big of body, and as strong as any two men. He was unhired and unmarried, and was looking for some employment, as he was penniless. Thorhall rode to the ship, and found Thorgaut there. He asked him whether he would enter his service. Thorgaut answered that he might

well do so, and that he did not care much what work he did.

'You must know, however,' said Thorhall, 'that it is not good for any faint-hearted man to live at my place, on account of the hauntings that have been of late, and I do not wish to deceive you in any way.'

'I do not think myself utterly lost although I see some wretched ghosts,' said Thorgaut. 'It will be no light matter for others if *I* am scared, and I will not throw up the place on that account.'

Their bargain was quickly made, and Thorgaut was to have charge of the sheep during the winter. The summer went past, and Thorgaut began his duties with the winter nights, and was well liked by everyone. Glam began to come again, and rode on the house-top, which Thorgaut thought great sport, and said that the thrall would have to come to close quarters before he would be afraid of him. Thorhall bade him not say too much about it. 'It will be better for you,' said he, 'if you have no trial of each other.'

'Your courage has indeed been shaken out of you,' said Thorgaut, 'but I am not going to fall dead for such talk.'

The winter went on till Christmas came again, and on Christmas Eve the shepherd went out to his sheep. 'I trust,' said the goodwife, 'that things will not go after the old fashion.'

'Have no fear of that, goodwife,' said Thorgaut; 'there will be something worth talking about if I don't come back.'

The weather was very cold, and a heavy drift blowing. Thorgaut was in the habit of coming home when it was half dark, but on this occasion he did not return at his usual time. People came to church, and they now began to think that things were not unlikely to fall out as they had done before. Thorhall wished to make a search for the

shepherd, but the church-goers refused, saying that they would not risk themselves in the hands of evil demons by night, and so no search was made.

After their morning meal on Christmas Day they went out to look for the shepherd. They first made their way to Glam's cairn, guessing that he was the cause of the man's disappearance. On coming near to this they saw great tidings, for there they found the shepherd with his neck broken and every bone in his body smashed in pieces. They carried him to the church, and he did no harm to any man thereafter. But Glam began to gather strength anew, and now went so far in his mischief that everyone fled from Thorhall-stead, except the yeoman and his wife.

The same cattleman, however, had been there for a long time, and Thorhall would not let him leave, because he was so faithful and so careful. He was very old, and did not want to go away either, for he saw that everything his master had would go to wreck and ruin, if there was no one to look after it.

One morning after the middle of winter the goodwife went out to the byre to milk the cows. It was broad daylight by this time, for no one ventured to be outside earlier than that, except the cattleman, who always went out when it began to grow clear. She heard a great noise and fearful bellowing in the byre, and ran into the house again, crying out and saying that some awful thing was going on there. Thorhall went out to the cattle and found them goring each other with their horns. To get out of their way, he went through into the barn, and in doing this he saw the cattleman lying on his back, with his head in one stall and his feet in another. He went up to him and felt him and soon found that he was dead, with his back broken over the upright stone between two of the stalls.

The yeoman thought it high time to leave the place now, and fled from his farm with all that he could remove. All the livestock that he left behind was killed by Glam, who then went through the whole glen and laid waste all the farms up from Tongue.

Thorhall spent the rest of the winter with various friends. No one could go up into the glen with horse or dog, for these were killed at once; but when spring came again and the days began to lengthen, Glam's walkings grew less frequent, and Thorhall determined to return to his homestead. He had difficulty in getting servants, but managed to set up his home again at Thorhall-stead. Things went just as before. When autumn came, the hauntings began again, and now it was the yeoman's daughter who was most assailed, till in the end she died of fright. Many plans were tried, but all to no effect, and it seemed as if all Water-dale would be laid waste unless some remedy could be found.

All this befell in the days of Grettir, the son of Asmund, who was the strongest man of his day in Iceland. He had been abroad at this time, outlawed for three years, and was only eighteen years of age when he returned. He had been at home all through the autumn, but when the winter nights were well advanced, he rode north to Water-dale, and came to Tongue, where lived his uncle Jökull. His uncle received him heartily, and he stayed there for three nights. At this time there was so much talk about Glam's walkings, that nothing was so largely spoken of as these. Grettir inquired closely about all that had happened, and Jökull said that the stories told no more than had indeed taken place; 'but are you intending to go there, kinsman?' said he. Grettir answered that he was. Jökull bade him not to do so, 'for it is a dangerous undertaking, and a great risk for your friends to lose you, for in our opinion there

is not another like you among the young men, and "ill will come of ill" where Glam is. Far better it is to deal with mortal men than with such evil spirits.'

Grettir, however, said that he had a mind to fare to Thorhall-stead, and see how things had been going on there. Jökull replied: 'I see now that it is of no use to hold you back, but the saying is true that "good luck and good heart are not the same".' Grettir answered: '"Woe stands at one man's door when it has entered another's house." Think how it may go with yourself before the end.'

'It may be,' said Jökull, 'that both of us see some way into the future, and yet neither of us can do anything to prevent it.'

After this they parted, and neither liked the other's forebodings.

Grettir rode to Thorhall-stead, and the yeoman received him heartily. He asked Grettir where he was going, who said that he wished to stay there all night if he would allow him. Thorhall said that he would be very glad if he would stay, 'but few men count it a gain to be guests here for long. You must have heard how matters stand, and I shall be very unwilling for you to come to any harm on my account. And even although you yourself escape safe and sound, I know for certain that you will lose your horse, for no man that comes here can keep that uninjured.'

Grettir answered that there were horses enough to be got, whatever might happen to this one. Thorhall was delighted that he was willing to stay, and gave him the heartiest reception. The horse was strongly secured in an out-house; then they went to sleep, and that night passed without Glam appearing.

'Your coming here,' said Thorhall, 'has made a happy change, for Glam is in the habit of riding the house every

night, or breaking up the doors, as you may see for yourself.'

'Then one of two things will happen,' said Grettir; 'either he will not restrain himself for long, or the hauntings will cease for more than one night. I shall stay for another night, and see how things go.'

After this they went to look at Grettir's horse and found that he had not been meddled with, so the yeoman thought that everything was going on well. Grettir stayed another night, and still the thrall did not come about them. Thorhall thought that things were looking brighter, but when he went to look to Grettir's horse he found the outhouse broken up, the horse dragged outside, and every bone in it broken. He told Grettir what had happened, and advised him to secure his own safety, 'for your death is certain if you wait for Glam.'

Grettir answered: 'The least I can get for my horse is to see the thrall.' Thorhall replied that it would do him no good to see him, 'for he is unlike anything in human shape; but I am fain of every hour that you are willing to stay here.'

The day wore on, and when it was bedtime Grettir would not take off his clothes, but lay down on the floor over against Thorhall's bed-closet. He put a thick cloak above himself, buttoning one end beneath his feet, and doubling the other under his head, while he looked out at the hole for the neck. There was a strong plank in front of the floored space, and against this he pressed his feet. The door-fittings were all broken off from the outer door, but there was a hurdle set up instead, and roughly secured. The wainscot that had once stretched across the hall was all broken down, both above and below the cross-beam. The beds were all pulled out of their places, and everything was in confusion.

A light was left burning in the hall, and when the third part of the night was past Grettir heard loud noises outside. Then something went up on top of the house, and rode above the hall, beating the roof with its heels till every beam cracked. This went on for a long time; then it came down off the house and went to the door. When this was opened Grettir saw the thrall thrust in his head; ghastly big he seemed, and wonderfully huge of feature. Glam came in slowly, and raised himself up when he was inside the doorway, till he loomed up against the roof. Then he turned his face down the hall, laid his arms on the cross-beam, and glared all over the place. Thorhall gave no sign during all this, for he thought it bad enough to hear what was going on outside.

Grettir lay still and never moved. Glam saw that there was a bundle lying on the floor, and moved further up the hall and grasped the cloak firmly. Grettir placed his feet against the plank, and yielded not the least. Glam tugged a second time, much harder than before, but still the cloak did not move. A third time he pulled with both his hands, so hard that he raised Grettir up from the floor, and now they wrenched the cloak asunder between them. Glam stood staring at the piece which he held in his hands, and wondering greatly who could have pulled so hard against him. At that moment Grettir sprang in under the monster's hands, and threw his arms around his waist, intending to make him fall backwards. Glam, however, bore down upon him so strongly that Grettir was forced to give way before him. He then tried to stay himself against the seat-boards, but these gave way with him, and everything that came in their path was broken.

Glam wanted to get him outside, and although Grettir set his feet against everything that he could, yet Glam succeeded in dragging him out into the porch. There they had

a fierce struggle, for the thrall meant to have him out of doors, while Grettir saw that bad as it was to deal with Glam inside the house it would be worse outside, and therefore strove with all his might against being carried out. When they came into the porch Glam put forth all his strength, and pulled Grettir close to him. When Grettir saw that he could not stay himself he suddenly changed his plan, and threw himself as hard as he could against the monster's breast, setting both his feet against an earth-fast stone that lay in the doorway. Glam was not prepared for this, being then in the act of pulling Grettir towards him, so he fell backwards and went crashing out through the door, his shoulders catching the lintel as he fell. The roof of the porch was wrenched in two, both rafters and frozen thatch, and backwards out of the house went Glam, with Grettir above him.

Outside there was bright moonshine and broken clouds, which sometimes drifted over the moon and sometimes left it clear. At the moment when Glam fell the cloud passed off the moon, and he cast up his eyes sharply towards it; and Grettir himself said that this was the only sight he ever saw that terrified him. Then Grettir grew so helpless, both by reason of his weariness and at seeing Glam roll his eyes so horribly, that he was unable to draw his dagger, and lay well-nigh between life and death.

But in this was Glam's might more fiendish than that of most other ghosts, that he spoke in this fashion: 'Great eagerness have you shown to meet me, Grettir, and little wonder will it be though you get no great good fortune from me; but this I may tell you, that you have now received only half of the strength and vigour that was destined for you if you had not met with me. I cannot now take from you the strength you have already gained, but this I can see to, that you will never be stronger than you

are now, and yet you are strong enough, as many a man shall feel. Hitherto you have been famous for your deeds, but hence forth you shall be a manslayer and an outlaw, and most of your deeds will turn to your own hurt and misfortune. Outlawed you shall be, and ever have a solitary life for your lot; and this, too, I lay upon you, ever to see these eyes of mine before your own, and then you will think it hard to be alone, and that will bring you to your death.'

When Glam had said this the faintness passed off Grettir, and he then drew his dagger, cut off Glam's head, and laid it beside his thigh. Thorhall then came out, having put on his clothes while Glam was talking, but never venturing to come near until he had fallen. He praised God, and thanked Grettir for overcoming the unclean spirit. Then they set to work, and burned Glam to ashes, which they placed in a sack, and buried where cattle were least likely to pasture or men to tread. When this was done they went home again, and it was now near daybreak.

Thorhall sent to the next farm for the men there, and told them what had taken place. All thought highly of the exploit that heard of it, and it was the common talk that in all Iceland there was no man like Grettir Asmundarson for strength and courage and all kinds of bodily feats. Thorhall gave him a good horse when he went away, as well as a fine suit of clothes, for the ones he had been wearing were all torn to pieces. The two then parted with the utmost friendship.

Thence Grettir rode to the Ridge in Water-dale, where his kinsman Thorvald received him heartily, and asked closely concerning his encounter with Glam. Grettir told him how he had fared, and said that his strength was never put to harder proof, so long did the struggle between them last. Thorvald bade him be quiet and gentle in his conduct,

and things would go well with him, otherwise his troubles would be many. Grettir answered that his temper was not improved; he was more easily roused than ever, and less able to bear opposition. In this, too, he felt a great change, that he had become so much afraid of the dark that he dared not go anywhere alone after night began to fall, for then he saw phantoms and monsters of every kind. So it has become a saying ever since then, when folk see things very different from what they are, that Glam lends them his eyes, or gives them glam-sight.

This fear of solitude brought Grettir, at last, to his end.